BLURB

When death claimed my parents, fate delivered me to him—my protector, my damnation, my foster brother.

At nine years old, I lost everything to a drunk driver's careless actions. Thrust into the Wilson's foster home, I found an unlikely guardian in Talon, whose fierce eyes and protective nature became my anchor in a world of chaos.

As years passed, our bond deepened into something darker, more possessive. But when they caught us together, they made sure our separation was absolute.

Now I'm at MIT, trapped in an engagement to a man whose true nature emerges behind closed doors. But Talon lurks in the shadows, his obsessive love a dangerous promise of salvation. His protection comes at a price, one collected in broken bones and fresh graves.

Some of the most beautiful love stories are written by the most damaged souls. Welcome to ours.

In a world built on control and manipulation, sometimes the only way to find love is to let the monsters win.

GRAVE INTENTIONS

SELENA WINTERS

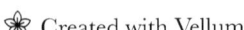 Created with Vellum

PLAYLIST

<u>Grave Intentions Playlist</u>

"Paranoia Agent"— Savage Gasp, Lil Darkie, KAMAARA
"On My Own"—Darci
"Kiss me"—Le Flex
"Come Through"—Rui
"Obsessed"—Zandros, Limi
"Eve"—Kat Cunning
"Aphrodisiac"—KIRRA47, Desire4u
"In For It"—Tory Lanes, RL Grime
"Redemption"—Drake
"Persephone"—PierceTheSkies
"Closed"—ONEIL, Titov
"I Crave Blood"—HALLOW, Shelley
"The Hills x Where Have You Been"—Noturgf

You can find the playlist on Spotify here

To all the naughty book whores dreaming of a dangerous protector who'd kill for you then fuck you in the blood of your enemies——your ultimate anti-hero has arrived. Embrace your darkest impulses. It's time to let your freak flag fly.

AUTHOR'S NOTE

Author's Note

This story explores dark romance and contains explicit content that may not be suitable for all readers. It includes themes of dominance, psychotic behavior, possessiveness, and explicit mature scenes presented alongside delicate subject matters that may be distressing or triggering for some individuals.

Please refer to the comprehensive list of warnings on my website for detailed information on this book's triggers.

I advise reader discretion and recommend only proceeding if you're comfortable with the mentioned themes. Rest assured, the story ends in a HEA with no cliffhanger or cheating between the main characters.

LENA

NINE YEARS OLD

I'm sitting on the bench outside my school, waiting for my mom and dad to pick me up. All my friends have already gone home, but that's okay because my parents always come for me, no matter what.

Mrs. Jacobs walks over with a sad face as the last teachers leave. My tummy feels funny. I'm scared.

"Lena, sweetie, can you come inside with me for a second?" she says, putting her hand on my shoulder.

I nod and follow her into the quiet school. We go to the principal's office, and he's looking really serious.

Mrs. Jacobs points to a chair in front of the desk. "Sit here, Lena," she tells me.

"Lena," the principal says softly, "I have bad news. There was an accident. Your parents were taken to the hospital."

My heart starts racing, like when I run too fast, and

my hands get sweaty. "Are they okay?" I ask, my voice shaky.

He looks at Mrs. Jacobs, and they share a look that hurts my stomach. "Lena, I'm so sorry. The accident was really bad. Your parents... they didn't make it."

I can't think straight. This must be a mistake. My mom and dad would never leave me!

"No! That's not true!" I yell, hot tears streaming down my cheeks. "You're lying! They're coming to get me!"

Mrs. Jacobs bends down and hugs me tight while I cry and cry. The principal looks sad, but I can't believe what he's telling me.

My parents can't be gone. They promised they'd always be here. They *promised...*

Time feels like it's moving slowly. I try to understand what's happening. I feel so alone. Who will tuck me in at night or kiss my bumps and scrapes? Or tell me they love me?

It hurts so much like something inside me is torn apart. I wrap my arms around my knees while I sit in the chair, feeling like the world is crashing down on me.

Dead means that my mom and dad are never coming back. I'm all alone.

The principal asks, "Lena, do you have any family we can call? Aunts, uncles, grandparents?"

My eyes are all blurry with tears. "N-no, it's just my mom and dad." My voice is so quiet.

Mrs. Jacobs looks at the principal, and he asks, "What about your mom's parents?"

"They died before I was born," I whisper, holding my knees tight.

The principal sighs. "And your dad's parents?"

I remember how my dad hadn't talked to them since he met my mom. "My dad didn't want to see them anymore."

Mrs. Jacobs pats my shoulder gently. "Oh, sweetie, I'm so sorry." Her eyes are full of tears, too.

The principal's face is serious now. "That means we'll have to call social services. They'll need to find you a place to stay."

My heart drops. Social services? Foster care? That's not what I want. The thought of going away from my home, from everything I know, terrifies me. I can't lose my mom and dad and then lose my home, too.

"No, please!" I beg, more tears coming. "I want to stay here! I don't want to go!"

Mrs. Jacobs hugs me again, her hand running through my hair. "I know, honey. I know it's so hard. But you need to be safe."

The principal nods. "I'm sorry, Lena. We have to do what's best for you."

I squeeze my eyes shut, wishing I could wake up and everything would be okay. But this is real and hurts too much. I'm all alone now.

The adults look at each other sadly as they prepare to call for help. My heart races with fear. What will happen now?

I'm sitting in the chair, my tears slowing down, but that feeling of fear is still there.

After what feels like forever, a lady in a gray suit walks in. She looks serious and not nice at all.

"Lena Graves?" she asks coldly.

I nod my head, feeling all trembly.

"I'm from social services. We talked to your grandparents, and they said they can't take you in." She stops for a second, her mouth tight. "You have no other family, so we'll need to find you a foster home."

It feels like she just punched me in the stomach. My grandparents don't want me? More tears fill my eyes.

"But... they're my family," I whisper, my voice shaky. "They can't just leave me..."

The lady doesn't show any feelings. "I'm sorry, but that's what they decided. Now, let's get you ready for your new home."

I look at Mrs. Jacobs and the principal, hoping they will help me, but they look sad.

Slowly, I get up from the chair, my legs feeling like jelly. The lady reaches for my hand, but I pull away and hug myself. I don't want to hold her hand. I want my mom and dad back. I want to go home.

As we leave the school, I look back one last time. This place, these people, they were my whole world. And now it's all taken away.

The lady helps me into the backseat of her car, which feels like sitting on rocks. I look out the window as my school disappears, and tears keep coming down my cheeks.

I don't know where I'm going or what will happen, but I know one thing: I've lost everything. My parents, my home, my life. And now my grandparents don't want me either.

The car starts moving. Fear grips me. What is going to happen to me?

2

LENA

NINE YEARS OLD

I'm staring out the car window, watching the little town of Stockbridge disappear. It feels heavy inside my chest, like I'm carrying a big rock. I'm holding onto a thin blanket that the nice lady, Emily, gave me, but it doesn't make me feel any better. I miss my mom's hugs.

Emily, my social worker, sits next to me. "It won't be too long until we're there," she says with a smile and puts her hand on my arm. "I know it's all scary, but the Wilsons are the family you'll be staying with. They're nice people. I think you'll like them."

I nod, but I can't talk. It's a long ride, and my heart feels stuck in a muddy pit. The Wilsons live in Salem, which is far away—like another planet. I've never been anywhere else. How can anyone replace my family? I feel tears starting to come again, so I blink fast.

The car slows down after what seems like forever,

and Emily gives me a hopeful smile. "Are you ready to meet your new foster family?" she asks.

I take a big breath and nod. I know I can't fight it—I've learned about all this foster care stuff in the last few weeks. When the car stops at a busy parking lot, I get out and follow Emily to a nearby car. A nice-looking couple is waiting for us. The lady, who I think must be Mrs. Wilson, comes over and wraps me in a big hug that makes my shoulders stiffen.

"Welcome, Lena," she says softly. "We're so happy to have you with us."

I'm not used to being hugged by strangers, so I freeze for a second. Mrs. Wilson notices and lets go, giving me a kind smile.

"Let's get you settled in, okay?" she says, leading me to the car. "You've had a long day, and I bet you're very tired."

When I climb into the backseat, Emily follows and settles in beside me, giving me a reassuring smile. Mr. Wilson starts the car, taking me farther away from my old life.

I gaze out the window, watching everything zoom by. This is supposed to be my new home, but I don't know anyone here. A shiver of fear zips down my back, and I wonder if I'll ever feel like I belong.

The car finally stops outside a regular two-story house. Mrs. Wilson helps me carry my few things inside, and I feel a chill. This is it—my new home, where there won't be any of the love I used to know.

"Welcome to your new room, Lena," Mrs. Wilson says, guiding me upstairs. She opens the door to a little bedroom that's tidy but plain. It doesn't feel cozy at all, not like my old room did.

I nod, but my heart feels heavy as I drop my bag and sit on the edge of the bed. The mattress is hard, and the sheets are stiff. Nothing feels like home.

"I'll let you get settled," Mrs. Wilson says while Emily talks to her about boring adult stuff. She gives me a nice smile. "Dinner will be ready soon. Why don't you come down and meet everyone then?"

As she walks out, I feel a wave of worry. I'm going to meet a whole bunch of strangers, and I'm scared they won't like me. I want to disappear.

Suddenly, I hear a soft creak at the door. I turn around and see a tall boy standing there. His dark hair covers part of his face, and his blue eyes look serious and scary. This must be Talon, the other foster kid Emily told me about.

"Hi," I say, trying not to sound too freaked out.

He doesn't say anything, staring at me and making me feel weird. It's like he can see right through me.

After a moment that feels like forever, he finally says, "You're the new girl."

"Yeah, I'm Lena. Nice to meet you," I say, smiling a little.

Talon smirks, and it feels like he's up to something. "Nice to meet you, huh?" He steps closer, looking at me like he knows something I don't. "You have no idea what you're getting into."

Before I can say anything, I hear a loud voice from downstairs, calling us to dinner. Talon gives me another look before fading back into the shadows of the hallway.

I sit still for a second, my heart racing, and I feel kind of scared about what will happen next.

Taking a big breath, I head down the stairs, even though my tummy feels funny and twisted. I can smell something yummy in the kitchen, but I am too nervous to be hungry.

When I stroll into the dining room, everyone from the Wilson family sits at the table. Mrs. Wilson smiles at me and waves me over to sit by her. I feel their eyes on me, which warms my cheeks.

"Lena, this is my husband, Mr. Wilson, and our son, Jamie," Mrs. Wilson introduces, her voice still nice.

Mr. Wilson nods and gives me a serious look like he's not too happy to see me. Jamie glares at me like I did something wrong.

"Great, another one," Jamie says, rolling his eyes. "As if we don't have enough problems already."

I shrink a little inside. Is this how it will be—people who don't want me here?

Mr. Wilson clears his throat and looks right at me. "I expect you to help out here, girl. We're not running a charity."

I nod, my voice almost a whisper. "Yes, sir."

While they talk, Mrs. Wilson's quiet, looking down at her plate. I can't help but think she might be scared of Mr. Wilson, too, just like I am.

Across from me, Talon's still staring at me without saying anything. It's like he's studying me, but it feels creepy, like he knows more than he's letting on.

The food goes mostly untouched, and silence fills the air except for the clanking of forks and spoons. I pick at my plate, not hungry, and try to ignore how mad Mr. Wilson and Jamie look.

After dinner, Mrs. Wilson gets up to clear the table. "Lena, why don't you head to your room and rest? You must be so tired after today," she suggests.

I nod, relieved to escape the awkwardness. When I head back upstairs, I can feel Talon's eyes on me again, making me think about the darkness that's hanging around in this house.

3

TALON

THIRTEEN YEARS OLD

Through narrowed eyes, I watch the new girl from my spot on the stairs. She's crossed-legged in front of the TV, her dark hair falling around her tiny shoulders like some innocent little halo while she colors in her book. She has a naive vibe, like she doesn't know what will hit her.

Heavy footsteps thud from the kitchen. Mr. Wilson's shadow stretches across the doorway, and I notice Lena tense up. Smart move. She's already picking up on the vibe but not learning fast enough.

"What're you doing there, girl?" His voice has that sharp edge that makes my jaw clench tight.

"Just coloring, sir," she says, sounding small and unsure.

"Shouldn't you be doing something useful? These floors won't sweep themselves!"

I grip the handrail, watching as she scrambles to

gather her stuff and drops her red crayon in a panic. It rolls under the couch, forgotten.

"I'm sorry. I'll clean right away." She almost trips over herself getting to the utility closet.

Mrs. Wilson appears behind Mr. Wilson, her smile so fake it could be used in a horror movie. "Now, dear, don't be too hard on her. She's still adjusting."

Yeah, right. I know her sweet act is just another weapon. I've seen how quickly it turns into something nasty when no one's looking.

Jamie stomps down the stairs, shoving into my shoulder on purpose. "Watch it, freak," he mutters.

I don't even flinch. My eyes stay locked on Lena, who's struggling to hold onto the broom that's too big for her. She doesn't belong here in this den of wolves. She's too pure, too untouched by the kind of darkness festering in these walls.

A week is all it took for the Wilsons to show their true colors. But Lena doesn't get it yet. She still believes Mrs. Wilson's fake nice touches and whispers mean something. She thinks Mr. Wilson's anger can be dodged if she's good, quiet, and useful enough.

But she doesn't realize that it will never be enough.

I lean back against the stairs, memories rushing in. Sarah was the first one—they had her broken in six months. I found her crying in the bathroom one night, blood dripping down her wrists. Then there was Maya, who tried to run three times before they sent her back. And Emma... Emma just faded into nothing over time, like a lightbulb burning out.

The broom gets snagged on the rug, and Lena stumbles. Her face goes red as Mr. Wilson scoffs from his armchair. She quickly rights herself, determination carved into her small frame as she keeps sweeping.

There's something different about her, though. The others would cry themselves to sleep, but Lena? She's quiet. I've seen her at dinner, how she watches everything, taking mental notes. The way her eyes narrow when Mrs. Wilson gives Jamie extra while we get scraps. The timing of her bathroom breaks to avoid Jamie's stupid pranks.

But will it be enough? This house has a way of smashing spirits, turning light into shadow. I've seen it happen too many times.

Mrs. Wilson walks past Lena, her heels clicking on the floor, not even looking at her. "Make sure you get under the furniture, dear," she says, her voice dripping with fake sweetness.

Lena drops down to her knees, peering under the couch. I catch a glimpse of defiance when she reaches for the red crayon, pocketing it instead of putting it away like Mrs. Wilson would expect.

Maybe this girl's got what it takes to stick around.

4

TALON

THIRTEEN YEARS OLD

One month later...

*L*ena dutifully scrubs the kitchen floor on her hands and knees. Her movements are already wearying, a resigned acceptance of her fate. I recognize that feeling. I've felt it myself ever since I can remember.

My parents never gave a shit about me. To them, I was a burden, an inconvenience. They neglected me, leaving me to fend for myself while they drowned themselves in booze and drugs. And when they did pay attention to me, it was only to unleash their rage. I learned quickly to make myself scarce and avoid them.

The few times I dared to reach out for help, I was met with indifference or disbelief. Adults are useless, untrustworthy. They only pretend to care, but they'd always look the other way when push comes to shove. I learned that the only person I could count on is myself.

So I've toughened up and built walls around my heart. Emotions are a weakness I couldn't afford. I've focused on survival, on making it through each day. The foster system wasn't much better than my parents' house. Different faces, same bullshit.

Lena still hasn't witnessed the true ugliness in this house. The Wilsons put on a good show, but beneath the surface, they're just as rotten as the rest. She'll learn, just like I did. She'll have to if she wants to survive.

I catch Mr. Wilson's glare from across the room. His beady eyes narrow as he takes in my idle stance, lips curling into a sneer. I brace myself, knowing what's coming.

"Get your lazy ass over here, boy!" he snarls, words slurred from drinking too much whiskey.

I stay rooted to the spot, not obeying. I've learned it's better to take the beating stoically than to show fear. It appears today that Lena will finally see Mr. Wilson's true colors.

He staggers toward me, fists clenched. The stench of stale booze wafts off him in thick waves. "You think you can just stand around while the rest of us do your work?"

The first blow catches me in the gut, knocking the wind out of me. I double over, gasping for air, but I don't make a sound. Never let them see you're hurting.

"Answer me, you worthless piece of shit!" Another punch, this time to my jaw.

I taste blood in my mouth but keep my eyes trained on the floor. Don't give him a reason to escalate things further.

From the corner of my eye, I see Lena. Her face is pale, eyes wide with horror. This is her first time witnessing Mr. Wilson's violence.

He grabs a fistful of my hair, yanking my head back. I'm forced to meet his bloodshot gaze, his breath hot and rancid on my face. "You're gonna learn some respect, boy."

The blows keep raining down, but I barely feel them anymore. I've endured worse, much worse. This is just another day in the life.

When he's finally spent, Mr. Wilson releases me with a shove. I crumple to the floor, ribs aching, blood trickling from my split lip. But my expression remains impassive, unflinching.

Lena's hands are trembling as she watches the aftermath.

I lay on the floor, blood pooling in my mouth, as Mr. Wilson's heavy footsteps retreat. The bastard will probably drink himself into a stupor, like always. I spit out a glob of blood and slowly push myself up, ignoring the pain shooting through my ribs.

That's when I see Lena approaching me, her eyes wide with concern. "Talon, are you okay? Let me help you."

She reaches out to me, but I jerk away from her touch. I don't need her pity or her help. I've survived worse than this on my own.

"Don't touch me," I growl, my voice low.

Lena flinches, hurt flashing across her face. "I... I just wanted to make sure you were alright."

I release a harsh laugh, the sound grating even to my

own ears. "Alright? You think anything about this is alright?"

I push myself to my feet, ignoring the way my body screams in protest. I stalk toward Lena, invading her personal space until she's forced to take a step back.

"Listen up, princess. This is the real world, not some fairy tale where everyone holds hands and sings kumbaya. The sooner you learn that, the better."

Lena's lower lip trembles, but she holds my gaze. "I know about the real world, but we could help each other. We don't have to be alone in this."

I scoff, shaking my head. "You don't get it, do you? There is no 'we.' There's only survival. You're on your own here, just like I am." I lean in closer, my voice dropping to a whisper. "You want my advice? Toughen up. Don't let them see you cry. Don't let them see you're hurting. They'll only use it against you."

Lena's eyes search mine as if trying to find some shred of humanity buried beneath the surface. She won't find any. I made sure to bury that weakness a long time ago.

"I'm sorry you've been hurt, Talon. But I won't believe that kindness is a weakness. It's better to be nice than mean."

I stare at her, marveling at her naivety. She still clings to hope, believing that people are inherently good. I almost envy her innocence.

Almost.

"You'll learn, Lena. You'll see the truth soon enough. And when you do, remember what I told you. Toughen up, or this place will eat you alive."

With that, I brush past her, leaving her alone in the kitchen. She'll have to find her own way, just like I did. There's no room for softness or sentiment in a place like this.

The only person you can count on is yourself.

5

LENA

NINE YEARS OLD

I walk quietly to where Talon is sitting alone in the backyard. His face looks hurt from what happened yesterday, and even though he seems cold and mean, I want to help him feel better. "Hey, Talon," I say softly as I sit beside him on the grass. "I'm sorry about what happened yesterday. Are you okay?"

He scoffs, turning his ice-blue eyes on me like a glare. "I don't need your pity, kid. Just leave me alone."

His words sting a bit, but I want to keep trying. "I just thought we could be friends," I say, hoping he won't be so mean.

Talon stands up suddenly, towering over me. "Listen, Lena, I don't do friends. I don't need anyone, especially not some little girl who thinks she can fix everything with a few kind words."

Tears well in my eyes, but I blink them away so he won't see me cry. "I was just trying to be nice," I mumble, my lip quivering.

"Well, don't bother. Nice gets you nowhere in this world." He walks away, leaving me all by myself.

I sit on the grass and hug my knees, feeling super lonely. I don't understand why Talon is so mean. I only want a friend to talk to and maybe even play with. But he just wants to push me away.

My heart feels heavy, and tears spill down my face while I think of my parents. I remember how my mom hugged me tight, and my dad made the silliest jokes that always made me giggle. And now they're gone forever, and I'm stuck in this strange place where nobody seems to care about me.

I miss my old school with its bright colors and friendly teachers. I think about my best friend, Emily, and how we used to whisper secrets to each other during recess. Ever since I got taken into foster care, I haven't been allowed to see any of my friends. I even miss the boys who pulled my pigtails. At least they were familiar faces in a world I understood.

Now, everything feels different. The Wilsons' house is cold, and it doesn't feel warm or welcoming at all. Mrs. Wilson barely even looks at me, and Mr. Wilson dislikes me. Jamie, their son, isn't around much. Then there's Talon, with his scary eyes and mean words that hurt my heart.

I try to hold back my tears and be strong, but the sadness feels too big. I bury my face in my hands, letting the sobs shake my shoulders as I cry and cry.

I don't know how long I sat there. My eyes feel all sore and puffy, and my throat hurts, but eventually, I'm just left empty and tired. I wipe my face with my hand and take a shaky breath to get it together.

Jamie clears his throat behind me. "You should be careful sitting out here doing nothing."

I swallow hard. Jamie isn't exactly friendly to me or Talon, but I notice he's meanest when he's with his father. "Why?" I ask.

He looks toward the house and then back at me. "If my dad sees you lounging around out here…" He trails off because we both know what happens. I'll get the same treatment Talon got yesterday.

I know I can't let Mr. Wilson see me like this; crying out here. I don't want him to think I'm weak or that he can pick on me more. It's become clear already that they don't like weakness.

I stand up, brush the grass off my jeans, and take deep breaths to calm myself down. "Why warn me?"

Jamie shrugs. "I know I'm mean to you sometimes, but it's what my father expects. He expects me to be on his side." I notice the way his shoulders slump. "The best thing to do is keep busy and try and stay out of his way."

"I'll remember that," I murmur before returning inside.

I know I can't let the Wilsons see me like this. I don't want them to think I'm weak or that they can pick on me more. It's become clear already that they don't like weakness. So I stand up, brush the grass off my jeans, and take deep breaths to calm myself down.

As I turn to go back inside, I catch a glimpse of Talon watching me from the kitchen window. I freeze for a second, and our eyes meet. I think I see a flicker of something in his gaze—maybe sympathy or understanding? But then he looks away, and the moment fades.

I lift my chin and walk back into the house, determined to find a way to get through this strange new life, even if it means being alone.

I try to be super quiet when I step inside, but I almost run right into Mr. Wilson when I turn the corner. He glares down at me, his eyes narrow, and his face gets all red like a volcano about to erupt.

"What were you doing outside, girl?" he growls, his voice dripping with angry words. "There are chores to be done in this house, and you're just wasting time!"

My heart races, and I stammer out an apology. "I-I'm sorry, Mr. Wilson. I just needed some air. I didn't mean to—"

But he interrupts me with a hard slap across my face that sends me stumbling backward. Tears spill out as I clutch my stinging cheek, too shocked to even cry out right away.

"You ungrateful little brat," he hisses, raising his hand again like he's going to hit me more. "I'll teach you to slack off."

I brace myself, expecting it to hurt again, but it doesn't happen. Instead, I hear a loud breath and a smack. I open my eyes and see Talon standing before me, looking all tense with his fists balled up at his sides.

"Leave her alone," he growls, his voice deep and protective. "She didn't do anything wrong."

Mr. Wilson's face turns an even darker shade of red, and he spins around to yell at Talon. "You dare to defy

26

me, boy?" he shouts, grabbing Talon by the collar. "I'll teach you respect!"

He pushes Talon against the wall, hitting him in the face hard. Talon grunts but doesn't cry. He just keeps his eyes glued to Mr. Wilson.

I'm frozen in shock, while Mr. Wilson repeatedly hits Talon. It feels like forever, and even though it's horrible, Talon just takes it. He's really tough, but it hurts me to see him getting hurt for me.

Finally, Mr. Wilson steps back, all huffy like he's just run a race. "Let that be a lesson to both of you," he spits, wiping his bloody knuckles. "Now get back to work."

He stomps away, leaving Talon and me alone in the hallway. I rush over to Talon, my hands hovering over his bruised face.

"Why did you do that?" I whisper, my voice shaky. "I thought you hated me. You told me to toughen up but jumped in to protect me twice. I don't get it."

Talon looks at me, and I see something I don't understand in his eyes. "I don't hate you, Lena," he says, wincing as he tries to sit up. "I just don't want you to get hurt."

I watch him walk away, his shoulders bent and fists clenched tight. I want to thank him for standing up for me, but the words get stuck in my throat. One minute, he's all cold and pushing me away, and the next, he's taking a beating for me. It's confusing.

I get to my feet, wincing because my cheek still hurts where Mr. Wilson slapped me. I remember that short moment when I thought he understood how I felt. Maybe Talon isn't just mean—maybe he's alone, too.

A tiny spark of hope fills my heart. Could he be my friend, after all? We could help each other in this scary new world. It won't be easy—Talon seems to want to keep me away, and I'm still so sad about my parents—but having someone who gets what I'm going through makes me feel a little better.

6

TALON

FOURTEEN YEARS OLD

One year later...

$\mathcal{I}$ watch Lena from across the yard as she hangs laundry, her dark hair catching the sunlight. A year has passed, yet she's still here, still standing. Most foster kids break within months under the Wilsons' abuse, but not her.

My ribs ache from last night's beating—another one I took in her place when Mr. Wilson caught her reading past curfew. The pain is familiar now, almost comforting. I've lost count of how often I've stepped between them, drawing his rage onto myself instead.

"You dropped some socks." Mrs. Wilson's saccharine voice drifts through the open window. Lena's shoulders tense, but she doesn't flinch like she used to. She's learned to weather the constant criticism.

I shift in my hiding spot behind the oak tree, ready to intervene if needed. This protective instinct confuses me. Jamie surprises me by grabbing the socks and taking them to Lena. He's one year younger than me and has always been a complete asshole. But, he seems to have a slight soft spot for Lena, even if he acts the part of bully when Mr. Wilson is around. And I don't understand why I hate seeing him talk to her as she gives him a shy but sweet smile.

I've never cared about anyone before—caring gets you hurt. Yet whenever Mr. Wilson raises his hand to her, my body moves all by itself.

The screen door creaks. Mr. Wilson stumbles out, reeking of whiskey even at this hour. My muscles coil as he approaches Lena. But she handles him perfectly— eyes down, voice soft, movements quick and efficient. She's learned the dance of survival.

Still, I stay close. Because even though she's stronger now, even though she's mastered the art of becoming invisible when needed, I can't risk it. Can't let them break her like they broke the others.

Perhaps it's because she still has light in her eyes despite everything. Or because she's the only one who's ever tried to reach past my walls. Or maybe I'm tired of watching things get destroyed in this hellhole.

Whatever the reason, I'll keep taking the hits. Keep standing between her and them. It's become as natural as breathing, this role of protector. Even if I don't understand why.

I trail behind Lena as she heads inside, keeping my footsteps silent. She pauses in the kitchen, reaching for a glass of water. Her small hand trembles slightly—after-effects of dealing with Mr. Wilson's drunken presence.

"You handled that well." My voice makes her jump, water splashing over the rim of her glass.

She turns, those hazel eyes widening. "I learned from watching you."

The words hit something raw inside me. I lean against the doorframe, maintaining distance as I want to move closer. "Good. Keep learning. Keep surviving."

"Why do you help me?" She sets the glass down, fidgeting with the hem of her dress. "You take beatings for me. But you never talk to me."

"Talking gets people hurt."

"Not talking hurts, too." Her chin lifts, defiant despite her fear. It's that spark that draws me, that refuses to die no matter what the Wilsons do.

I cross the kitchen, stopping beside her. She doesn't back away anymore, not like she used to. "Being alone is safer."

"Is it?" She looks up at me. "You're alone. Are you safe?"

The question catches me off guard. This ten-year-old girl sees too much and understands too deeply. It's dangerous. She's dangerous.

"Safer than caring about someone who'll end up broken or dead." I grab her glass, dumping the remaining water in the sink. "Stop trying to understand me, Lena. Stop trying to be my friend."

"I won't." Her voice is quiet but firm. "You're not as scary as you pretend to be."

"You should be scared of me." I turn back, towering over her small frame. "I'm not good, Lena." I step closer, forcing her to tilt her head back to maintain eye

31

contact. "There's nothing but darkness inside me. My parents made sure of that before I even got here."

Her small frame refuses to retreat despite my looming presence. The stubborn light in her eyes makes my jaw clench. She needs to understand—she needs to stay away.

"The things I've done, the things I'm capable of..." I grip the counter, knuckles white. "You think you know darkness because of the Wilsons? They're nothing. I've seen real monsters. Been shaped by them. Become one."

"You protect me," she whispers.

"Because I'm possessive. Obsessive. It's not kindness driving me—it's something darker." The truth spills out, raw and ugly. "When I hurt people, I enjoy it. When I take those beatings meant for you? Part of me loves the pain and craves it. That's not normal. That's not good."

"But—"

"No." I slam my hand on the counter, making her jump. "Stop trying to find light where there isn't any. I'm telling you what I am. A creature full of violence and rage. The only difference between me and them is that I've chosen you as mine to protect. That doesn't make me better. It makes me worse."

Her eyes shimmer with unshed tears, but she doesn't run. Still, she looks at me like I'm worth saving.

"You should fear me more than them," I growl. "Because at least they're honest about their cruelty. I hide mine behind protection. But it's still there, Lena. Always there. Growing stronger every day."

The innocence in her eyes cuts deeper than any of

Mr. Wilson's blows. She reaches for my hand, her small fingers barely covering my palm.

"We could help each other," Lena says, her voice carrying that childish hope I lost years ago. "Like... like when you share cookies at lunch. The hurt gets smaller when you share it."

My chest constricts. Such simple logic. Such dangerous thinking.

"You can't fix me, Lena." I pull my hand away. "I'm not some broken toy that needs putting back together. I was never whole to begin with."

"But—" She wrings her hands, searching for words too big for her ten-year-old vocabulary. "But you're nice to me. Even when you pretend not to be. And I could be nice back."

The urge to touch her face, to memorize every detail of her innocent expression, surges through me. That's exactly why I need to stay away. These possessive thoughts aren't normal—especially not toward a child. I'm fourteen, old enough to recognize the darkness of my obsession.

"Stop." I back away, forcing steel into my voice. "I'm not nice. I'm not your friend. And if you're smart, you'll keep your distance."

"But—"

"No." I cut her off, hating how my harsh tone makes her flinch. "This ends now. We're not having cookies together. We're not sharing our pain. We're not anything."

Tears well in her eyes, but I force myself to turn away. Every protective instinct screams at me to stay, to comfort her. But that's the problem. My version of protection is twisted, warped by years of abuse and neglect. She deserves better than my corrupted form of care.

I stride away. Behind me, I hear her quiet sniffle, and my fists clench. But I keep walking because the alternative—giving in to this obsessive need to possess and protect her—would destroy us both.

7

LENA

THIRTEEN YEARS OLD

Three years later…

The hallway bustles with high school drama, but I keep my head down, clutching my books. Four years with the Wilsons have taught me how to stay invisible.

"Hey, charity case!" Jessica Martin's shrill voice cuts through the crowd. "Where'd you get those shoes? The dumpster?"

Heat rises to my cheeks as I glance down at my worn sneakers. The other girls snicker, forming a circle around me.

"I heard her parents were drunks who crashed their car," one of them whispers loud enough for me to hear.

My throat tightens. "That's not true."

Jessica steps closer, her perfectly manicured nails reaching for my textbook. "What are you going to do about it, orphan?"

A shadow falls over us. The temperature in the hallway drops ten degrees.

"Back off." Talon's voice is quiet but carries an edge that makes Jessica's hand freeze mid-grab.

I don't need to turn around to know it's him. After four years, I can sense his presence like a storm rolling in.

Jessica's face pales. "We were just talking."

"No, you weren't." Talon takes another step forward, towering over her. His presence fills the space, dark and threatening. "Touch her again, and you'll regret it."

The girls scatter like leaves in the wind. Even the other students press against the lockers, giving him a wide berth. Nobody meets his eyes.

Talon doesn't look at me, but his hand brushes my shoulder as he passes. It's the closest thing to comfort he allows himself to show in public. The touch sends warmth through my body, chasing away the chill of Jessica's words.

I watch him disappear down the hallway, his tall frame cutting through the crowd like a knife. Other students whisper about him—the troubled foster kid, the one who gets into fights, the one to avoid. But they don't know him like I do. They don't see how he continues to take beatings meant for me or how he leaves half his dinner by my door on nights when Mr. Wilson sends me to bed hungry.

I lean against my locker, watching Talon's retreating form. The crowd parts for him like he's Moses, and they're the Red Sea. My heart still races from the confrontation, but a different kind of flutter takes over when I think about how he stepped in.

"Thank you," I whisper, knowing he can't hear me from this distance. But I'll tell him later like I always do. And like always, his response will be the same.

During lunch, I spot him at his usual table in the far corner of the cafeteria. No one sits within twenty feet of him. I slide into the seat across from him, pushing my apple toward his tray. This is the first time we've attended the same school, and I've only been here for a few weeks.

"You didn't have to do that this morning."

His blue eyes flash up at me, cold and distant. "Don't."

"Don't what?" I ask, even though I know Talon hates it whenever I thank him for anything.

"You know what. I don't need your thanks," he growls.

"But you keep protecting me. That means something."

"It means nothing." He pushes my apple back. "I do what I want when I want. Don't mistake it for kindness."

His constant pushing me away stings, but I've grown used to it. Talon may say he doesn't care or isn't one of the good guys, but I know deep down he's got a soft side.

"Whatever, you like me, really," I tease.

A muscle ticks in his jaw. "I've gotta stick up for you because you're my foster sister."

"I don't believe that's the only reason," I retort. "You

stand up for me *all the time*. Even at school. It means you care."

He glares at me. "I have my own reasons for my actions, not because I care."

"Which are?"

"Selfish ones." His voice drops lower, taking on that dangerous edge. "I'm not your guardian angel, Lena. The sooner you understand that, the better."

But I've seen the way his hands shake after defending me. I've noticed how he positions himself between me and danger without hesitation. There's something beneath that spiky exterior, which he wraps around himself like armor.

"I don't believe you," I say quietly.

His eyes meet mine, and something flickers in their depths for a split second—an emotion I can't name. Then it's gone, replaced by that familiar coldness.

"That's your first mistake." He stands, leaving his untouched lunch behind. "Don't make me prove you wrong."

The plastic lunch tray scrapes against the table as Angela drops into Talon's vacant seat. Her curly red hair bounces as she settles in, unwrapping her sandwich.

"What were you two talking about?" She takes a bite, watching me with curious green eyes.

I poke at my untouched apple. "Nothing, really. Just thanking him for this morning."

"What happened this morning?"

"Jessica Martin and her minions cornered me in the hallway. Started saying stuff about my parents." My fingers clench around the apple. "Talon stepped in and made them back off."

"Aww, that's so sweet!" Angela's face lights up. "He's your guardian, big brother, always looking out for you. Must be nice having someone protect you like that."

My stomach twists at her words. If she only knew what our home life was really like. The bruises Talon hides under his long sleeves. The sounds of Mr. Wilson's belt late at night.

"Yeah," I force a smile. "Like a brother."

But the word feels wrong on my tongue. Brother doesn't explain the electricity when his hand brushes mine. Brother doesn't account for how my heart races when our eyes lock. Brother definitely doesn't cover the dreams I've been having lately of him kissing me.

"You're so lucky," Angela continues, oblivious to my discomfort. "My brothers just pull my hair and steal my stuff. Talon actually keeps the bullies away."

I nod, not trusting myself to speak. How can I explain that Talon's protection feels nothing like brotherly love? That there's something more intense and taboo brewing between us?

But Angela wouldn't understand—no one would. So I let her believe what she wants while that forbidden truth burns in my chest like a secret flame.

8

TALON

EIGHTEEN YEARS OLD

One year later…

I lean against the lockers, my jaw clenching as I watch that pathetic freshman, Brad Thompson, hover around Lena. His letterman jacket marks him as one of those entitled jocks who think they own the school. The way he runs his fingers through his hair to impress her makes my blood boil.

Lena's grown so much these past few years. Her dark waves cascade down her back, and her smile lights up the hallway. That fierce spirit I saw in her as a child now radiates through every graceful movement. But the months are counting down until I graduate. Until I'm no longer here to protect her from scumbags like Brad or assholes like Jessica Martin.

Brad steps closer to her, and my fingers curl into fists. He has no right to breathe her air, let alone try to make her laugh. I know his type—seen plenty of them come and go through the foster system. All charm on the surface, rot underneath.

"Come on, just one date," Brad says, blocking Lena's path to her next class. "Friday night, after the game?"

My vision blurs red at the edges. I imagine wrapping my hands around his throat, watching the light fade from his eyes. It would be so easy. One quick move behind the bleachers after practice...

But I can't. Not just because it would draw attention but because of her. Lena's fourteen—still so young, still finding her way. And I'm eighteen now, practically a man. These feelings I have, this possessive rage that consumes me when others get close to her—I have to control it for her sake.

I watch her give him attitude as she confidently declines Brad's invitation and heads to class. My chest aches with a familiar mix of pride and pain. She's blossomed into a confident, strong woman I can't help but care for. The Wilsons have tried to break her, but she's unbreakable. In four months, I'll have to leave high school and the thought of not being near her tears me apart.

For now, I memorize every detail of her—how she tucks her hair behind her ear, how her bag bumps against the curve of her hip as she walks. I'll carry these images with me when I go.

Later that day, I walk the hallway after the last bell, tracking Brad's movements. The idiot isn't giving up. He corners Lena by her locker, his hand against the metal beside her head.

"Just one date. Stop playing hard to get." His voice carries down the hall.

"I said no." Lena's voice is sharp and defiant.

My feet move before I can think. In three strides, I'm there, yanking Brad back by his collar. He stumbles, face draining of color when he sees me.

"She said no." I lean close, letting him see the darkness in my eyes. "Leave."

Brad scrambles away, nearly tripping over his own feet. Pathetic.

"I didn't need your help." Lena slams her locker shut, glaring at me. Gone is that sweet little girl who used to follow me, trying to "save my soul." Now she's all fire and spite. Ever since she turned thirteen, things changed between us.

"Really? Looked like you needed it to me, princess."

Her eyes narrow at the nickname. "Stop calling me that. And stop acting like my guardian angel. You don't need to be my protector anymore, Talon."

I step closer, backing her against the lockers. "No? Then why do I keep chasing off guys who have the hots for you?"

"Because you're a controlling asshole who can't mind his own business." She tilts her chin up, defiant. The gesture sends a thrill through me.

"Better an asshole than a naive little girl who thinks she can handle everything alone."

"Fuck you." She tries to push past me, but I don't budge.

"Such language, princess. What would Mrs. Wilson say?"

Her cheeks flush with anger. It's intoxicating, watching her lose control like this. The fiercer she gets, the more I want to push her buttons.

"Get out of my way," she hisses.

I lean down until my lips nearly brush her ear. "Make me."

Her sharp intake of breath hits my ears like a drug. I pull back just enough to study her face, catching how her pupils expand in those mesmerizing hazel eyes. The hallway feels electric, charged with something dangerous and raw.

My body cages her against the lockers, close enough to catch the scent of her strawberry shampoo. The same cheap brand Mrs. Wilson has begrudgingly bought for her since she arrived. The familiarity of it twists something deep in my gut.

"Not so brave now, are you, princess?" I trace one finger along her jawline, then the column of her neck, feeling her pulse race beneath my touch. Her skin is soft, perfect. Everything about her is perfect.

She tries to maintain that fierce glare, but I see right through it. See the way her breath catches, how her lips part slightly. The darkness that lives in me calls to something hidden deep inside her, something equally as dark.

"I hate you," she whispers, but there's no conviction. Her eyes drop to my mouth for a fraction of a second.

"No, you don't." I lean closer, letting my breath fan across her face. "You're afraid of how much you don't hate me."

Her fingers curl into the fabric of my shirt, but she doesn't push me away. Instead, she holds on like she's drowning. Like I'm both the waves pulling her under and the life vest keeping her afloat.

The desire rolling off her is intoxicating. It matches the hunger that has eaten me alive ever since I became aware she's not that little girl anymore—ever since I noticed how she'd grown into this fierce, beautiful creature that haunts my every waking moment.

I rip myself away from her, my hands clenched with the effort it takes. Every cell in my body screams to go back, to claim what's mine. But she's fourteen. Just fourteen. Reality hits me like ice water.

"Talon?" Her voice is small, confused.

I can't look at her. Can't trust myself if I do. My feet carry me down the empty hallway, each step feeling like I'm dragging lead weights. The exit sign glows red ahead, matching the haze of want clouding my vision.

The metal door slams behind me as I burst into the parking lot. Cold air bites at my face, but it's not enough to cool the fire under my skin. I slam my fist into the brick wall, welcoming the sharp pain that shoots up my arm. Again. And again. Until blood trickles down my knuckles.

Four years. Four fucking years until she's eighteen. The thought of anyone else touching her before then makes me want to burn this whole town to the ground. But I can't touch her. If I do, I'll destroy her. Turn her into something as twisted and broken as me.

My bloody hand leaves a smear on my bike handles as I pedal out of the parking lot. I don't look over my shoulder. Don't check to see if she followed me out. I just cycle, pushing myself as fast as I can, trying to outrun the memory of her pulse racing under my touch.

9

TALON

EIGHTEEN YEARS OLD

Three months later…

Two weeks. Fourteen days until I graduate and have to leave my princess behind. My locker door creaks as I slam it shut, jaw clenched at the thought.

Lena's strong—stronger than anyone gives her credit for. But the idea of leaving her here with these animals is infuriating. Especially that piece of shit, Brad, who can't handle rejection like a man.

Speak of the devil. His voice carries down the hall, that smug tone that makes me want to break his jaw.

"Look who it is, boys, the resident cock tease."

My fingers curl into fists. Through the crowd, I glimpse Lena trying to hurry past Brad and his crew of mindless followers.

"What's wrong, slut? Too good to say hello?" Brad's hand shoots out, grabbing her backpack.

The world goes red. Before I realize I'm moving, my feet carry me through the crowd. Brad's smirk disappears when my fist connects with his face. The satisfying crunch of cartilage fills my ears as blood sprouts from his nose.

"Touch her again, and I'll break more than your nose." My voice comes out in a growl as I tower over him.

Brad's friends charge forward like rabid dogs. "You're dead, freak!"

James's fist flies at my face. I catch it mid-swing, twisting until bones crack. The owner howls. Good. Pain is what they deserve for threatening what's mine.

Derek tackles me from behind. We hit the lockers with a metallic clang. My elbow snaps back, connecting with his solar plexus. As he doubles over gasping, I grab his hair and slam his face into my rising knee.

Aaron, the last one standing, circles, looking for an opening. "Fucking psycho!"

My lips curl into a snarl. The rage pumps through my veins like poison, demanding blood. I welcome it. This is who I am—what I am. A monster wearing human skin.

He throws a wild haymaker. Amateur. I duck under and drive my fist into his kidney. Once. Twice. Three times until he crumples.

Brad tries crawling away, leaving a trail of blood from his nose. I stalk after him, every muscle coiled tight. The crowd parts like water, their fear tangible.

"Please..." he whimpers.

My boot connects with his ribs. The crack echoes through the silent hallway. "I warned you."

Another kick. His pitiful attempts to shield himself only fuel my fury. How dare he touch her? How dare any of them look at her?

"Talon, stop!"

Lena's voice cuts through the haze. My fist freezes mid-swing, Brad's collar twisted in my other hand. Her small fingers wrap around my arm, and reality comes crashing back.

Four bodies on the ground. Blood on my knuckles. Teachers shouting in the distance.

"They're not worth it," she whispers.

I release Brad, watching him scramble away like the coward he is. The rage still burns, demanding more violence, more pain. But Lena's touch anchors me, keeping the monster at bay.

Mrs. Reynolds's shrill voice pierces through the hallway. "What in God's name is going on here?"

The crowd scatters like roaches, leaving me standing over Brad's whimpering form. My knuckles throb, sticky with his blood. Worth it.

"All of you. Principal's office. Now." Her face pales as she takes in the carnage—Brad's broken nose, Derek clutching his ribs, James nursing his arm, and Aaron barely conscious.

Lena's hand slips from my arm. The loss of contact sends the rage surging back, but I force it down. Can't lose control again.

"Mr. Voss, help Mr. Thompson up." Mrs. Reynolds's voice shakes.

I bare my teeth. "He can crawl there himself."

Brad flinches when I step over him. Pathetic. His friends stumble to their feet, using the lockers for support. They give me a wide berth as we trudge toward the office.

Principal Matthews is going to have a field day with this. Four against one, and I'm the only one without a mark on me, except for these bloody knuckles that prove exactly what I did to them.

The walk feels endless. Every step echoes with Mrs. Reynolds's heels clicking behind us. Lena follows, too, probably to give her statement. My chest tightens because this is the first time she's witnessed this side of me. The monster I try so hard to cage.

But they touched her. Threatened her. The rage builds again, demanding more violence.

I flex my fingers, watching the blood crack and flake. Two weeks until graduation. Two weeks until I have to leave. And now, I might not even make it that far.

Worth it. They'll think twice before going near her again.

Brad stumbles, and I resist kicking his legs out from under him. Mrs. Reynolds clears her throat nervously. Smart woman. She knows what I'm capable of now.

We reach the principal's office, and she gestures to us inside. "Sit. All of you."

I claim the chair furthest from the others, my bloody hands resting in plain sight on my lap. Let them see. Let them remember.

LENA

FOURTEEN YEARS OLD

I stand beside Talon outside Principal Matthews's office, my heart racing. Blood stains his knuckles, his chest rising and falling with each breath. The image of him destroying those guys plays over in my mind—the raw power, the violence, the way his muscles flexed as he threw each punch. Heat rushes to my face.

"You shouldn't have done that." My voice comes out breathier than intended.

His blue eyes lock onto mine, dark and intense. "They deserved worse."

A shiver runs through me. I squeeze my thighs together, ashamed of how my body responds to his protective rage. He's my foster brother. These feelings are wrong on so many levels.

"Two weeks suspension." He wipes his bloody knuckles on his jeans. "Could've been worse."

"Matthews is giving you a chance to graduate." I

lean against the wall, needing its support. "You're lucky."

"Lucky?" He steps closer, towering over me. His scent—sweat and something darker—fills my lungs. "Those assholes threatened you. They're the lucky ones that I didn't—" He cuts himself off, jaw clenching.

My skin prickles with awareness. I've noticed these reactions more lately—the way my pulse quickens when he's near, how I catch myself staring at his lips, the heat that pools low in my belly when he gets protective.

The tension in the hallway thickens as we wait. My foster parents' muffled voices drift through Principal Matthews's door, mixing with his stern tone. Talon's presence burns against my skin—he's close, too close, yet not close enough.

"They'll blame me for this." I wrap my arms around myself, fighting a shiver when his fingers brush my elbow.

"No." His voice drops lower, turning rougher. "I won't let them."

I turn to face him, my back against the wall. A mistake. His broad chest blocks my view of the hallway, caging me in. My breath catches as his palm presses flat against the wall beside my head.

"Talon—"

"Don't." The muscle in his jaw ticks. His gaze drops to my lips, then snaps away. He pushes off the wall, creating distance between us. "Just don't."

The loss of his warmth hits like a physical blow. I hate how my body craves his proximity, how my skin tingles where he almost touched me. He runs a hand through his dark hair, messing it further.

"You're only fourteen," he mutters, more to himself than me.

Heat floods my cheeks. We never acknowledge this thing between us—this electric current that charges the air whenever we're alone. He's eighteen, legally an adult. I watch his shoulders bunch under his shirt as he paces, three steps away, three steps back.

The door handle rattles. Talon freezes mid-step, his expression shuttering closed. Mr. Wilson's voice grows clearer as he approaches the door. My foster brother shoots me one last heated look before moving further away, leaving me trembling against the wall.

The office door swings open. Mr. Wilson's face is red with rage as he storms out, followed by Mrs. Wilson wringing her hands. Principal Matthews stands in the doorway, his expression grim.

"We'll make sure he understands the gravity of his actions," Mr. Wilson says, his voice dripping with barely contained fury.

My stomach twists. I know that tone—it used to precede the worst beatings. But something's different now. Mr. Wilson's hands shake as he gestures at Talon, and he keeps his distance. The memory of those bullies' broken bodies flashes through my mind.

Talon towers over our foster father, his shoulders broad, arms corded with muscle. The last time Mr. Wilson tried to hit him was over a year ago. The bruises on Mr. Wilson's ribs took weeks to fade.

Mrs. Wilson touches her husband's arm. "Richard, perhaps we should—"

"Shut up, Margaret." He jerks away from her, but his eyes never leave Talon. There's fear there, buried under the anger. He's realized what I already know—Talon could kill him with his bare hands.

Talon stands perfectly still, but tension radiates from every line of his body. His eyes are cold, calculating, fixed on Mr. Wilson's throat. The air crackles with violence, waiting to explode.

"Let's go," Mr. Wilson barks, but he backs away first, creating distance between himself and Talon. His attempt at authority falls flat, undermined by his obvious fear.

I hold my breath, watching Talon's face. Will this be the day he snaps? The day he finally gives Mr. Wilson what he deserves? Part of me hopes he does, which terrifies me more than anything.

11

LENA

FIFTEEN YEARS OLD

One year later…

The fluorescent lights of JJ's Grocery Store buzz overhead as Angela, Kelly, and Helen toss snacks into our cart. I trail behind them, my heart racing every time we turn down a new aisle.

"We need chips. The good ones, not those cheap knock-offs," Kelly says, pushing her blonde hair behind her ear.

"And don't forget ice cream." Helen grabs a bag of M&Ms. "Movie night needs chocolate."

I scan the store, catching glimpses of dark hair and broad shoulders stocking shelves. Talon. My stomach twists.

"Earth to Lena." Angela waves her hand in front of my face. "You've been quiet."

"Just tired." I force a smile.

We round the corner to the chip aisle, and there he

is. Talon's muscles flex under his black t-shirt as he arranges bags on the shelves.

"Oh my God, he's so hot," Kelly whispers. "That's your foster brother, right?"

I nod, unable to speak. Talon's eyes flick our way for a fraction of a second before returning to his task. No acknowledgment. No hint of recognition. Just like every time I've seen him this past year. Despite aging out of the system, he rents a room from the Wilsons. God knows why considering they still treat him like shit and overcharge him for the room, which he's rarely even in. And when he is at the house, he's like a ghost.

"He used to be different," I mumble.

"What do you mean?" Helen asks.

How can I explain the way he used to look at me? The electricity when our eyes met across a room? For a while now, I haven't looked at Talon as a brother. Especially as I got older and started to have dreams about him—sinful dreams. My stomach flutters even though I know it's wrong. We've grown up in the same house as kids, but I guess being in such an abusive situation has twisted me up in ways I never imagined.

"Let's just get the chips and go." I grab two bags of Doritos and toss them in the cart.

As we pass him, his shoulder brushes mine. The contact sends sparks through my body, but Talon doesn't flinch. He might as well be stocking shelves next to a stranger.

"Cool Ranch? Really?" Angela examines my chip choice, oblivious to my internal turmoil. "Get the Nacho Cheese ones instead."

I let them drag me toward the checkout, but I can't shake the chill of Talon's indifference. The boy who once warned me to fear him more than anyone else now acts like I don't exist.

"Wait!" I call to my friends. "I forgot the French onion dip."

Angela rolls her eyes. "Hurry up. We're next in line."

I sprint down the aisle, my shoes squeaking against the linoleum floor. As I round the corner, I slam into what feels like a brick wall. Strong hands grip my shoulders to steady me, and I look up into piercing blue eyes.

Talon.

My breath stalls in my throat. This close, I catch his familiar scent—pine and a scent that's uniquely him. His hands drop from my shoulders like I've burned him.

"Hey," I whisper, the word escaping before I can stop it.

He grunts, jaw clenched, and steps back.

"Why are you being like this?" The question bursts out of me. "You won't even look at me anymore."

Talon's silence stretches between us like razor wire. His cold, unreadable eyes bore into mine.

"What do you want me to be like?" His voice comes out low.

Heat floods my cheeks as memories of that day at school flash through my mind—his body pressing me against the lockers, his breath hot on my neck, the way my heart raced. I drop my gaze to the floor, unable to meet his eyes.

"I—" The words stick in my throat. How can I tell him I miss his protection? That the house feels emptier, colder without him there the way he used to be? That Mr. Wilson's fists find me more often now?

I tug at my sleeve, a nervous habit I've developed to hide the evidence of Wilson's anger. But Talon catches the movement. His hand shoots out, gripping my wrist. I wince as his fingers brush against fresh bruises.

He yanks up my sleeve, exposing the mottled purple and yellow marks that paint my skin. A growl rumbles deep in his chest, animalistic and raw. His grip tightens, and tremors run through his body.

"He did this?" The words come out between clenched teeth.

I try to pull away, but he holds me firm. "It's nothing. I dropped a plate and—"

"Don't lie to me." His fingers trace the distinct shape of fingerprints wrapped around my wrist. "Mr. Wilson did this because I wasn't there."

"Yes." The admission comes out barely above a whisper. "He's gotten worse since you stopped being around."

Talon's face contorts with regret, his fingers gentling on my wrist. "I'm sorry, Lena. I never meant for this to happen to you."

"It's not your fault." I step closer, drawn to his warmth like a moth to a flame. "You've aged out of the system, so… I get it. You're on your own."

I shrug. I guess he's lucky the Wilsons still let him call their house "home," even though the government checks for fostering Talon stopped when he turned eighteen.

His thumb traces circles on my pulse point. The

fluorescent lights cast shadows across his face, high-lighting the sharp angles of his jaw. The air between us crackles with unspoken words and suppressed feelings.

"Why aren't you home at least sometimes, anyway?" I search his eyes, desperate for answers. "I barely see you."

Talon drops my wrist and takes a step back, breaking our connection. "I pick up every extra shift I can get here. Need the money."

"What for?"

"Saving up." He runs a hand through his dark hair. "As soon as I have enough, I'm leaving."

The words hit me like a physical blow. Leaving. Talon's leaving. My chest tightens at the thought of facing the Wilsons alone all day, every day, of living in that house without his presence lurking in the shadows.

"Oh." It's all I can manage past the lump in my throat.

"Lena! What's taking so long?" Angela's voice cuts through the tension. She appears at the end of the aisle, hands on her hips. "We're waiting at checkout."

My cheeks burn. "Sorry! I got distracted."

I glance back at Talon, whose expression has hard-ened into that familiar mask of indifference. "I'll see you around."

He doesn't respond. His blue eyes track my move-ments as I grab the French onion dip from the shelf. My fingers tremble as I clutch the container to my chest and hurry toward the checkout, feeling the weight of his stare on my back until I round the corner.

12

LENA

SIXTEEN YEARS OLD

Ten months later...

The day I turn sixteen, I wake up to the familiar silence that has become the norm in the Wilson household. There are no cheerful birthday greetings, no presents waiting to be unwrapped, just the heavy weight of another year gone by, another milestone reached without my parents by my side. When Jamie was still here, he had given me a hand-drawn card each year, but he's been at college now for a year and rarely visits.

I spend the morning going through the motions, doing my chores, and trying not to dwell on the ache in my chest. As evening falls, I retreat to my room, curling up on my bed and hugging my knees to my chest. A soft knock at the door startles me, and I quickly swipe at the tears on my cheeks.

"Come in," I call out, my voice thick with emotion.

To my surprise, the door opens, and Talon enters the room. He's graduated high school, yet he's agreed to rent a room from Mr. Wilson at a ridiculous rate. Why he stays, I'll never understand.

He looks as brooding as ever, but there's something different in his expression, a flicker of hesitation that's unusual for him.

"What do you want?" I ask, unable to keep the defensiveness from creeping into my tone.

Talon crosses the room and sits on the edge of my bed, his movements slow and deliberate. Finally, he reaches into his pocket and pulls out a small object, holding it out to me.

It's a delicately carved bird, intricately detailed and clearly handmade. I stare at it, my breath catching in my throat.

"For your birthday," Talon says gruffly, his gaze fixed on the ornament. "I made it."

Slowly, I reach out and take the ornament from him. Our fingers brush together, and a spark shoots through me. It's the same every time we accidentally touch, not that I see him very often.

Gazing down at the ornament, I realize that Talon crafted it himself, that he put time and effort into creating something for me, and I feel a warmth I haven't felt in years.

Tears prick my eyes, and I blink rapidly, trying to hold them back. Talon's jaw tightens, and he leans forward, eyes boring into mine.

"Don't cry," he says, his voice low and intense. "Be strong for me, Lena."

His words should sound harsh, but an undercurrent of concern, maybe even affection, beneath them catches me off guard. I nod, swallowing hard and clutching the ornament tightly.

At that moment, despite the years of aloof detachment from him, I feel a deeper, more emotional connection with Talon that I haven't experienced before. A shared understanding of what it means to be alone, to have suffered loss and hardship. And in his own way, he's offering me a lifeline, a reminder that I'm not entirely alone in this world.

I meet his gaze, my heart pounding in my chest. "Thank you, Talon," I whisper, pouring every ounce of sincerity into those two simple words.

He steps closer, and suddenly, it feels like all the air in the room is gone. My heart pounds harder and faster.

I stare at the intricately carved bird in my hand, marveling at the delicate details Talon managed to capture. It's a testament to his skill and dedication, and the fact that he made this for my birthday sends a flutter through my chest.

I glance at him, taking in his appearance. In the past year, Talon has changed. He's taller now, his shoulders broader, and his features have a roughness that wasn't there before. But what catches my eye are the tattoos peeking out from beneath his shirt sleeves.

"When did you get those?" I ask, gesturing to the ink adorning his skin.

Talon shrugs, a smirk playing at the corner of his mouth. "A while ago. The Wilsons don't know."

I can imagine their reaction if they found out. They're strict and conservative, and tattoos don't fit into their idea of proper behavior.

"They suit you," I say, my cheeks heating.

Talon looks amused, and he leans in closer, his gaze intense. "You think so?"

I nod, my heart hammering in my chest. There's a tension between us, a crackling energy that makes me clench my thighs together. For a while now, I've seen Talon in a light no foster sister should see her foster brother. Dreams haunt me of his touch on my skin, his lips on mine. It's both thrilling and terrifying.

I feel my breath catch in my throat as Talon leans in even closer, his eyes dark and intense. The air between us is charged with a tension I can't quite name. I've never been this close to him before, never noticed the flecks of gold in his blue eyes or the way his lips curve into a smirk.

It's wrong; I know it is. Talon is my foster brother, someone I've grown up with since I was nine, someone I should see as family. But at this moment, with his gaze locked on mine and his presence overwhelming my senses, I can't deny the attraction that simmers beneath the surface.

Talon reaches out, his fingers brushing against my cheek. His touch is electric, sending sparks through my veins. I know I should pull away and put some distance between us, but I find myself leaning into his touch instead.

"Lena," he murmurs. "Do you feel it, too?"

I swallow hard, my mouth suddenly dry. I know

what he's asking, what he's implying. And as much as I want to deny it, to push him away and pretend this moment never happened, I can't lie to myself any longer.

"Yes," I whisper, my voice barely audible over my heart pounding. "I feel it."

Talon's eyes darken, and he leans in even closer, his breath ghosting over my lips. For a moment, I think he will kiss me, and a part of me wants him to. But instead, he pulls back, a small smile tugging at the edge of his mouth.

"Happy birthday, Lena," he says softly before standing up and walking out of the room, leaving me alone with my racing thoughts and the lingering heat of his touch on my skin.

I look down at the little bird in my hand, tracing my finger over its smooth, polished surface. It's the most beautiful thing I've ever seen, a tiny piece of art crafted just for me. And it came from Talon, the boy who has always been so cold and distant, who seems to hate the world and everyone in it.

But maybe he doesn't hate me. Maybe, in his own way, he cares.

13

TALON

TWENTY YEARS OLD

One month later…

$\mathcal{I}$ watch Lena from the shadows, my eyes never straying far from her delicate form. She moves through the house, her steps light and graceful, even as she carries out the endless chores our foster parents assign her. I can see the strain in the set of her shoulders, the weary resignation in the downcast tilt of her head. But beneath that docile exterior, I know there burns a fierce determination.

Lena may play the obedient foster child, but I've seen the small acts of rebellion: how she lingers too long in the bathroom, savoring each rare moment of solitude, and the defiant tilt of her chin when Mrs. Wilson berates her. And I can't help but admire her spirit, her refusal to be broken by the cruelty of our surroundings.

It's that same stubborn resilience that draws me to her. I should keep my distance to avoid the inevitable pain of caring for another human being. But Lena...Lena is different. She's a beacon in the darkness, a fragile yet unyielding light that calls to the deepest, most primal part of me.

So I watch, and I wait, and I plan. I've learned to navigate the shadows, blend in, and observe without paying attention to myself. And slowly, methodically, I begin to insert myself into Lena's life, offering her small, unexpected kindnesses.

A stolen chocolate bar was left on her pillow. A gentle touch that lingers just a fraction too long when I pass her in the hallway. Subtle glances that convey an unspoken understanding, a silent promise that she is not alone in this hell we call home.

I know my actions confuse her, that the contrast between my harsh words and these tender gestures must seem jarring. But I can't help myself.

So I continue to lurk in the shadows, watching, waiting, biding my time. Because one day, Lena will understand. She'll see the depths of my devotion and my love's ferocity. And when that day comes, I'll be there, ready to claim her as my own.

The shrill sound of Mrs. Wilson's voice grates on my nerves. For some unknown reason she's calling us down to dinner, even though we never have dinner together. I brace myself, steeling my expression into an impassive mask before heading to the dining room. The sight that greets me makes my blood boil. Mrs. Wilson's friends, the Collins family, are here. A perfectly coiffed couple with sickly-sweet smiles plastered across their faces. And beside them, their son. David.

I study him through narrowed eyes, taking in the arrogant set of his broad shoulders and how his gaze lingers a little too long on Lena's curves. He's exactly the type of entitled prick I despise—rich, cocky, and undoubtedly used to getting his way.

But the calculating gleam in Mrs. Wilson's eyes truly sets me on edge. I've seen that look before how she sizes people up and makes her plans. And as her gaze flits between Lena and David, the realization hits me.

They're trying to set them up.

Lena's only just hit the legal age of consent in Massachusetts, and they're trying to set her up with a scumbag like David.

A low growl rumbles in my chest as possessive fury claws through my veins. How dare they? How dare they parade Lena in front of this pompous asshole as if she's a prize to be won?

The darkness swirls within me, an inky, viscous thing threatening to consume me whole. My fingers curl into fists as I fight the urge to lash out and tear this charade apart with my bare hands.

Because Lena is mine.

She may not understand the depths of my obsession, but that doesn't change the reality of its existence. It's why I'm still living under the Wilsons' roof. Why I'm handing over half my paycheck to an asshole who spent years beating me, and now that I'm too big for him, he has turned his attention to Lena when I'm not around. From the moment I first saw her, a scared, vulnerable girl thrust into this hellish existence, she became the center of my universe.

Mrs. Wilson's grating voice cuts through the tension like a dull knife. "Lena, David, you two probably have so much in common. Why don't you sit together at the table?"

She gestures for Lena to sit beside that smug bastard, David. I can see the hesitation flicker across Lena's delicate features as she eyes the empty chair. Her lips part, no doubt to protest, but one stern look from Mrs. Wilson has her mouth snapping shut.

Glowering at Mrs. Wilson, she hesitates and places her hands on her hips. When she doesn't sit, Mr. Wilson moves to stand and she immediately sinks into her chair, the fear of what he might do driving her. But I don't miss how her shoulders hunch inward ever so slightly, bracing herself. Nor do I miss the way David's gaze rakes over her petite form, his eyes lingering on the gentle swell of her breasts beneath her modest sweater.

Rage surges through me, a white-hot inferno that sears my veins. How dare he look at her like that? Like she's just another pretty little thing to be leered at and devoured. Lena is no one's plaything. She's too pure, too precious for the likes of an arrogant prick like David Collins.

I dig my nails into my palms to keep from launching across the table and wiping that look off his face. The sharp sting of broken skin does little to dull the anger coursing through me.

David leans closer, his bulky frame practically dwarfing Lena's slight figure. "So, Lena," he drawls, his voice dripping with an arrogance that makes me want to vomit. "I hear you like reading."

Lena tenses and her knuckles whiten as her hands clench. "I do, yes."

"That's cute." David chuckles, the sound grating on my ears. "You could read me a bedtime story sometime."

The implication in his words is clear, and bile rises in my throat. I can see how Lena shrinks away from him, her cheeks flushing with embarrassment and discomfort.

Anger and something else, something darker and more primal, swirls within me. I have this all-consuming need to protect her from people like David. My fingers itch to reach across the table and wrap around his neck, to squeeze until that lecherous grin is wiped clean off his smug face and he's no longer breathing.

Instead, I remain still, my body taut as a bowstring as I watch the scene unfold. Lena may not realize it yet, but she needs me. Needs someone to keep the monsters at bay, to guard her light from being snuffed out.

And I will be that someone. No matter what it takes, I'll ensure her safety and happiness, even if it means embracing the darkness within myself and giving in to the twisted desires that churn in the depths of my soul.

Because Lena Graves is mine. And I'll be damned if I let anyone, especially some entitled prick like David Collins, lay a single finger on her.

LENA

SEVENTEEN YEARS OLD

Eleven months later…

$\mathcal{I}$ sit beside David in the darkened movie theater, trying to focus on the film. His arm rests on my seat, and I catch the scent of his expensive cologne. He's attractive, the kind of guy any girl would want—successful, from a good family, interested in me. I should feel lucky.

But my thoughts keep drifting to Talon. The way his blue eyes pierce through me. The bird ornament he gave me one year ago is still perched on my dresser. The electricity whenever we're close.

David's hand slides onto my thigh, jolting me from my thoughts. I shift uncomfortably. After a rather awkward meeting eleven months ago around the dinner table at the Wilsons and constant badgering from Mrs. Wilson, I've finally agreed to a date with him.

"David, stop," I whisper, moving his hand away.

He chuckles softly, his fingers creeping back. "Come on, baby. No one can see."

My stomach churns. "I said no." I keep my voice firm but quiet.

His grip tightens, fingers digging into my leg as his hand moves higher. The movie's dialogue fades to background noise as panic rises in my chest.

"David, please." I grab his wrist, but he's stronger.

"Don't be such a prude," he hisses in my ear. "Your foster parents want us together. You should be grateful I'm interested in you at all."

His words sting, but the fear overwhelms the hurt. I try to stand, but his other hand clamps down on my shoulder, keeping me in place. The darkness that once felt cozy now feels suffocating. Other moviegoers remain oblivious, absorbed in the film playing before us.

"Stop it," I say again, louder this time. A few heads turn in our direction.

David's fingers dig deeper into my shoulder. "Shut up and sit still," he growls, his charming facade completely gone.

I freeze as David's hand slides higher, my throat tight with fear and disgust. Tears burn behind my eyes as I realize he won't listen to me.

A shadow falls over us. I look up to see Talon's tall frame, his presence commanding even in the darkness.

"We're leaving." His voice is low but sharp.

David's hand stills on my thigh. "Back off. This is none of your business."

"Get your hands off her." Talon's words carry deadly intent.

"She's my girlfriend. You're just some foster kid who—"

"Shut up!" Someone behind us whispers harshly.

"Yeah, keep it down," another voice adds.

Talon's hand wraps around my arm, yanking me to my feet. David tries to hold onto me, but Talon's grip is stronger. He pulls me past the other seated viewers, ignoring their grumbled complaints.

"You can't just take her," David whisper-shouts after us.

"Watch me," Talon growls back, leading me up the theater steps.

I stumble beside him, relief flooding through me as we escape the suffocating darkness of the theater. My legs shake with each step, but Talon's firm grip keeps me moving forward.

The cool night air hits my face as we exit the theater. My heart still pounds from what happened inside. Talon's grip on my arm loosens, but he keeps me close as we walk toward his black car.

"How did you find me?" My voice trembles.

"I'll always find you, Lena." His blue eyes lock onto mine, intense and unwavering. "Always."

He opens the passenger door, and I slide into the leather seat. The car smells like him—a mix of pine and leather. Talon gets in beside me, his presence filling the small space. His knuckles are white on the steering wheel.

"Were you watching the movie too?" I ask, rubbing my arms where David's touch still burns. "I didn't see you inside."

"No." His jaw clenches. "I wasn't inside."

"Then how—"

"Does it matter?" He cuts me off, turning to face me. The streetlight catches his profile, highlighting the sharp angles of his face. Electricity crackles between us in the confined space. I can't look away from him.

"You were following me," I whisper, the realization hitting me. Something warm unfurls in my chest at the thought.

"Following. Watching." His voice is rough. "Call it what you want."

My breath catches as his hand reaches across the console, fingers ghosting over where David grabbed my thigh. Unlike David's forceful grip, the touch is gentle but sends sparks through my entire body.

"I saw what he did to you," Talon growls. "How he put his hands on you like he had the right. It took every ounce of my self-control not to snap his wrist right then and there."

His eyes meet mine, smoldering with a dangerous intensity. "I'll always be watching, Lena. I'll be the shadow that follows you, the whisper in the dark that keeps you safe. And if anyone tries to lay a finger on you again, they'll have to answer to me."

"For how long?" I ask, knowing that Talon has been working to save up enough to leave, or at least, that's what he says. It still doesn't make sense. He could sleep in his car for a month or two to get enough for a deposit on a place. Instead, he's stuck in an abusive home where he used to be beaten on the regular. Mr. Wilson won't dare raise a hand to him now, not with how stacked out he is.

Talon's hand drops from my thigh, and he leans back in his seat. The loss of his touch leaves me cold.

"If you mean me getting enough to move out, the Wilsons are making it impossible." His fingers drum against the steering wheel. "Takes more than half my paycheck for 'rent.' I owe him for all the years he put up with me, even though the state paid for my 'care.'"

"That's not fair." I shift in my seat to face him. "You're barely making minimum wage at the grocery store. Why don't you just leave?"

"Life isn't fair, Lena." He turns those piercing blue eyes on me. "You and I, we've seen the worst of it. The Wilsons are just another reminder that the world doesn't care about people like us."

"There has to be something—"

"Listen to me," he interrupts. "I know what they're capable of. They'll break you down, piece by piece, until there's nothing left. And they'll enjoy every fucking minute of it."

He leans closer. "I won't let that happen to you. I've been saving up and planning my escape. And when I'm ready, I'm taking you with me. We'll leave this shithole behind and never look back."

His hand finds mine, his calloused fingers intertwining with my own. "But until then, we have to be smart. We have to play their game, even if it kills us inside. Because the alternative..." He trails off with a haunted look. "Trust me, Lena. You don't want to know what they'll do if they think you're trying to cross them."

The silence stretches between us, heavy with unspoken words. Through the windshield, I watch a couple exit the theater, holding hands and laughing. They look carefree and normal. Everything we're not.

"How much have you saved?" I ask.

"I've only got fifteen hundred saved so far. There should be thousands by now, but..." He shakes his head. "Whenever I get close, Mr. Wilson finds a reason to take more. Broken window, damaged furniture, missing food."

"But you didn't—"

"It doesn't matter if I did or didn't. His house, his rules." Talon's knuckles whiten on the steering wheel. "And he knows exactly what he's doing."

I gently place my hand on Talon's thigh, wanting to comfort and show him he's not alone. The gesture feels natural, right—like my hand belongs there.

His entire body goes rigid. The muscles beneath my palm tense, hard as steel. His jaw clenches, the sharp line of it more pronounced in the dim light. His knuckles whiten further on the steering wheel, and I hear the leather creak under his grip.

My breath catches as I notice the growing bulge in his jeans right beside my hand. Heat floods my cheeks, but I can't look away. The air in the car becomes thick, charged with electricity.

"Lena," he says, his voice rough and strained. "Move your hand."

I should listen. Should pull away. But something keeps my hand in place, my fingers curling slightly into the denim of his jeans.

"Why?" I whisper.

His chest rises and falls with rapid breaths. "Because if you don't, I might do something we'll both regret."

The haunting tone of his voice awakens something deep inside me that I've tried to ignore.

"What if I don't regret it?" The words slip out before I can stop them.

Talon's head snaps toward me, his blue eyes blazing. The streetlight catches his face, highlighting the sharp angles of his features.

My hand trembles on his thigh, but I don't move it. "I turned seventeen last month."

"You're still too young." Talon's voice comes out strained, his muscles taut beneath my touch.

"The age of consent in Massachusetts is sixteen." Heat floods my cheeks at my boldness, but I press on. "I looked it up."

His head turns sharply toward me, those piercing blue eyes searching my face. "You looked it up?"

"Yes." My heart pounds so hard I wonder if he can hear it. "I wanted to know... for us."

"For us," he repeats, his voice dropping lower. "You've thought about this."

"Haven't you?"

The silence stretches between us, charged with years of unspoken desire. His hand covers mine on his thigh but doesn't push it away.

"Every day for longer than you know," he admits roughly. "That's why I've been distant. I couldn't trust myself around you."

My breath catches at his confession. All this time, I thought he was being distant because he didn't care.

"I'm not a kid anymore," I whisper.

"No. You're not." Talon's hand tightens over mine, but then he gently lifts it off his thigh. The loss of contact leaves me cold.

"We can't," he says, his voice rough. "Not yet."

"Why not?" I hate how young and petulant I sound. "I told you, I'm legal—"

"This isn't about legality, Lena." He turns in his seat to face me fully. "You're seventeen. Your hormones are driving you right now, making you think you want this."

"That's not true." I cross my arms over my chest. "I know what I want."

"Do you?" His blue eyes pin me in place. "Do you understand what it means to be with someone like me? Someone broken?"

I swallow hard. "I'm not afraid of your jagged edges."

"You should be." He leans closer, his presence overwhelming in the confined space. "If we cross that line, if I let myself have you, I'll never let you go. You'll be mine completely, corrupted by me. There won't be any going back."

His words send a shiver down my spine—part fear, part desire.

"I need you to wait," he continues. "Until you're eighteen. Give yourself time to really think about what you're asking for. What you're willing to give up."

"And if I still want this when I'm eighteen?"

His eyes darken. "Then nothing will stop me from making you mine."

The intensity in his voice makes my breath catch. I want to argue, to convince him I'm ready now, but I see the resolve in his expression.

"Fine," I whisper. "I'll think about it."

"Good girl." He pulls back onto the road, breaking the tension between us. "Now, let's get you home."

"One condition," I say, my heart racing. "Kiss me now."

Talon's eyes narrow. "Lena..."

"I want you to be my first kiss." I twist in the seat to face him fully. "Not David or some other guy. You."

His jaw clenches the muscle ticking. "That's not a good idea."

"Please." I lean closer, emboldened by the desire I see flickering in his eyes. "I don't want anyone else to take this from me."

A low groan escapes him like he's in physical pain. "You're making this very difficult."

"Good." I reach for his hand. "So, is that a yes?"

His fingers thread through my hair, gripping the back of my head. The touch sends electricity down my spine. His eyes lock onto mine, intense and burning.

"Just one kiss," he growls.

Then his mouth crashes into mine and it feels like the world stands still. His lips are firm and demanding, claiming me with a possessiveness that makes me gasp as a shock travels straight to my core.

He takes advantage of my parted lips, deepening the

kiss. And it feels like my entire body is burning from the inside out as his tongue tangles with mine.

I grip his shirt, pulling him closer as the sensation between my legs heightens. He tastes like mint and something more addictive. His hand tightens in my hair, tilting my head to get a better angle.

A whimper escapes me as my core throbs, and he groans in response. The sound vibrates through me, and then he bites my lip hard enough to draw blood before licking it.

"Fuck," he groans. "Mine. All fucking mine." His kiss deepens as if he's trying to imprint himself on me. Mark me as his forever, and I want that. I've never been so desperate in my entire life for something. What, I'm not sure. I'm aching deep within.

This is nothing like I imagined a first kiss would be. It's not sweet, gentle, or tentative. It's consuming, passionate, almost violent in its intensity. Talon kisses my neck and then sucks hard like he's trying to mark me, brand me, make sure I'll never want anyone else's lips on mine.

And he's succeeding.

I break away from the kiss, gasping for air. My whole body thrums with an unfamiliar energy, a pulsing need centered between my thighs that makes me squirm in my seat. My lips feel swollen, tingling from the pressure of his kiss.

Talon's breathing comes in heavy pants, his chest rising and falling rapidly. His blue eyes are dark, pupils blown wide with desire. I can't help but notice the prominent bulge in his jeans. He groans, running a hand over it.

"Fuck," he swears under his breath, shifting in his seat.

My cheeks burn hot, but I can't look away. The knowledge that I affect him strongly sends another wave of heat through my body. My heart pounds so hard I'm sure he can hear it in the confined space of the car.

The tension between us is thick enough to cut with a knife. Every breath feels charged with electricity. I press my thighs together, trying to ease the unfamiliar ache there.

"We need to stop," Talon says through gritted teeth, though he makes no move to start the car. "This is already more than I should have allowed."

"A deal's a deal," I say, my voice still shaky from the kiss. "I'll wait until I'm eighteen to decide."

Talon nods, adjusting in the seat.

"But I want you to know something." I gather my courage, heart pounding against my ribs. "I'm saving myself for you. Only you."

His breath catches, and those intense blue eyes lock onto mine. "Don't make promises you can't keep."

"I mean it." I touch my lips, still tingling from his kiss. "After that... I'll never want anyone else. Not David, not any other guy. Just you."

A low growl rumbles in his chest. "You don't know what you're saying."

"I do." I meet his gaze steadily. "That kiss proved everything I've been feeling. Everything I want."

Talon's jaw clenches as he turns the key in the ignition. The engine roars to life, breaking the heated silence between us. He shifts the car into drive, his movements precise and controlled. And we return to the Wilsons' house in charged silence, everything between us altered forever.

15

LENA

SEVENTEEN

Two months later…

I creep down the hallway, my heart pounding as I approach the living room. The muffled voices of the Wilsons drift out from behind the closed door, their words laced with disdain.

"That boy is nothing but trouble. An absolute disgrace covered in tattoos. He's twenty-one now, and it's time he gets out of here." Mr. Wilson's gruff tone sends a chill down my spine.

"I don't know how long we can keep him under control," Mrs. Wilson replies. "He's becoming more and more unhinged."

My stomach twists with fear. They can't send Talon away. Not when I've finally started to see him in a different light. I need to do something. Sighing heavily, I turn and head toward Talon's room.

I take a deep breath and push open the door, stepping into Talon's dimly lit room.

He sits on the edge of his bed, his gaze fixed on the floor. At the sound of my footsteps, he lifts his head, piercing blue eyes locking onto mine.

"Lena," he murmurs, his voice low and rough. "What are you doing here?"

I swallow hard, suddenly acutely aware of how his muscles ripple beneath his shirt. Ever since our kiss, I can hardly look at him without my pussy getting wet. "I heard the Wilsons talking. They want to kick you out, Talon."

He arches one dark brow. "And so what if they do?"

I take a step closer, my fingers twisting nervously in the hem of my shirt. "I don't want them to send you away. I—" My voice trails off, the words catching in my throat.

Talon rises from the bed, his movements fluid and graceful. He towers over me, his presence filling the small space. "You what, Lena? Can't stop thinking about our kiss?" he questions.

The air crackles with tension, and I find myself captivated by the intensity of his gaze. "I... I want you to stay. We made a deal. Once I'm eighteen," I whisper.

Talon's lips curl into a slow smile. "We did. But if they kick me out before, it won't change a thing." He takes a step closer, and the warmth of his body radiates towards me. "They can't keep us apart, princess."

I stand there, paralyzed by his closeness, his intensity. A part of me wants to shrink away, to put distance between us. But another part, a deeper, darker part, longs to lean in closer, to lose myself in the depths of his eyes.

"Do you promise?" I stammer, hating how my voice trembles with uncertainty.

Talon reaches out, his calloused fingers brushing a stray lock of hair from my face. "I swear to you that nothing on this earth can keep me away from you."

I fight against the dizzying effect of his touch. "Talon," I breathe his name, almost moan it.

He takes another step closer, backing me up against the wall. "Yes, princess?" he murmurs, his lips almost brushing mine. "What do you want?"

Heat floods my cheeks as I meet his piercing gaze. "Kiss me again, please," I demand.

His jaw clenches. "Lena," he says my name in a warning tone, but I'm so needy for him. I wake most mornings panting his name. And if he doesn't kiss me again soon, it feels like I'll combust.

"Please," I push.

His lips brush against mine barely as he shuts his eyes and growls softly. "This is a bad idea. Do you know how fucking close I am to snapping?"

I lick my lips, wanting him to snap and give me what I want.

"No, Lena," he says, pushing away from me. "We made a deal. You stick to it. Got it?"

His refusal hurts, even though I know he doesn't want to touch me until I'm eighteen. Talon must see the hurt in my eyes because his expression softens slightly. "I won't risk it until you're eighteen. The age of consent may be sixteen, but you know how much sway Mr.

Wilson has in this town. He's got a buddy at the precinct, and if Mr. Wilson told him I touched you when you were seventeen, he'd try to say I groomed you or something."

He's right. The Wilson family has a lot of connections in Salem, and I know it's the kind of thing Mr. Wilson would do. "You're right," I admit.

His jaw clenches. "I overheard them also."

Confusion washes over me as I stare at him. "Overheard them saying what?"

He draws in a deep breath. "I overheard the Wilsons talking to the Collins family about you and David's engagement."

Engaged? To David Collins?

I've gone on a few dates with him since the movie theatre because Mrs. Wilson insisted. And thankfully, I've been able to ward off his continued sexual advances. But I assumed I'd be free of him when I left for college since I secured a full-ride scholarship to MIT.

"That can't be right," I stammer. "I would never agree to that."

Talon laughs. "You really think they care what you want, Lena?" He grabs my hips hard, the sensation sending a bolt of lightning to my core.

I know they don't care. Mrs. Wilson wouldn't care if I told her how David always tries to make a move on me, even when I say no.

"Once I've graduated high school, I've aged out of the system and don't have to answer to them. How do they expect to force me to marry David?"

Talon's gaze hardens. "I don't know exactly," he admits. "But I know the Wilsons, and they will have some way of making you do what they want. Maybe they'll find a way to use your scholarship at MIT against you."

I open my mouth to protest, but Talon speaks first.

"Don't try to tell me they wouldn't do that," he says. "I heard it with my own ears. Your future is sealed."

Tears spill down my cheeks as the weight of his words settles over me. Trapped. That's what I am. A prisoner in my own life, with no say in my own future.

Talon's expression softens ever so slightly as he takes in my distress. "Hey," he murmurs, brushing the tears from my cheeks. "It's not too late. I told you I'll take you away once I've saved enough. I'm in line for assistant manager at JJ's, so I'll earn more."

I blink up at him, my heart fluttering with fear and hope. "You want me to leave with you still?"

The corner of Talon's mouth curves upward in a crooked smile. "Of course. We can start over somewhere new, somewhere they can't control us." He pauses, his gaze boring into mine. "Just you and me, Lena. Together."

I stare at him, unblinking. Leave everything behind? With Talon? The idea is equally terrifying and exhilarating, and I am drawn to his promise of freedom.

Before I can respond, Talon leans in closer, his lips a breath away from mine. "I want you by my side, Lena," he whispers, his voice sending a shiver of anticipation through me.

And with that, he pulls away, leaving me trembling

and utterly confused, torn between the life I've grown comfortable with and the tantalizing promise of something new, something dangerous...something with Talon.

I stare at Talon, my heart racing as I process his words. Should I leave everything behind? Should I start a new life with him?

But as much as I long for freedom, for a chance to escape the suffocating control of the Wilsons, I can't just run away. I'm going to MIT. I have my whole future in front of me.

"It depends when you leave," I whisper, my voice trembling as I force the words out. "I can't leave everything behind before finishing high school."

Talon's eyes flicker with anger. "So even if they kick me out before then, you'll stay?" he growls. "If you stay here, they'll only use you."

"I... I know," I whisper, my voice barely audible. "But I need...I need time to think. To figure out what I want."

Talon scoffs. "You're a fool, Lena," he spits, his words cutting deep. "You think you have a choice in any of this? You think they'll ever let you be free?"

I swallow hard. "I have to believe that there's another way. I can find a path that doesn't involve running away or giving in to their demands."

Talon stares at me for a long moment, his eyes boring into mine. "Fine," he says. "Have it your way. But don't come crying to me when they break you. When you realize the only way out is the one I offered you."

With that, he strides out of his own room, leaving

me alone with my heart aching. I know he's right on some level. Staying here means subjecting myself to the Wilsons' control for a future I never wanted.

But I can't bring myself to take the leap, to abandon everything I've worked for. Not yet. Not until I've exhausted every other option.

With a heavy sigh, I return to my room, my mind whirling with the implications of Talon's revelation and the weight of the choice that lies before me.

16

TALON

TWENTY-TWO YEARS OLD

Ten months later...

*L*ena is eighteen now.

I'm close to having enough money to get us out of here; whether she agrees to come with me is another matter, especially since she was not up for it when I suggested it ten months ago.

Another year of saving since we first kissed and a promotion to assistant manager at JJ's means I've accumulated the measly sum of four thousand dollars. It's enough to strike out on our own, and I'll find a job quickly wherever we go.

It's been three days since Lena's birthday. Thankfully, the Wilsons have gone on vacation out of state to visit family, leaving us alone.

I'm sure Lena's been thinking about the deal we struck. She's eighteen now, and it's hard to stop my mind wandering to all the dirty and depraved things I want to do to my little foster sister.

I watch Lena fidget with the hem of her shirt, her brow furrowed with worry. "Are you still planning to leave?" she asks, her voice small and uncertain.

I lean against the kitchen counter, crossing my arms over my chest. "I told you, I'm saving up enough money from my job at the grocery store. Once I have enough, I'm out of here."

Lena's shoulders slump, and she bites her lower lip. "But I thought... I thought you'd stay. For me."

I sigh, running a hand through my hair. "Lena, we've been over this. I can't stay here forever. The Wilsons are toxic, and I need to get away before they destroy me completely."

I watch Lena shift in her seat, her fingers twisting in her lap. The silence stretches between us, thick with tension.

"About our deal..." she whispers.

My cock twitches at her words. I've been waiting for her to bring this up since her birthday three days ago. "What about it?"

"I'm eighteen now."

I push off from the counter and stalk toward her. Her breath catches as I lean down, caging her between my arms against the kitchen table. "Are you saying you still want me to fuck you?"

Her cheeks flush pink. "Yes."

I drag my fingers along her jaw, tilting her face up. "You have no idea what you're asking for. The things I want to do to you would break most people."

"I'm not most people."

A dark laugh escapes me. "No, you're not. You're mine." I grip her chin harder. "But once I have you, there's no going back. I'll corrupt every innocent part of you. Mark you. Ruin you for anyone else."

Her pupils dilate, and it drives me fucking insane.

"I've thought about bending you over this table countless times. Watched you doing dishes, imagining how pretty you'd look with my hand around your throat while I fuck you senseless." I lean closer, my lips brushing her ear. "Is that what you want, Lena? To be destroyed by your psychotic foster brother?"

She shivers against me. "Yes."

"Say it properly."

"I want you to fuck me, Talon."

The taboo nature of our relationship only fuels my desire. She's off-limits, forbidden fruit, and I can't resist the temptation.

"Talon, I—" Her breath hitches as I press my body against hers.

"I will, but not right now." I want to draw this out and savor our forbidden desire in every torturous moment.

Lena's eyes widen at my response, her chest rising and falling sharply. She wants this, but I'm going to make her wait.

I step back, holding her gaze. "Come with me."

Confusion flickers in her eyes, but she follows obediently. I lead her to her bedroom, a place I've invaded so often without her knowledge. I close the door behind us, relishing the privacy. I spot a pair of her dirty panties crumpled on the floor and smirk.

I can feel Lena's eyes on me as I bend down to pick them up, inhaling her unique scent. It's heady and musky, filling my lungs and making my cock even harder.

Lena's breath catches, her cheeks flaming red as she realizes what I'm doing. I see the moment her eyes drop to the bulge in my pants, her gaze raking over me with a mix of desire and uncertainty.

"You have no idea how many times I've imagined this," I confess, my voice hoarse as I climb onto her bed. I kick off my shoes and loosen my belt, freeing my straining cock.

Lena watches, rapt, as I wrap her panties around my length, stroking myself slowly. "I'd imagine what it would be like to finally give in. For me to slide into that tight, innocent pussy of yours." I remember the countless nights I've tortured myself like this.

"Did you ever touch yourself with my underwear?" Lena's voice is barely a whisper.

I chuckle darkly. "So many times. I'd inhale your scent and imagine you were riding my cock." I lick my lips, keeping my eyes locked on hers as I stroke myself faster, the fabric of her panties soft against my skin. "You have no idea how much I've fantasized about defiling that sweet body of yours."

"Have you ever touched yourself thinking about me?"

Lena's eyes flicker with a mixture of desire and hesitation. I can practically hear the wheels turning in her head as she considers her response.

"Tell me the truth," I growl, my patience waning.

She takes a deep breath, her gaze dropping to the floor. "Yes."

Hearing that word leave her mouth sends a bolt of arousal straight to my cock. I'm rock hard, aching to be inside her.

"Show me," I command.

Lena's eyes widen, her face flushing a deep crimson. She shakes her head, her voice barely above a whisper. "I—I can't."

I climb off the bed and step toward her, relishing the fear and desire warring in her eyes. "You can, and you will." I place a hand on her hip, my thumb grazing the soft skin of her lower back. "Get on the bed and show me how you touch yourself when you think of me."

Lena bites her lip, hesitating momentarily before slowly lying on the bed. Her eyes are fixed on my cock, the tip glistening with pre-cum.

"Close your eyes," I instruct.

She does as she's told, her chest rising and falling rapidly.

"Now, show me," I demand.

Lena's hands tremble as she reaches down between her legs, her fingers ghosting over the fabric of her shorts. A whimper escapes her lips, and her hips buck involuntarily.

"That's it," I encourage, my voice low and rough. "Such a good girl."

Lena's fingers slip under the waistband of her shorts

to drag them down along with her panties, her breath hitching as she touches her bare skin. She moans, a soft, breathy sound that goes straight to my cock.

I watch, utterly transfixed, as she reveals her tight, pink cunt. Her fingers tease her clit, circling it slowly.

Her hips buck off the bed, and she throws her head back, losing herself in the sensation. "Talon," she moans.

My name falling from her lips is my undoing. I step forward, gripping her hips and pulling her to the edge of the bed. And then I kneel down so my head is between her thighs.

"You're so fucking beautiful," I murmur, my breath ghosting over her sensitive skin. "I've imagined tasting you so many times."

Lena whimpers, her hips bucking involuntarily as I blow warm air over her swollen clit. "Please, Talon," she begs.

I chuckle darkly, relishing her desperation. "I've fantasized about this moment countless times. Wondering what you'd look like, spread out beneath me, begging." I run my tongue along her slit, relishing the sweet taste of her arousal.

Lena moans, her hands tangling in my hair as she tries to pull me closer. I growl in response, my hands gripping her thighs tightly.

"Not so fast," I warn, my voice husky. "I plan to savor every inch of you."

I lick her slowly, teasingly, from her entrance to her clit, delighting in the way her body trembles beneath my tongue. I hum in appreciation, the vibration sending her bucking against me.

"Oh God, Talon," she cries, her hips arching off the bed. "Please, more."

I chuckle, my breath hot against her sensitive skin. "You have no idea how good you taste, Lena. Like the sweetest candy." I lick her again, my tongue teasing her clit. "I could feast on you all day."

Lena whimpers, her fingers tightening in my hair. "Please, I need——"

I suck her clit into my mouth, swirling my tongue around it, and her hips buck wildly. "Yes, just like that," she moans.

I suck harder, my tongue working relentlessly as I drive her closer to the edge. Her breath comes in sharp gasps, her body tensing as she teeters closer and closer to the precipice.

"Come for me, Lena," I command, my mouth never leaving her core. "Let me taste you."

Lena cries out, her body arching off the bed as her orgasm washes over her. I moan in response, the vibrations of my voice sending her even higher. Her juices coat my tongue, and I groan in satisfaction, utterly addicted to the taste of her.

I continue to lick her slowly, drawing out her pleasure, until her body finally relaxes, spent. I kiss her inner thighs gently, my hands caressing her soft skin.

Lena lies there, breathless and dazed, her chest rising and falling rapidly. "Oh my God, Talon," she whispers.

I smirk up at her, my lips glistening with her arousal. "Your brother's good with his tongue, huh?"

Lena whimpers, her cheeks flushed with a mix of shame and desire. "Yes," she whispers, her voice thick with need. "You're so good at that."

I chuckle, my thumb brushing her swollen lower lip. "You haven't seen anything yet, princess." I climb up her body and kiss her quickly, allowing her to taste herself on my tongue. And then, I pull away. "Sweet dreams."

I slip out of Lena's room, my body still humming with satisfaction. I should feel guilt, remorse, or, at the very least, a sense of shame for what transpired. But all I feel is a deep, primal satisfaction. She's mine now, marked by my touch, my tongue.

Returning to my room, I know she'll have conflicting emotions. She'll regret what we did, especially since it's so taboo. She'll question her morals, values, and desire for me. But I won't let her push me away, not ever.

The Wilsons are gone for the week, leaving Lena and me alone in this house. It's the perfect opportunity to explore the simmering tension between us. I won't let her deny what's building between us any longer. She may feel like it wrong, twisted, or sick, but it doesn't change the facts. She wants me as much as I want her.

I want her cherry. Her first time should be with me, not some douchebag who won't appreciate her the way I do. I know she's thought about it, fantasized about me taking her virginity. I've seen the longing in her eyes when she looks at me, the desire that flames in her cheeks.

I'll start slow, seducing her with soft touches and whispered words, and then I'll take her. I won't stop

until I've claimed every inch of her body, marked her as mine.

Lena's a smart girl, and she'll likely regret giving in to me. But I'm not giving her a choice this time. I won't be gentle or kind. I'll take what's mine by force if I have to.

Because underneath that innocent exterior, Lena's a wildcat, and I intend to unleash her. I'll show her the darkness within; once she embraces it, she'll be mine forever.

Sweet dreams, Lena. Tomorrow, your life changes forever.

LENA

*M*y body is heavy with sleep as I wake with a start. The events of last night play in my mind. The careful plan we devised together in secret, the thrill of anticipation, and then...the act itself. I curl my fingers around the bedsheet, feeling excitement and unease.

Was it a mistake? I'd wanted it, craved it even, but now...now, I can't shake the feeling that we're teetering on the edge of something dangerous. My body still hums with the memory of Talon's touch and our shared intimacy. A part of me yearns for more and wants him to claim me fully and make me his. But there's a voice of caution whispering in my ear, warning of the potential consequences.

I bury myself under the covers, hoping to escape the dilemma by hiding from the morning light. But my quiet refuge is soon disrupted by a familiar knock. Talon enters, clad only in boxer briefs. My gaze drops, and I see the outline of his erection, prominent and demanding. I'm shocked by his boldness and the raw desire it ignites.

My mouth goes dry as I take in his form, every muscle sculpted by years of enduring silent abuse. And now, despite my lingering doubts, I want to explore every inch of him.

He strides toward me, each step confident and purposeful. His gaze holds mine, challenging, alluring. This is Talon, always pushing boundaries, always unafraid. He stands tall even in the face of our foster parents' wrath. And now, here he is, offering himself to me.

I swallow hard, fighting the urge to look away. My heart pounds in my chest as I realize the power I hold now. I could accept him, embrace our shared darkness, or step back, reigniting our tension.

"Are you ready, princess?" he asks, his voice laced with challenge.

"What for?" I ask, feigning ignorance. I already know the answer, but I want to hear him say it.

A slow, confident smirk spreads across his face, and a spark of triumph glints in his eyes. "You know what for, Lena."

My pulse quickens as he hooks his thumbs under the elastic of his boxer briefs and pushes them down just enough to free his cock. It springs out, hard, veiny and thick.

My breath catches in my throat as heat coils low in my belly. A familiar ache pulses between my legs, and I shift uncomfortably, feeling vulnerable and exposed. My body betrays me, yearning for something I've never experienced.

I glance up at his face, searching for a sign of hesitation, a hint that this is all moving too fast. But his expression is impassive, his eyes fixed on me.

Without speaking, he steps closer, his intent clear. Warmth radiates from his body along with the scent of his skin, a mix of musk and something uniquely him. He towers over me, powerful and commanding, a force of nature that cannot be stopped.

My mouth waters, and my rational mind fades into the background. I need to feel him inside me, stretching me, claiming me as his own. I don't care that it's my first time or that I'm still unsure where this leaves us. My body has a mind of its own, and it craves Talon.

"I'm ready," I whisper, my voice trembling with anticipation. "I want you to be my first."

A deep growl rumbles in Talon's chest. "And you'll be mine."

I freeze, processing his words. "What? But I thought..."

"You thought wrong." His blue eyes lock onto mine with fierce intensity. "It's always been you, Lena. Only you. I've been waiting."

My heart pounds against my ribs. All this time, I'd assumed... The boys at school used to talk about Talon's conquests, about how many girls he'd been with. But they were wrong. He'd been saving himself, just like me.

"But last night..." I trail off, remembering how skillfully his mouth had worked between my legs. "You seemed to know exactly what you were doing."

A dark smile plays across his lips. "I made sure I knew how to please you. Studied everything there is to know about making you feel good." His fingers trace along my collarbone. "But no, I've never tasted another woman before you."

The possessiveness in his voice sends shivers down my spine. Everything about him—his touch, words, and presence—speaks of ownership. And somehow, that knowledge that I'm the only one he's ever wanted this way makes me want him even more.

"Then prove it," I demand, my eyes daring him to do it. I'm trembling, unsure if it's from anticipation or fear. I'm inviting something wild and untamed into my life—something that might consume me entirely.

Talon doesn't reply; he simply grabs my wrists and pushes me back onto the bed. I land with a soft bounce, my hair cascading around me. His eyes burn with desire as he takes in the sight of me splayed out before him.

"God, you're beautiful," he murmurs, his voice rough with need.

His gaze rakes over my body, and I feel it like a physical touch. I want to cover myself, but I force my hands to stay by my sides. This is what I asked for, what I wanted. I will not shy away now.

He leans over me, and his lips hover just above mine for a moment. I catch my breath, expecting a kiss, but instead, he speaks, his warm breath ghosting over my lips. "You want me, Lena?"

"Yes," I whisper, meeting his eyes. "I want you."

"Say it again," he commands, his voice low and demanding.

"I want you," I repeat, my voice stronger this time.

"Good." His lips curve into a wicked grin. "But the question is, can you take me?"

My heart pounds as he finally releases my wrists, and his hands wander over me. He traces the strap of my tank top, his eyes never leaving mine.

His fingers find the hem, and he pulls it over my head, leaving me bare from the waist up. I resist the urge to cover my breasts, feeling vulnerable but strangely powerful at the same time. Talon's eyes move hungrily over my exposed skin.

He leans in, his lips brushing mine, but then he pulls back. "Are you sure about this, Lena? Once I'm inside you, there's no going back."

I swallow, my throat dry. "I'm sure," I say. "I want you to take my virginity, Talon."

He groans at that, and all restraint seems to leave him. He moves his body over mine, his erection pressing against my core. "Then take me, baby," he growls.

His mouth crushes down on mine, stealing my breath away. I moan into the kiss as he grips my hips, grinding his length against my damp panties. My body moves with his, begging for friction, for release.

His lips trail kisses along my jaw and neck until he reaches the sensitive spot above my collarbone. I arch my back, offering myself to him, needing more. His mouth latches onto the tender skin, sucking gently as his hands slip under my panties. With one swift motion, he rips them off, baring me to his gaze.

"So fucking beautiful," he murmurs, his breath hot against my skin.

Talon hovers over me, his eyes blazing with a fierce light that sends shivers down my spine. Desire pools low in my belly as I feel his hardness against my core. His mouth, fierce and demanding, covers mine, and I moan into the kiss. His tongue tangles with mine, tasting heat and need, stoking the flames burning inside me.

I'm aching, throbbing for him, and when he pulls away, I feel a moment of loss. But then he teases my earlobe with his teeth, his breath hot against my skin. "You have no idea how long I've wanted this," he growls. "How many nights I've dreamed of having you beneath me, soft and willing."

His words send a rush of liquid heat between my legs, and I shift beneath him, longing for relief. Talon chuckles a sound that seems to vibrate through my core. His hand reaches down, his fingers stroking my sensitive clit, gently at first and then more firmly. I cry out, the pleasure shooting through me like lightning.

"Please..." I don't even know what I'm begging for, but I need something to ease this sweet torture.

Talon doesn't answer with words. Instead, he begins to move against me, his hard cock sliding against my wetness. His precum mixes with my arousal, providing just enough lubrication as he rubs himself over my swollen clit.

I moan, my back arching off the bed as sensation after sensation washes over me. His movements are deliberate and purposeful, driving me to the edge and then pulling back, teasing me with the promise of release. I'm gasping, clawing at his back, desperate for more.

"That's it, baby," he whispers, his lips brushing my ear. "Come for me."

His words push me over the edge, and my body convulses, wave after wave of pleasure crashing over me. I cry out, my voice hoarse with need, my body shaking.

He continues to thrust against my clit as my orgasm washes over me.

"You ready for the main event, princess?" Talon's voice is gravelly, his eyes focused on mine. I feel his hard length pressing against me, and my breath catches in my throat.

"Yeah," I breathe, suddenly nervous. This is it—the moment I cross the point of no return. Once he takes my virginity, I know a part of me will belong to him forever. Even if we go our separate ways, I'll never forget him.

He chuckles, his breath hot against my ear. "You sure about that? Because once I've had you, I'll never be able to stop."

I sink my teeth into my bottom lip, my eyes flitting to his. "That's what I want," I whisper.

A feral grin stretches across his face, and he grips my hips, holding me in place. "Hold tight, baby, because I'm not holding back."

My heart stutters in my chest as I brace myself for his invasion. I feel the thick head of his cock pressing against my entrance, and I suck in a breath. This is it.

With a low growl that sounds more animal than human, Talon begins to push inside me. I feel the stretch of my untried channel as he fills me inch by inch. His eyes close, his jaw clenches, and I know he's struggling to maintain control.

"Fuck," he grits out, his eyes flying open. "You're so tight, so fucking tight, Lena."

I whimper as he slides deeper, a combination of pleasure and pain washing over me. I can feel every thick vein on his length as he pushes further, claiming me, marking me as his.

"Please," I whisper. I want him to stop, and at the same time, I want him to keep going. I want to feel him buried to the hilt, completing the union of our bodies.

"You want more?" he asks, his voice harsh.

"Yes," I gasp, surprising myself with my boldness. But it's the truth. I need all of him.

His eyes darken with desire, and he pulls out slightly before thrusting back in, harder this time. "Fuck, you're so wet," he groans, his eyes glued to where we're joined. "You have no idea how good this feels."

I can't answer; I'm too lost in the sensation of him moving inside me. It's overwhelming, all-consuming. I've never felt so full, so exquisitely possessed.

Talon's control snaps, and he begins to move with purpose, his hips pistoning as he sinks deep into me with each thrust. I cry out with each impact, my body rocking with the force. It's a blur of sensation, my nerves alight with pleasure.

"Take all of me," he growls, gripping my hips tightly.

His pace is relentless, and heat coils in my belly again, building toward another climax. Talon's breathing is harsh, his eyes fixed on mine.

"Look at me, Lena," he commands, his voice hoarse. "I want to watch your pretty eyes when you come again."

I force my heavy-lidded eyes open, meeting his fierce gaze. He pounds into me with abandon, each thrust pushing me to the edge. I feel the familiar coiling in my core, tightening like a spring.

"I'm close," I gasp, unable to look away from the raw hunger in his eyes.

The primal intensity in his eyes knocks the breath from my lungs. Everything but this moment fades away as Talon gives in to his most basic urges, and so do I.

His mouth finds mine again, and our tongues battle for dominance. It mirrors the erotic dance of our bodies, our rhythm fast and fierce. He withdraws only to slam back into me, causing my back to arch and my legs to wrap around his waist. I'm desperate for this—for him —in a way I never imagined.

My nails dig into his back as he picks up the pace, thrusting relentlessly. "Fuck, baby, you feel so good," he grunts against my mouth. "Your tight little pussy is made for me."

His words thrill me. I bite my lip to hold in a whimper as he hits a spot deep inside that has me seeing stars. "Yes," I moan.

"I got you, baby," he murmurs, his hips snapping as he drives into me. "I'm gonna fill you up, mark you as mine."

My whole body goes rigid as the pleasure peaks. "Talon... I—I can't—"

"Let go, Lena," he commands. "Come for me."

His rough voice breaks my restraint, and I shatter around him, crying out his name. Wave after wave of ecstasy washes over me. He groans, his body going taut as he thrusts through my orgasm. I feel him throbbing inside me, and warmth spreads through my core as he fills me with his release.

His hands grab my hips, burying himself as deeply as possible, his forehead resting against mine. We're both breathless, sweating, sated.

I'm the first to break the silence. "That was..." I can't even find the words to describe it.

He chuckles, his breath tickling my ear. "Fucking incredible? Mind-blowing? Life-changing?"

I laugh, feeling light and giddy in a way I've never experienced before. "All of the above."

Talon lifts his head, his eyes locking with mine in a gaze that burns through me. "This is more than just a moment, Lena. What we just shared is a promise. A vow. I'll be your shield against the world, your anchor in the storm. And you'll be my reason to keep fighting, to never give up."

His hand slides into my hair, his fingers tangling in the strands as he pulls me closer. "From now on, it's you and me against the world. No matter what they throw at us, we'll face it together. Because what we have—it's unbreakable. It's forever."

I swallow, my pulse quickening as the weight of what we've just done sinks in. I'm bound to him forever. The thought should scare me, but it fills me with a heady sense of satisfaction.

"I know," I whisper, my eyes never leaving his. "And you're mine."

Something vulnerable flickers in his eyes, and his fierce expression softens. "Always, baby."

His lips capture mine, and our kiss is slower this time, sweet and tender. He's still inside me, and I feel him twitch, causing a ripple of pleasure to course through me. I smile against his mouth, my body already responding to his.

His hands reach up to cup my breasts, thumbs brushing my sensitive nipples, sending sparks of pleasure through me. "You're so responsive," he murmurs, his eyes darkening with desire again. "I love how you react to my touch."

I shiver as he teases my nipples, rolling them between his fingers. "They're sensitive," I breathe, arching into his touch.

"Yeah?" He plucks at them, grinning when I mewl softly. "You like that, baby?"

"Mmm," I hum my agreement. "Don't stop."

His low chuckle vibrates against my chest. "Not a chance."

His mouth closes over one tight bud, sucking gently as his hand moves to tease the other. Heat spreads through my core, desire already building again. How is this possible? I just climaxed, and now my body is ready for more.

Talon pulls away, a hint of teeth scraping my sensitive flesh. "You have the most gorgeous tits," he growls. "I could play with these all day."

Heat creeps up my neck, and my nipples pebble

even tighter beneath his worship. I'm feeling emboldened by his praise. "They're yours to play with," I offer shyly. "Anytime you want."

I see the words affect him; his eyes darken further, and his cock twitches inside me. "Damn right, they are," he growls. "All of you belongs to me."

His possessiveness gives me goosebumps, and I get even wetter. This primitive side of him feeds something deep within me, something that yearns to be owned and dominated by this man who has always protected me.

He pulls out of me slowly, his eyes smoldering as he takes in the sight of his still-hard cock sliding out of my well-used pussy. My inner walls feel tender, and my thighs tremble slightly, but I'm already eager for more.

He chuckles, noticing my hungry gaze. "Hungry, baby?"

"For you," I breathe, meaning every word. "Always."

He grins, predatory and sexy. "Turn over."

I do as he says, getting on my hands and knees and offering myself to him. Talon moves behind me, his hands caressing my hips before gripping them roughly. "You ready for round two?"

"Yes, please," I beg, my voice thick with need. "I need you, Talon."

He leans over me, his hot breath fanning the back of my neck. "You're so fucking greedy, Lena," he growls in approval. "Just the way I like you."

And then he fills me again, making me scream in a mix of pleasure and pain as my world fades to just the two of us.

18

TALON

*L*ena descends the stairs, and I take a deep, steadying breath. Her dress clings to her curves in all the right places, the soft fabric accentuating her delicate beauty. My eyes drink in every inch of her, and I feel my control slipping.

Her voice pulls me from my trance. "You cooked?" she asks, her tone laced with surprise. I nod, gesturing to the table I've set with a simple but elegant meal. "I, uh, had to learn when I got here," I admit, the memory of Mrs. Wilson's lessons still fresh in my mind.

She moves closer, her hazel eyes searching mine. "It looks amazing, Talon." She offers me a small smile, and I feel my chest tighten. This woman, this beautiful, captivating woman, is the only light in my bleak existence. She's the one thing I can't bear to lose, the one person who makes me feel alive in a world that's tried to break me.

The fierce desire to shield her from harm, to keep her safe from the cruelty we've both endured, consumes me. I want to wrap her in my arms, to promise her that I'll always be there, no matter what. The intensity of my feelings for her is both terrifying and exhilarating, a powerful force that drives me to be better, to be stronger, for her. I pull out Lena's chair, waiting for her to sit before taking my place across from her. We eat silently; the only sound is the soft clink of silverware against China. I can't tear my eyes away, mesmerized by how she delicately lifts each bite to her lips.

"This is really good, Talon," Lena says, breaking the silence. "I didn't know you could cook."

I shrug, trying to appear nonchalant. "There's a lot you don't know about me, Lena." My voice drops to a low, intimate register, and I see her shiver.

Lena sets down her fork, her gaze locked with mine. "Then tell me," she whispers. "Tell me everything."

I lean forward, my eyes narrowing as I study her face. "Are you sure you're ready to know, Lena?" I reach across the table, my fingers grazing the soft skin of her hand. "You're mine. And I'm not about to let you go."

I lean back in my chair, my fingers drumming against the tabletop as I consider how much to reveal. Lena deserves to know the truth and understand the darkness within me. But part of me wants to keep her innocent, to protect her from the horrors of my past.

"My childhood wasn't exactly...easy," I begin, my voice low and gruff. "My parents were..." I pause, searching for the right words. "Neglectful, to say the least. The abuse..." I trail off, my jaw clenching as the memories flood my mind.

Lena's eyes widen, her hand reaching across the table to cover mine. "Talon, I'm so sorry—"

I cut her off with a sharp shake of my head. "Don't," I snap, my tone harsher than intended. "Don't apologize. It's not your fault."

Lena flinches at my words, her hand retreating back to her lap. I exhale slowly, trying to rein in my temper. "I've never told anyone about this before," I admit, my voice softening. "Not even the social workers or any of my foster parents. It's..." I pause, searching for the right word. "Private."

Lena nods, her gaze locked with mine. "I understand," she murmurs. "Thank you for telling me."

I reach out, my hand covering hers and stilling her nervous movements. "Lena, I..." I hesitate, unsure of how to express the depth of my feelings. "You're the only one I've ever trusted with this."

Her eyes widen, a faint blush coloring her cheeks. "Talon, I—"

I silence her with a gentle squeeze of her hand. "Shh," I murmur, my thumb caressing the soft skin of her knuckles. "Just... let me have this moment, okay?"

Lena nods, her lips curving into a small smile. She's never looked more beautiful with the soft candlelight flickering across her features. I find myself leaning closer, drawn to her like a moth to a flame.

"Lena," I breathe, my free hand reaching up to trace the delicate line of her jaw. "You have no idea how much you mean to me."

"Why?" she asks, her voice trembling. "Why be so distant all these years?"

I avert my gaze, unable to meet the intensity of her stare. "Because I liked you so damn much, Lena," I admit, the words tumbling out before I can stop them. "And that scared the hell out of me."

Lena's brow furrows, her lips parting as if she's about to speak. But I raise a hand, silencing her.

"You have to understand," I continue, my voice low and gruff. "Growing up, I... I never knew what it was like to have someone care about me. Everyone I loved either left or hurt me." I swallow hard, my childhood memories still a raw, visceral wound.

"When you came into my life, I..." I pause, struggling to find the right words. "You were a light in the darkness, Lena. And I was terrified of letting you in, of letting myself feel..." I trail off, my fingers flexing against the tabletop.

Lena reaches across the table, her small hand covering mine. "Talon," she murmurs, her voice gentle. "I'm right here. You don't have to be afraid anymore."

I laugh. "You don't get it, Lena. I'm always going to be afraid of getting close to someone. It's who I am." I turn my hand over, lacing my fingers with hers. "You deserve so much better than me. Someone who can give you the world, not just a broken, damaged—"

"Stop," Lena interrupts, her grip tightening on my hand. "You're not broken, Talon. And you're not damaged goods, either." She shifts in her chair, leaning closer. "You're the strongest person I know. And you've always protected me."

I open my mouth to protest, but Lena presses a finger to my lips, silencing me.

"I'm not going anywhere, Talon," she murmurs, her eyes shining with a fierce determination. "You're stuck with me whether you like it or not."

I stare at her. "Lena, I..." I swallow hard, the words catching in my throat. "I don't deserve you."

Lena's lips curve into a soft smile. "No, you don't," she concedes. "But you're the only one I want."

I can't take my eyes off her as Lena pushes her plate aside, her gaze locked with mine. "I'm finished with dinner," she murmurs, her voice low and sultry. "But I think I'm still hungry for something else."

My breath catches in my throat at her suggestive tone, and I feel the familiar heat of desire coiling in the pit of my stomach. Lena has always had a way of getting under my skin, of stirring the darkness within me.

"Is that so?" I rasp, my fingers tightening around the edge of the table. "And what exactly did you have in mind?"

Lena rises from her chair, her hips swaying as she moves around the table. "I was thinking..." She trails off, her fingertips grazing my shoulder as she stops behind me. "Maybe you could satisfy my craving."

I can feel the heat of her body radiating against my back, and I struggle to resist the urge to pull her into my lap. "Lena," I warn, my voice strained. "Be careful what you wish for."

She leans in close, her lips brushing the shell of my ear. "I know exactly what I'm wishing for, Talon." Her breath fans across my skin, sending a shiver down my spine. "So, why don't you come and get it?"

That's all the invitation I need. In one swift motion, I push back from the table and pull Lena onto my lap, her thighs straddling my hips. She releases a soft gasp of surprise, her hands gripping my shoulders for balance.

"Talon," she breathes, her eyes wide and pupils dilated. "What are you—"

I silence her with a searing kiss, my hands sliding around her waist to pull her flush against me. Lena melts into my embrace, her lips parting in a soft sigh. The taste of her, the feel of her body pressed against mine, it's intoxicating. I can feel the darkness within me surging, demanding that I claim her as my own.

But I force myself to slow down, to savor this moment. Lena is mine, and I'll be damned if I rush this. I pull back, my fingers tracing the delicate line of her jaw.

"You drive me crazy, Lena," I whisper against her lips, my hands sliding up her thighs. "Can you feel what you do to me?"

Lena's eyes flutter closed as I grind against her, her hips moving in a slow, torturous rhythm. "Yes," she moans, her breath coming in short gasps. "I can feel you, Talon."

I nip at her lower lip, my hands tightening on her thighs. "Show me," I demand, my voice harsh with need. "I want you to take it all off, Lena. Every. Single. Piece."

Lena's eyes snap open, desire and a hint of uncertainty flashing in their depths. She stands without hesitation, reaching up to pull the dress over her head, baring her body to me. I take a moment to admire the swell of her breasts, the narrow line of her waist, and the curve of her hips. She's perfect, an ethereal goddess standing before me, offering herself up.

"Keep going," I growl, unable to tear my eyes away.

Lena's cheeks flush as she bends to step out of her underwear, leaving her naked before me. I let my eyes wander, taking in every inch of her, committing this moment to memory.

"Now me," I announce, my voice hoarse with need. I stand, pull my shirt over my head, and quickly shed my jeans, kicking them aside.

Lena's eyes roam over my body, her breath quickening as her gaze lands on the evidence of my arousal. I step closer, my bare chest brushing against hers, and reach down to take her hands in mine. "Look at what you do to me, Lena," I whisper, pressing her palm against my hard cock. "You make me insane."

Lena moans, her eyes fluttering closed as she strokes me through my boxers. "Talon—"

I silence her with a kiss, my tongue tangling with hers as I savor the taste of her. My hands move to the waistband of my boxers, slowly sliding them down my hips, eager to feel the full extent of her touch.

"You like this, don't you?" I murmur against her lips, relishing the feel of her soft skin against mine. "Getting me all worked up."

Lena whimpers, her hands exploring my body with a boldness that matches my own. "You know I do, Talon," she breathes, her lips trailing my jaw. "I love knowing that I affect you this way."

I chuckle, low and deep in my throat. "Oh, you

affect me, Lena. More than you know." I slide my hands into her hair, tilting her head back to expose the delicate line of her neck. "And I plan on returning the favor."

Lena's eyes flutter open, her gaze locking with mine as her fingers trace patterns across my skin. "I want that," she whispers, her voice thick with desire. "I want all of you, Talon."

I lean in, my lips brushing against hers as I savor the moment. "And you'll have it," I promise, my voice gravelly. "Every inch of me is yours, Lena. Always."

And with that, I surrender to the moment, letting Lena's touch consume me as much as I want to consume her.

19

LENA

The house is quiet. The sun is still bright outside, but in the living room, the curtains are drawn, casting the room in a sensual, dusky light. My heart is pounding as I lie beneath him on the couch.

Talon's eyes are hungry as they rove over my body, and his lips curl into a devastating smile. I can feel the hard planes of his chest against mine, his skin damp with sweat, and his breath hot on my neck.

"You have no idea what you do to me," he murmurs. "You're so beautiful when you let go, Lena."

I shiver at the sound of my name on his lips. His hands grip my thighs, squeezing gently, and he lifts me slightly, positioning me just right.

"Look at me," he commands, and I open my eyes, meeting his intense gaze. His eyes are dark and stormy, and I'm lost in them. "You're mine, aren't you? Can't get enough."

I nod, unable to speak, as he lowers me onto him. "That's it," he growls. "Take what you need."

I move with him, my body instinctively matching his rhythm. His hands move to grip my hips, guiding me, and his mouth finds my neck, kissing and sucking gently.

"You're so tight, Lena. So perfect," he whispers.

I moan softly, my breath coming in sharp gasps as pleasure coils within me. Talon's fingers dig into my skin, his movements becoming more frantic. His desire fuels mine, and I surrender to the sensations, letting the pleasure consume me.

Talon's thrusts become more urgent, and he buries his face in my neck, his breath hot against my skin. "You feel so damn good," he groans. "I'm close, baby."

His words send me over the edge, and my body tightens around him as I climax, crying out his name. Talon follows soon after, his body tensing as he fills me, his breath a ragged mix of grunts and curses.

We lie tangled together for a moment, our hearts pounding in unison. I can feel his heavy breaths against my skin, and I know he's looking at me, but I keep my eyes closed, still riding the wave of pleasure.

"You're incredible," he says softly, tracing lazy patterns on my back with his fingertips.

I smile, feeling a warmth spread through me. "You too," I whisper back, turning my head to kiss his shoulder softly.

The warmth of Talon's body against mine is suddenly shattered by Mr. Wilson's bellow from the doorway. "What the fuck is going on here?"

My blood runs cold. I freeze, unable to move, as if staying still might make this moment disappear. But Mr. Wilson's face is turning an alarming shade of purple, and Mrs. Wilson behind him lets out a horrified gasp.

"You disgusting pieces of shit!" Mr. Wilson storms into the room.

Talon moves fast, wrapping a blanket around me as we scramble up from the couch. My hands shake as I clutch the fabric to my chest, my heart hammering against my ribs.

"This is sick. You grew up together!" Mrs. Wilson's voice quivers with revulsion. "Like brother and sister!"

"Get your fucking clothes and get out!" Mr. Wilson advances on Talon, who positions himself between me and our foster father. "You want me to call the cops? Tell them about all the shit you've broken? The windows? The car? How you've been grooming her?"

"That's not—" I protest, but Talon cuts me off with a sharp look.

"I'm leaving," Talon says, his voice steady despite the tension crackling through the room. He's already pulling on his jeans, movements precise and controlled. "Give me five minutes to pack."

"Three," Mr. Wilson spits. "Or I'm calling them right now."

My hands tremble as I clutch the blanket tighter around my body. Talon's jaw clenches, his muscles tense as he faces Mr. Wilson.

"And if I ever see you within a hundred yards of this property again, I'm calling the cops." Mr. Wilson's face is still purple with rage, spittle flying from his lips. "You hear me, boy? I never want to see your face again."

Talon's eyes flick to mine for a split second, and I see

something dark pass through them. But he says nothing, just nods and heads upstairs.

Mrs. Wilson grabs my arm, her nails digging into my skin. "Get dressed," she hisses. "You disgusting little whore."

The words cut deep, but I lift my chin, refusing to let her see how much they hurt. I gather my scattered clothes from the floor, my cheeks burning with humiliation as Mr. Wilson's eyes follow my every move.

The stairs creak under my feet as I hurry to my room. Through the thin walls, I hear Talon moving around in his room, shoving things into his duffel bag. The sound makes my heart ache. After everything we've shared, after finally giving in to our feelings, it's all falling apart.

I want to run to him, to beg him to take me with him, but Mr. Wilson follows me up the stairs. He stations himself in the hallway between our rooms, arms crossed, ensuring we can't communicate.

"Three minutes," he barks.

This isn't right—what we have isn't wrong. We both wanted this. But the words stick in my throat as I walk toward my room.

I watch Talon throw his duffel bag into his car through my bedroom window. He doesn't look back as he peels out of the driveway, leaving me alone with the Wilsons and their disgust.

I collapse onto my bed, pulling the covers tight around my trembling body. I was wrapped in Talon's arms just minutes ago, feeling complete, whole, and loved. Now, there's nothing but emptiness and the echo of Mr. Wilson's rage.

My skin still burns where Talon touched me, a ghost of his fingers tracing patterns of desire. The memory feels surreal now, like a beautiful dream shattered by the harsh light of reality. My chest aches, and tears slip down my cheeks as I replay those final moments.

The look in Talon's eyes before he left—there was something there, something fierce and determined. But he didn't fight to stay. He just... left. Again. Just like when he turned eighteen.

Mrs. Wilson's words ring in my ears. "Like brother and sister." But she's wrong. Talon and I were never that. From the first moment I saw him, there was always something else between us—something inevitable. As if we're soulmates and were destined to end up together, but now he's gone.

I curl tighter into myself, my body still humming from our encounter. How can something that felt so right be treated as so wrong? The warmth of the afternoon sun streams through my window, but I feel cold inside. Empty.

The happiness of mere minutes ago seems like a cruel joke now. I can still taste him on my lips, feel the weight of his body against mine, and hear his whispered promises. All of it is gone instantly, scattered like ashes in the wind.

My fingers clutch at the sheets, and I catch the lingering scent of his skin. Fresh tears spill over as reality crashes down around me. I'm truly alone now, trapped in this house with people who see our love as something twisted and wrong.

TALON

Sitting in my car, I unzip the worn duffel bag holding my meager belongings. My fingers grab the photo album with a photo of Lena and me on the front that she gifted me for my seventeenth birthday.

It was the first gift I'd ever received and the most precious thing I own. Flipping through the photo album, memories come flooding back—the rare moments of lightness in our dark childhoods captured forever on these pages.

The first photo shows Lena and me as kids, sitting on the rickety swing out back. She's grinning from ear to ear while I wear my usual brooding scowl. But her smile is infectious, and I can't help the tiny quirk of my lips in response.

I turn the page, and there she is again—hair tousled by the wind, eyes sparkling with mischief as she points her ancient camera at me. God, how that thing used to drive me crazy. I'd duck and dodge, growling at her to leave me alone. But she never listened, always insisting on documenting every mundane moment of our lives.

At the time, I cursed her obsession with that damn camera. But now, as I flip through this album, I'm struck by a profound gratitude. These photos are all I have left of the rare moments of peace we found together amid the chaos and misery. Lena's gift has preserved those precious memories, immortalizing our bond in a way I never imagined.

My fingers trace the outline of our faces in one particular snapshot—Lena and I sitting side by side on a park bench, our shoulders brushing. I'd, as usual, been in a foul mood that day, but Lena's warmth and light had slowly melted away the ice encasing my heart. This photo captures that moment perfectly—the slight upward curve of my mouth, the way I'm leaning ever so slightly into her orbit.

I toss the photo album onto the passenger seat and lean back, running my hands through my hair. The decision weighs on me like a lead blanket. Boston's calling—I must establish myself there before Lena arrives at MIT. Seven months will feel like an eternity, but I refuse to let her think I've abandoned her again.

Grabbing my phone, I pull up the feed from her bedroom camera. She's curled up in bed, clutching the pillow I used last night. The sight of her tears makes my chest tighten. Three other camera feeds show different angles of the house—the hallway, living room, and back door. I've ensured complete coverage in an attempt to keep her safe.

My fingers hover over my burner phone. I could text

her and let her know I'm watching. But that might spook her. No, better to be subtle. Opening my glove compartment, I pull out a small package wrapped in brown paper. Inside is a delicate silver chain with a bird pendant—matching the wooden one I carved for her sixteenth birthday.

I slip out of my car and move through the shadows toward her window. The Wilsons are asleep. With practiced ease, I scale the drainpipe and perch on the narrow ledge outside Lena's room.

I watch her chest rise and fall through the glass with each breath. Carefully, I wedge the package through the slight gap in her window—the one I'd loosened months ago. It lands silently on her desk.

She'll find it in the morning. She'll know I haven't left her unprotected. The pendant will remind her that she's mine and I'm always watching and waiting. Eight months isn't so long when you have eyes everywhere.

With one final glance, I climb back down the drainpipe and get back into my car. I have work to do—plans to make, traps to set.

As I walk, the darkness stirs within me, coiling and pulsing with a primal need. It's a hunger only Lena can sate, a craving that has consumed me for years. But now, it's more than just a desire. It's a promise I'll stop at nothing to fulfill.

Lena Graves is mine. My obsession, my salvation, my everything.

And I'll gladly burn the world to keep it that way.

LENA

One month later…

J grab a glass from the cabinet, the house eerily quiet at this late hour. Mrs. Wilson is already in bed, leaving me alone downstairs. My hands shake as I fill the glass with water.

The floorboard creaks behind me. My spine stiffens as the sour stench of whiskey fills the air.

"Well, well. Look who's up late." Mr. Wilson's slurred voice makes my stomach turn.

I grip the counter, knuckles white. The glass slips from my trembling fingers, shattering at my feet. Water spreads across the tile floor.

"I-I'll clean it up." My voice comes out as a whisper.

"Don't move." His heavy footsteps draw closer. "Wouldn't want you cutting those pretty feet."

My throat closes up as he corners me against the counter, pressing his bulk against my back. His hot breath hits my neck, and I squeeze my eyes shut. The memory of last week floods back—his rough hands, the pain, my muffled cries.

"Been thinking about our little... chat." His fingers trail up my arm. "Since that boy's gone, someone has to keep you satisfied."

I can't breathe. Can't move. My body betrays me, frozen in terror as his hands roam where they shouldn't. The kitchen walls close in, trapping me in this nightmare.

"Please," I whisper, but the word catches in my throat.

His grip tightens painfully on my hip. "Shut up. You're mine now."

My mind screams for Talon, but he's gone. I'm alone with this monster and can do nothing to stop what's about to happen.

His sweaty palm slides up my thigh as he presses me harder against the counter. The smell of cheap whiskey and stale cigarettes makes bile rise in my throat. Mr. Wilson's beer belly crushes against my back, his labored breathing hot and wet on my neck.

"Such a pretty little thing." His words slur together, his thick fingers digging into my hip. "Always prancing around in those tight clothes."

I try to twist away, but he's too strong, too heavy. My bare feet crunch on broken glass. The pain barely registers through my panic.

"Get off—" My plea cuts short as he clamps his other hand over my mouth.

"Dad? What the fuck?"

Jamie's voice slices through the kitchen. Mr. Wilson

stumbles back, releasing me. I gasp for air, wrapping my arms around myself.

"The hell are you doing?" Jamie stands in the doorway, his college backpack still slung over one shoulder.

"Just helping her clean up some broken glass." Mr. Wilson wipes his mouth, swaying on his feet.

"Bullshit." Jamie's face twists with disgust. "I saw what you were doing."

I slide along the counter, putting distance between myself and Mr. Wilson. My whole body trembles as Jamie steps between us.

"Go to bed, Dad. You're drunk." Jamie's voice is cold and firm. "And if I ever catch you touching her again, I'm calling the cops."

Mr. Wilson mumbles something unintelligible, shooting me a dark look before stumbling out of the kitchen. Jamie waits until his heavy footsteps fade up the stairs.

"You okay?" He turns to me, his expression softer.

I nod, unable to speak past the lump in my throat. Jamie grabs the broom from the corner and starts sweeping up the glass while I stand there, arms still wrapped around myself, trying to stop shaking.

I slide down to sit at the kitchen table, my legs too shaky to hold me up. Jamie pulls out a chair across from me, his eyes full of concern.

"Has he... has this happened before, Lena?"

The gentleness in his voice breaks something inside me. Tears spill down my cheeks as I nod, wrapping my arms tighter around myself.

"Three weeks ago. When your mom was at her book club." My voice cracks. "I tried to fight him off, but—"

"Fuck." Jamie runs his hands through his hair. "I'm so sorry. I should've been here."

"You were at college."

"Yeah, well, I'm back now." He leans forward, his expression serious. "Since I've graduated and didn't find a job in Providence, I'm taking a few months to figure out what I want to do next. But I'm not going anywhere for a while."

I wipe my eyes with trembling fingers. "You don't have to—"

"I do." Jamie's jaw clenches. "I won't let him touch you again. I should've spoken up more when we were younger. I was just a kid too, but... seeing how toxic my parents are now that I'm older..." He shakes his head. "It's not right. None of this is right."

"Thank you," I whisper, fresh tears falling.

"Don't thank me. I should've done something sooner." Jamie stands, grabbing a clean glass from the cabinet. He fills it with water and sets it in front of me. "Drink this. And if he ever tries anything again, you come straight to me. I mean it."

I push back from the table, my legs steadier now. "I should try to get some sleep."

Jamie nods, but I catch the worry in his eyes. He tears a corner from an old grocery list on the fridge and scribbles something down.

"Here's my cell." He slides the paper across the table. "I mean it—any time, day or night. If I'm not here, call me. I'll come right over."

My fingers close around the paper, this small lifeline. The Jamie I knew growing up would've walked away and pretended not to see. But the man sitting across from me now has changed. His eyes hold a determination I've never seen before.

"College opened my eyes to so many things," he says, as if reading my thoughts. "Made me realize how messed up everything was here. Still is." He runs a hand through his hair. "I can't change the past, but I can try to make things right now."

I tuck the paper into my pocket, touched by this unexpected alliance. "Thank you, Jamie. Really."

He waves off my gratitude, but I see the resolve in his expression. Whatever made him change his mind about our family's dysfunction, I'm grateful for it. Having someone else in this house who sees the truth and is willing to stand up against it since Talon was kicked out lifts a weight I didn't realize I was carrying.

22

LENA

Six months later...

I stare at my reflection in the mirror, trying to ignore the bruises hidden beneath my long-sleeved graduation gown. The beautiful bird pendant I know Talon left me sits around my neck. I never take it off.

Just one week ago, Mr. Wilson had beaten me for incorrectly sorting the trash, his drunken rage leaving its marks on my body.

I take a deep breath, focusing on the day ahead. I've worked hard for this moment, studying relentlessly and honing my coding skills. The full-ride scholarship to MIT is a testament to my dedication and natural talent. It means I get to leave this place. Unfortunately, David got into Boston University, meaning we're practically going to college together. And Mrs. Wilson has forced me to room with him at his apartment the Collins bought him.

The Wilsons practically blackmailed me into accepting him as my fiancé. They said if I didn't agree to marry David, they'd reveal the truth about Talon and me.

And while I'm not ashamed of what happened between us, most people would find it disgusting. They even threatened to tell MIT that I'd been fucking my brother to get me kicked out.

David's motivations, on the other hand, appear to be ego-driven. My constant refusal of his advances has only fueled his determination to have me. It's as if the challenge of breaking down my walls and bending me to his will has become an obsession for him, a twisted game that feeds his ego and makes him determined to make me his wife.

As I go downstairs, the Wilsons greet me with false smiles and empty praise. Mrs. Wilson fusses over my hair and gown while Mr. Wilson claps me on the shoulder, his grip a little too tight. I fight the urge to flinch, knowing that any sign of weakness will only fuel his cruelty.

"We're so proud of you, Lena," Mrs. Wilson gushes, her eyes shining with manufactured tears. "You've come so far." I hate how false she is. But the moment she realized how good a pupil I was, she always latched onto the hope I'd be a big achiever. It almost made me want to be shit at school to spite her, but I knew my only way out of this kind of life was to excel and get myself out. No one else would help me.

I force a smile, nodding along to their hollow words. She acts as if she's had a hand in my success, conveniently forgetting the years of neglect and abuse I've endured under her roof. And it's all for appearances. She likes to brag about me to her friends.

As we pose for photos, I can't help but think of Talon. His absence is a constant ache in my chest, a reminder of the one person who truly understood me. The man who took my virginity and then left like it meant nothing, and yet, I wonder where he is now… if he's found the freedom he so desperately craved.

The graduation ceremony passes in a blur of speeches and applause. As I cross the stage to accept my diploma, I glimpse a familiar figure in the shadows. My heart skips a beat, but when I blink, he's gone.

Later, as I'm getting undressed for bed, I find a small, handwritten note on my pillow. The words are simple, but they fill me with a sense of warmth and longing:

"I'm proud of you, princess. Keep shining. - T"

I clutch the note to my chest, a tear sliding down my cheek. Talon may be gone, but his presence lingers. I have no idea how he got in here to leave the note. But I wish he'd come and see me. Speak to me. Anything.

I stiffen at a knock on my door and turn to see David let himself in. His eyes roam over my body, and I instinctively pull my cardigan tighter around myself.

"What do you want, David?" I ask, trying to keep my voice steady.

He steps closer, invading my personal space. "I just wanted to see my beautiful girl before the big move," he says, his tone dripping with false affection.

I back away, but he follows, his movements predatory. "I'm busy packing. Please leave."

David's expression hardens, and he grabs my arm, yanking me towards him. "Don't be like that, Lena. We're going to be together forever. You should be grateful."

I struggle against his grip, fear spiking through me. "Let go of me! You're hurting me."

His hold only tightens, and he pulls me flush against him. "That's no way to talk to your future husband." His free hand trails down my side, and I shudder in revulsion.

Panic rises within me, and I cry out, "Stop! Get off me!"

David clamps a hand over my mouth, silencing my pleas. "Shh, it's okay, Lena. I'm just showing you how much I love you."

Tears stream down my face as he forces me onto the bed, using his body to pin me down. I try to fight him off, but he's too strong. The realization that I'm truly alone in this hits me hard.

I kick and scratch, desperately trying to break David's vise-like grip. He leers at me, his eyes gleaming with a mixture of lust and anger. As he moves to tear my blouse, my heart hammers in my chest. I know what's coming next, and I'm terrified.

Suddenly, the door bursts open, and Jamie strides into the room. "Get the hell out, David!" he barks.

David freezes, his hands still wrapped around my wrists. He looks like he might refuse for a moment, but then he seems to think better of it. With a final, venomous glare in my direction, he releases me and straightens his clothes.

"Go on, get out!" Jamie repeats, his stance threatening.

David's face twists with annoyance. With one last look at me, he stalks out of the room, slamming the door behind him.

"Are you okay?" Jamie's voice is gentle as he approaches me. "He didn't hurt you, did he?"

I nod. "I-I'm fine, though. Thank you, Jamie."

Jamie's eyes flicker with concern. "You sure? He didn't... you know..."

"No," I whisper, feeling relieved that Jamie arrived when he did. "I'm okay. Really."

"You've had it rough, Lena. I'm sorry. First Talon, then my dad." He shakes his head, anger, and shame written over his face. "And now that scumbag David."

My jaw clenches. "What do you mean by first, Talon?"

He tilts his head. "Well, my parents mentioned that they caught him forcing himself on you—"

"That's a lie," I hiss, shaking my head. "I was more than willing with him. I loved him."

Jamie's eyes widen. "Motherfuckers," he mutters, shaking his head. "I need to get the fuck out of here and soon. With you leaving, I can't stand being around their lies." He gives me a sad look. "I'm sorry for all of this, Lena. Just be careful around David. He's a piece of work."

I grip the edge of my bed, trying to steady my shaking hands. "I don't know how I will be careful when forced to live with him in Boston." The words tumble out before I can stop them.

Jamie's expression darkens. "They shouldn't force you to live with him." His voice is tight with barely contained anger. "I've tried talking some sense into my mom, but she's got this warped idea that you and him will make the perfect couple. And, of course, his family is rich as sin. My mom will brag about it to all her book club friends."

Of course, that's all this is to Mrs. Wilson—a means to an end, a way to claw her way into the upper echelons of society and brag about it. My well-being and happiness have never factored into her decisions and never will.

"I just..." Jamie runs a hand through his hair, his expression pained. "I wish there was something I could do to help you. You don't deserve this."

His words strike a chord deep within me, and I blink back tears. In all my years under this roof, Jamie is the only Wilson to show me a shred of kindness or basic human decency. He may have a rough exterior, but there's a gentle soul beneath it all.

"Thank you, Jamie," I whisper, offering him a tremulous smile.

He shifts uncomfortably as if unused to such open displays of emotion. But then he meets my gaze, his eyes filled with a fierce determination. "I promise, Lena. If that bastard hurts you, I'll make him regret the day he was born."

I nod, knowing Jamie isn't one for empty threats. Despite his flaws, he has grown into a man with a strong moral compass and a deep-seated need to protect those he cares about—a miracle considering who his parents are. And for some reason, he seems to have taken me under his wing ever since Talon left.

As he turns to leave, I call out to him. "Jamie?"

He pauses, glancing back at me.

"Thank you," I repeat.

A ghost of a smile tugs at his lips. "Don't mention it. Just... stay strong, okay?"

With that, he's gone, leaving me with my thoughts and a glimmer of hope that I'm not as alone as I feared.

23

LENA

One month later...

$\mathcal{I}$ drag my suitcase into the pristine Boston apartment, my stomach churning at the thought of living here with David. The place reeks of money—all gleaming hardwood floors and modern furniture that probably costs more than my scholarship.

"Let me help you with that, babe." David reaches for my bag, but I clutch it tighter.

"I've got it." My voice comes out sharper than intended. "Which room is mine?"

His jaw tightens at my rejection. "Down the hall, first door on the right. Though soon enough, you'll be in my room anyway."

I suppress a shudder and hurry past him, desperate to reach the sanctuary of my own space. The bedroom is beautiful, with large windows overlooking the city, but it feels like a prison cell. How did I end up here? The Wilsons orchestrated this entire thing—the engagement,

147

the shared apartment, and my upcoming marriage to their wealthy friend's son.

David appears in the doorway as I'm unpacking. "My parents are old-fashioned, insisting we have separate rooms until the wedding." He smirks. "But what they don't know won't hurt them."

"I prefer having my own space." I busy myself with arranging my clothes, avoiding his gaze. "And I respect their wishes."

"Come on, Lena." His voice takes on that wheedling tone I hate. "We're engaged. It's not like—"

"I said no." The words come out firm and clear. "Your parents' rules."

He stands there, radiating frustration, before stalking away. I shut the door behind him and press my back against it, releasing a shaky breath.

I sink onto the bed, touching the small bird ornament in my pocket. That and the pendant around my neck are the only pieces of Talon I have left. The only reminder that once, someone loved me for who I am.

I trace my finger along the wooden bird's delicate wings, remembering how Talon's hands carved each detail with such care. The pendant weighs heavily against my chest, a constant reminder of what we shared. I've checked my phone every day since he left, hoping to see his name flash across the screen.

Unpacking the last of my clothes, I discover a small red crayon at the bottom of my bag—the same one I pocketed years ago when I first arrived at the Wilsons' home. Back then, it represented a tiny act of defiance.

Now, it reminds me of how Talon protected me, taking beatings meant for me.

My hands shake as I sit at the window, watching people hurry past on the street below. Boston is full of possibilities. The Wilsons can't control me here, not really. Even with David watching my every move, I have more freedom than before.

Talon left no trace, and there was no way to contact him. Sometimes, I wonder if he's watching me the way he used to at the Wilsons'.

I pull out my phone again, scrolling through old numbers. His isn't there—it never was—but I can't stop looking. My finger hovers over the keypad. If I could just hear his voice...

The bird ornament catches the late afternoon light, casting strange shadows on my wall. Talon always said we were meant for each other, that nothing could keep us apart. I have to believe he meant it. He's also thinking of me somewhere out there, planning how to find me again.

A car door slams outside, and my heart jumps. I hope to see Talon standing on the sidewalk for a split second, looking up at my window. But it's just another stranger rushing past without a glance.

A knock at my door makes me quickly tuck away Talon's gifts.

"Hey, I ordered pizza." David leans against the doorframe. "Thought we could watch a movie and get comfortable in our new place."

I smile, knowing I must try to make this situation work. "Sure, what movie did you have in mind?"

"Something romantic?" He waggles his eyebrows, and my stomach turns. "Come on, the couch is way more comfortable than unpacking."

I follow him to the living room, keeping a careful distance. He sprawls across the leather sofa, patting the spot next to him. I choose the armchair instead.

"Lena." His voice carries that warning tone I've come to recognize. "Don't be like that. We're engaged."

Swallowing my discomfort, I move to the couch. He immediately wraps an arm around my shoulders, pulling me close. His cologne is too strong, nothing like Talon's natural scent.

"That's better." His fingers trail down my arm. "See? This isn't so bad."

The doorbell rings, and I practically leap up. "I'll get the pizza!"

David chuckles. "Always so jumpy. Relax, babe. We've got all the time in the world."

I busy myself with plates and napkins, trying to delay returning to the couch. But eventually, I have to sit back down. David starts some romantic comedy I immediately tune out, more focused on maintaining space between us without being obvious about it.

His hand finds my thigh. "We could be doing something more fun than watching this movie."

"I'm actually really hungry." I grab a slice of pizza, using it as an excuse to shift away. "And tired from the move. Maybe we could just focus on the film?"

He sighs but backs off slightly. I keep eating slowly, methodically, using the food as a shield. It's going to be a long night.

24

TALON

Three weeks later...

I've been watching her for weeks, tracking her every move like a predator stalking its prey. Lena Graves is the only light in my dark and twisted world. She's the reason I breathe, the reason I exist. And now, she's here in Boston, so close I can almost taste her.

I hate that she's being forced to live with that scumbag David. The thought of him touching her drives me insane. I can't stand the way he looks at her like she's a piece of meat for him to devour. It takes every ounce of self-control I have not to rip his fucking throat out.

But I bide my time, watching from the shadows. I memorize her schedule and her routines. I know when she leaves for class, goes to the library to study, and grabs coffee with her friends. I'm always there, just out of sight.

Sometimes, I get close enough to catch her scent,

that intoxicating blend of vanilla and jasmine that haunts my dreams. I imagine burying my face in her hair, inhaling deeply as I claim her as mine again. She belongs to me, even if she needs a reminder.

I slip into her apartment like a shadow, my heart racing with anticipation. The thrill of being surrounded by her things in her space is almost too much to bear. I move through the rooms silently, my fingers trailing over her belongings, memorizing every detail. I go to the kitchen and rearrange the mugs in her cupboard, placing her favorite one at the back. I imagine her frustration as she searches for it in the morning, a small reminder of my presence in her life.

Then, I head to her bedroom, the most intimate space. Her scent is strongest here, enveloping me like a warm embrace. I run my hand over her pillows, imagining her lying there, her dark hair fanned out around her like a halo.

I can't resist the temptation to touch her things. I open her dresser drawers, running my fingers over her soft, silky underwear. I pick up a lacy red thong, bringing it to my face and inhaling deeply. The thought of her wearing it, the fabric caressing her most intimate places, sends a shiver down my spine.

The heady scent of her fills my nostrils, and I feel my cock twitch in response. I ache for her, my skin buzzing with need for her.

I spot a laundry basket in the corner of the room and move towards it, my heart pounding. Digging through her dirty clothes, I feel like a fucking creep, but

I can't stop myself. I need to find something, anything intimate and hers.

Then I see a pale pink thong, slightly crumpled and scented with her musk. My breath catches as I bring it to my face, inhaling her unique fragrance. I groan, my hands tightening around the delicate fabric.

I kick the basket aside and unzip my pants, freeing my already hardening cock. I wrap her thong around my hand and start stroking, my eyes shut tight as I imagine her beneath me, crying out my name. Her scent surrounds me, fueling my fantasy, my need for her.

I work myself into a frenzy, my hips thrusting as I picture her looking up at me with those beautiful, haunted eyes. I want to dominate her, claim her, brand her as mine.

The soft and silky item in my hand brings me back to reality. I realize what I'm doing and where I am. I glance around, half-expecting to see her walk in and catch me in the act. But the room is empty and silent except for the sound of my own harsh breathing.

My heart is pounding, my body coiled tight with anticipation. I know I shouldn't be doing this, but I can't stop myself.

My eyes land on the pot of moisturizer on her nightstand. It's perfect. I twist off the lid, exposing the creamy, fragrant contents. Then, still holding her thong in one hand, I stroke myself harder, faster.

Her face fills my mind—her flushed cheeks, her lips parted in pleasure. I imagine her soft moans as I thrust into her, claiming her body, her soul. The thought pushes me closer to the edge, and I groan, my hand moving frantically now.

I glance down, watching my cock disappear into the soft fabric, and then back up at the pot of moisturizer. My eyes flick between the two, my heart pounding harder with each thrust. I'm so close now.

A strangled groan escapes me as I jerk my cock a few more times, aiming my release into the pot of lotion. I picture her rubbing it onto her skin, my cum soaking into her, marking her as irrevocably mine.

As the last spurt leaves me, I collapse back against the bed, my heart hammering in my chest. I'm breathing heavily, my body slick with sweat. I gaze down at the pot, half-filled with my release, and feel a sense of satisfaction mixed with a burning need for more.

My breath comes in ragged gasps as I use my finger to work the cum into the creamy lotion. I want her to wear this, to rub it all over her perfect body, unknow-ingly coating herself with me.

A noise in the adjoining apartment startles me, bringing me back to my senses. I need to get out of here. I tuck myself back into my pants, buttoning them hastily, and slip Lena's used panties into my jacket pocket. I glance around the room, making sure I've left subtle differences. Her underwear drawer is still slightly ajar, the thong on the top. Then, with one last look at the pot of moisturizer, I slip out of her bedroom, my pulse still racing.

I make my way back to the shadows, to the safety of the darkness that has become my home. But my mind remains with her, my Lena, and the scent of her that still lingers on my fingers from her dirty thong.

25

LENA

*M*y frustration mounts each second while I stare at my mugs in disbelief. They've been moved again, rearranged in a way that makes no sense. This is the third time this week, and I'm increasingly annoyed.

"David!" I call out, my voice sharp. "Did you move my mugs around?"

There's a pause, and his voice drifts from the living room. "No, why would I do that?"

I grit my teeth, resisting the urge to hurl one of the offending mugs across the room. He's lying, I'm sure of it. Ever since I moved in with him, little things have been going missing or getting shifted around. At first, I thought it was just my imagination, but now it's becoming a pattern.

"Well, someone's been messing with my stuff." I slam the cupboard door shut. "And I'm getting really tired of it."

Footsteps approach, and David appears in the doorway, his expression a mixture of annoyance and conde-scension. "Relax, Lena. Maybe you're just forgetting where you put things."

I whirl on him, my eyes narrowing. "I'm not forget-ting anything. This is your doing, isn't it? Some sort of power trip?"

He scoffs, rolling his eyes. "You're being paranoid. Why would I waste my time moving your stupid mugs around?"

"I don't know, David. Because you get some sort of sick pleasure from messing with me." I step closer, my voice low and challenging. "Or because you can't stand the fact that I'm not some submissive little plaything for you to control."

His jaw tightens, and for a moment, I see a flicker of rage in his eyes. But then it's gone, replaced by a sickly sweet smile that makes my skin crawl.

"You're right, Lena," he says. "I'm just trying to keep you on your toes. You know how forgetful you can be."

I open my mouth to retort, but he's already turning away, sauntering back into the living room. I'm left standing there, my hands clenched into fists, my heart pounding with anger and frustration.

I know he's lying. I know he's messing with my things, trying to assert some twisted dominance over me. But what can I do? He's always been able to wrap my foster parents around his finger, and they'll never believe me over him.

As I glare at the mugs, a strange feeling washes over me. A sense of being watched, eyes boring into the back of my skull. I whirl around, half-expecting to see David lurking in the doorway.

But there's no one there. Just an eerie silence that sends a shiver down my spine.

My eyes stare back at me through the mirror, dull and lifeless. I can't imagine spending the rest of my life like this, trapped in a loveless relationship with a man who sees me as nothing more than a warm body to satisfy his urges. Not that I've let him get that far yet, but I know it's only a matter of time until he snaps and fucks me. The thought makes my stomach churn, bile rising in my throat.

But then I remember MIT, the shining beacon of hope in my otherwise bleak existence. I feel alive again when surrounded by like-minded individuals who share my passion for learning. I've even made a few friends. People who see me for who I am, not just as David's possession.

Rachel, my lab partner, has become a confidante of sorts. She's the only one who knows the truth about my situation, the only one I can talk to without fear of judgment or pity. She's been there for me, offering a shoulder to cry on and a listening ear whenever I need it.

And then there's Alex, the quiet, unassuming guy who sits next to me in my coding class. He's always been kind to me, offering a smile or a word of encouragement when I'm feeling down. I've caught him looking at me a few times, his gaze lingering just a little too long, but he always looks away before I can meet his eyes.

I wonder what it would be like to be with someone

nice like him who likes me. To be honest, I can't imagine being with anyone by choice other than Talon. My heart still remains firmly in his hand, but where is he?

After a moment of reflection, reality comes crashing down, and I remember who I am, where I am. I'm stuck with David until I graduate from MIT, as Mrs. Wilson has assured me she'll find a way to get me kicked out if I don't play ball. Not to mention, they do supply me with a small amount of money each month for things like food and other necessities that my scholarship doesn't cover. I could get a job, but my course workload will be intense.

I grab my bag and head for the door, calling out to David over my shoulder. "I'm heading to class. Don't wait up tonight, I'm going out with Rachel and her friends."

David's head snaps up from where he's sprawled on the couch, his eyes narrowing. "What? You're not going anywhere without me."

I pause, my hand on the doorknob, and turn to face him. "It's a girls' night out, David. No guys allowed."

He scoffs, pushing himself up to a sitting position. "I don't care what it is. You're not going out without me."

I can feel my temper rising, my grip tightening on the strap of my bag. "I'm not asking for your permission, David. I'm telling you what I'm doing."

He's on his feet now, his face twisting into an ugly sneer. "You don't get to make decisions like that, Lena. I'm the one in charge here."

I release a harsh laugh. "In charge? Of what, exactly? My life? My choices? I don't think so."

He takes a step towards me, his fists clenching at his sides. "Don't test me, Lena. You know what happens when you disobey me."

For a moment, I feel a flicker of fear at his tone. But then I think of Rachel and her friends, the freedom and laughter awaiting me outside these walls.

I straighten my spine, meeting his gaze head-on. "I'm going out, David. And there's nothing you can do to stop me."

With that, I turn on my heel and march out the door, slamming it behind me. I half-expect him to come storming after me, to drag me back inside and make me pay for my defiance. But there's no sign of him as I hurry down the stairs and into the cool night air.

I let out a shaky breath, my heart pounding in my chest. I can't believe I just did that, that I finally stood up to him after all this time. It feels exhilarating, like a weight has been lifted off my shoulders.

As I make my way towards the campus, I feel uneasy. It still feels like there are eyes on me, watching my every move. I glance over my shoulder, but there's no one there, just the empty street and the distant sound of traffic.

I shake off the feeling, telling myself it's just my imagination. I'm just paranoid.

A nagging sense of unease persists as I turn the corner and approach the bus stop.

I quicken my pace, my heart hammering in my chest. I can see the bus stop up ahead, the bright lights of the campus beyond. In just a few more steps, I'll be safe, surrounded by people, noise, and life.

I hurry onto the bus, my heart racing from the confrontation with David. As I sink into a seat near the back, I let out a shaky breath, trying to calm my frayed nerves.

But even as the bus pulls away from the curb, I can't shake the feeling of unease that's been following me since I left the apartment.

I glance out the window, my gaze scanning the street outside. At first, I don't see anything unusual—just the usual mix of pedestrians and traffic, the city's bright lights blurring together as we speed by.

But then I see him. A dark figure standing to one side of the bus stop, his face obscured by the hood of his jacket. He's not moving, not even seeming to breathe, just standing there like a statue, his eyes fixed on the bus.

A chill runs down my spine, and I feel a sudden rush of fear, like a cold hand wrapping around my heart. Who is he? What does he want with me?

I try to get a better look at his face, but the bus is moving too fast, and the figure is soon lost in the darkness behind us. I sink back into my seat, my mind racing with possibilities.

Could it be David following me, trying to keep tabs on me even when I'm not with him? Or is it someone else, someone I don't know, someone with even darker intentions?

I push the thoughts away. I'm being paranoid, I tell myself. It's just some random guy, probably waiting for the next bus, nothing to worry about.

But even as I try to convince myself, I can't shake the

feeling that something's wrong. Someone is watching me, waiting for the right moment to strike.

I wrap my arms around myself, suddenly feeling cold despite the warmth of the bus. I try to focus on the journey ahead, on the night of fun and freedom that awaits me with Rachel and her friends.

But even as I close my eyes and try to relax, I can't escape the feeling of dread settling in my stomach. Like a storm is coming, and I'm caught in the middle with no way out.

TALON

I watch Lena intently from the shadows of the dimly lit club, my eyes narrowing beneath the mask obscuring my face. She's laughing, head thrown back in carefree abandon as her friends surround her, the flashing lights casting her delicate features in a kaleidoscope of colors.

My jaw clenches at the sight of her so unguarded, so vulnerable amidst the throngs of people. Any one of them could be a threat, their wandering gazes lingering too long on the swell of her hips, the curve of her neck. I stay still, resisting the urge to stride across the room and wrap her in my embrace, sheltering her from their prying eyes.

A possessive growl rumbles in my chest as a man approaches her, his hand brushing her arm in a blatant attempt at flirtation. Lena flinches, clearly uncomfortable, but her friend laughs it off, oblivious to the potential danger. I tense, every muscle in my body coiled and ready to strike if he takes one step too far.

But then Lena extracts herself gracefully, politely declining his advances with a shake of her head. Relief washes over me as she moves away, her discomfort evident in the furrow of her brow. She's stronger than they give her credit for, my fierce little warrior.

Still, I can't tear my eyes from her, drinking in every subtle movement, every fleeting expression that crosses her lovely face. I'll keep her safe, no matter what it takes.

The mask concealing my identity is stifling but a necessary precaution. It wouldn't do for her to recognize me, not yet. Not until I'm ready to reveal the depths of my obsession, to show her how far I'm willing to go to claim her more than just that week we had together. To claim her forever.

I watch, transfixed, as Lena starts to sway to the pulsing beat, her body moving with a sensual grace that sets my blood on fire. The way her hips undulate, the arch of her back as she loses herself in the music—it's a sight that sears itself into my mind, branding me with its beauty.

I imagine her pressed against me, our bodies moving in perfect sync as we dance. I can almost feel the heat of her skin, the softness of her curves molding to my hard planes.

But then a man steps behind her, his filthy hands gripping her waist as he grinds against her. Red-hot rage surges through me, a primal, possessive fury that demands retribution. How dare he touch what's mine?

Before I can think, I'm moving, shoving my way through the crowd with a single-minded focus. I reach them in seconds, my hand clamping down on the man's shoulder as I yank him away from her. He stumbles back, eyes wide with shock. There's fear etched into his expression as he takes in my imposing frame and the dark promise of violence radiating from me.

Seizing her by the hips, I yank her flush against me, my body molding possessively to hers. She gasps, lips parting in surprise, but I cut off any protest by swaying my hips in time with the pounding bass.

I keep her facing away, my arms wrapped around her waist as we sway together. A heady mix of adrenaline and desire flows through my veins. She feels right in my arms, like she was made for me.

I lean down, my lips brushing the shell of her ear as I speak, my voice a low, deep rumble through my voice distorter. "You looked like you needed saving."

She shivers, her breath catching in her throat. "Thank you," she murmurs, her words nearly lost in the pounding music.

I tighten my hold on her, savoring the feel of her soft curves against my hardened muscles.

"Don't fight it," I murmur in a low rasp, pitching my voice deeper to disguise my identity. "Just feel me."

I grind against her, savoring the soft curves that press into me with every sensuous roll of my hips. She's frozen, trembling in my embrace, but I can sense the flicker of dark curiosity beneath her fear.

Reaching up, I tangle my fingers in her silken hair, angling her head away so she can't see my face beneath the mask. Not yet. Not until she's ready to know the truth of who I am.

"Relax," I growl against the delicate shell of her ear.

"I've got you, baby. No one's gonna lay a hand on you as long as I'm here." I bite at the skin there, wanting to leave my mark on her.

She moans softly as my other hand splays across her stomach, pulling her back impossibly closer until there's not a breath of space between us. She's soft and pliant in my arms, and I revel in her body melting against mine.

This is where she belongs. With me, safe in the circle of my embrace, the heat of our bodies twining together in a sensual, primal dance. Soon, she'll understand. Soon, she'll crave my touch and possession as deeply as I crave hers.

But for now, I'll settle for this stolen moment, for the chance to hold her while she remains blissfully unaware of the depths of my obsession. She doesn't realize that the man holding her is the same man who took her virginity.

But she will. Soon, she'll know the truth of who I am, of the lengths I'll go to keep her safe. When that day comes, she'll be mine, body and soul.

LENA

$\mathcal{I}$ can't stop thinking about the mysterious stranger at the club. A shiver ran down my spine as soon as his strong arms pulled me close. There was something primal and captivating about the way he moved against me, like a predator claiming its prey.

The dim lighting obscured his face, but I caught glimpses of the skull mask he wore. It only heightened the sense of danger and intrigue surrounding him. I wanted to leave with the alluring stranger and surrender myself to him.

When the aggressive man hassling me approached, the stranger's reaction was swift and vicious. He shoved the man away with such force that I knew he was capable of great violence. Yet, in that moment, I felt safer than I ever had. This dark, powerful man shielded me, claiming me as his own.

I recall how the stranger had pulled me closer and his breath had tickled my ear.

I've got you, baby. No one's gonna lay a hand on you as long as I'm here.

The way he said my name sent a thrill through me. He knew who I was, but I had no idea who he was.

When the song ended, I turned to ask him to take me home, but he had vanished. I scanned the crowd, my heart pounding, but found no trace of him. It was as if he had slipped into the shadows, leaving me bereft and aching for more of his touch.

Now, back in my apartment, I can still feel the ghost of his hands on my body. The way he held me, possessive yet protective, has left an indelible mark. I've only ever experienced anything like that with Talon.

Who is this masked stranger? And why does the thought of him make my pulse race and my skin flush with desire? I want to know more, to uncover the mystery that surrounds him. There's a darkness to him that both terrifies and enthralls me. I should stay away; getting involved with someone I don't know could be dangerous. But something deep inside me yearns to throw caution to the wind and surrender myself to him completely.

David storms out of the bedroom, his eyes like ice. My heart sinks as I anticipate the familiar rage building within him. I know I'm already in trouble for being late —a valid concern given the neighborhood—but my mind has been miles away, consumed by thoughts of the masked man.

Before I can even apologize, he lunges at me, grabbing my arm with a force that makes me wince. "Where the hell have you been, Lena? Do you have any idea how worried I was?" His words slice through the air, sharp with accusation. I try to pull away, but he tightens his grip, his fingers digging into my skin.

The stench of alcohol clings to David's breath as he leans in close, his words slurring together. "You think you can just come and go as you please? I'm your fiancé, Lena. You belong to me."

I recoil from the venom in his voice, my heart pounding. "I was just out with some friends. I told you I would be out earlier."

His hand lashes out, gripping my chin in a viselike hold. "Don't lie to me, you little slut. I saw how that guy was all over you at the club."

Fear coils in my gut as I realize he must have followed me. "David, please, you're hurting me..."

The sting of his palm across my cheek steals my breath. I stare at him in shock, unable to process what just happened. He's never hit me before. Never.

David looms over me, his chest heaving with drunken rage. "That'll teach you to disrespect me."

I press a trembling hand to my stinging cheek, tears welling in my eyes. This can't be happening. Not David, the man I'm supposed to marry. The man my foster parents wanted me to be with.

"You're mine, Lena," he snarls, grabbing a fistful of my hair and wrenching my head back. "And I'll do whatever it takes to keep you in line."

David drags me towards the bedroom, his grasp like a vice. "You'll learn not to go out without me again or face the consequences." I stumble, his grip bruising my skin, but he doesn't care.

As he pushes me onto the bed, I beg him to stop, writhing beneath him. "Please, David, you're hurting me. Just let me go. I won't be late again." My pleas fall on deaf ears as he climbs on top of me, his weight pinning me down. I struggle, but it's no use; he's too strong.

"Shut up, Lena," he snarls, his face contorting with anger. "You're mine, and you'll do as I say. You'll learn your place, and you'll learn to like it." He rips at my clothes, exposing my skin, while I squirm beneath him, desperate to escape. I knew this time would come. His hands are everywhere, claiming me like a possessive, ruthless conqueror.

"No, David, stop! Please, I don't want this!" My words fall on deaf ears as he continues, his breath heavy and his eyes cold. I feel trapped, suffocated by his presence, his body overpowering mine.

Through my tears, I catch a glimpse of the masked stranger in my mind's eye, and an overwhelming sense of longing washes over me. Even as David continues, my thoughts drift to Talon and his promise to keep me safe before he left.

Where is he now?

TALON

 y movements are silent and efficient as I break into the apartment. I can't shake the obsession that consumes me, the need to keep Lena safe from that snake, David. As I navigate the rooms, I expertly install the hidden cameras, positioning them to capture every inch of her living space.

First, the kitchen, tucked away in the corner where it will go unnoticed. Then, one in the living area is angled to monitor the entire room.

My heart drums erratically against my rib cage as I slip into Lena's room. The moonlight casts an ethereal glow over her sleeping form, making her look like an angel. I approach her bed, transfixed by the gentle rise and fall of her chest. I want to touch her, but I remain still. For now, I'll just watch.

Working quickly and quietly, I place the cameras, ensuring they have the optimal vantage point. I need to be able to see her, to watch over her, to protect her from that bastard David. The thought of him touching her, defiling her, makes my blood boil.

I step back, surveying my handiwork. Now I can keep a constant vigil, my eyes never straying from the footage that will stream in. I'll know her every move, her every interaction. Nothing will slip by me.

I sit on the edge of her bed, careful not to make a sound. My eyes trace the delicate lines of her face, drinking in her beauty. I reach out and tuck a stray lock of hair behind her ear, my fingertips brushing her soft skin. She stirs slightly but doesn't wake. I lean closer, inhaling her sweet scent. My mouth waters at the thought of tasting her. I want to brand her as mine, mark her skin with my lips and teeth.

I know I shouldn't, but I can't help myself. I reach under the covers, my hand gliding over her smooth skin. She murmurs something unintelligible but doesn't wake. My fingers find the hem of her nightgown and slowly inch it upward, baring her legs to my hungry gaze. I let out a sharp breath, wanting so desperately to touch her, to feel her wet cunt.

I gaze down at her sleeping form, my eyes trailing over her body longingly. My cock aches and throbs with longing, needing release. I know I shouldn't, but the temptation is too much.

I free my aching cock from the confines of my pants, stroking it slowly as I gaze at Lena. Her skin glows in the moonlight, her breasts rising and falling with each breath. I want to touch, taste, and feel her softness against me. I want to hear her moan my name as I fuck her into the mattress.

I stroke myself harder, imagining what it would be like to climb on top of her and slide into her warmth. She would be so tight around me, her legs wrapping around my waist as I thrust into her over and over. I'd feel her walls clench around my cock, milking me as I pounded into her.

The thought drives me wild, and I let out a strangled groan. My eyes flicker to her face, half-expecting her to wake up, but she sleeps on, oblivious to my presence.

I lean down, my breath ghosting over her ear. I whisper her name, my voice hoarse and full of need. "Lena," I breathe. "Baby, I need you."

I don't know if I intend to wake her. Part of me wants her to open her eyes and see the desperate longing in my gaze. But another part wants to keep her sleeping, to take her like this, with her innocence and trust laid bare.

I continue to stroke myself, my eyes glued to her body. I can't get enough of her. I want to hear her cry out my name as she comes, her body shaking with the pleasure I gave her.

I let out a harsh breath as pleasure coils in my gut. I'm close now, so fucking close. I tighten my grip on my cock, pumping it harder, faster. I bite my lip to stifle my moans, not wanting to wake her. I want to come all over her perfect tits, cover her in my cum, and then wake her up to lick me clean.

The image is too much, and I lose control, bucking my hips as I shoot rope after rope of hot cum into the air. It lands on her chest, a pearlescent streak against her creamy skin. I let out a shuddering breath, my body trembling with the force of my release.

I look down at her, my heart pounding in my chest. Lena moves, a soft sound escaping her throat. And then she simply turns over, continuing to sleep. She always could sleep fucking deeply.

She'll wake up with my cum on her chest, and that thought alone has my dick twitching with anticipation. It's wrong, I know, but I can't resist marking her. She's mine, and I need her to know it—to feel it. I want her to wake up and wonder who was in her room, touching her while she slept. The power of that thought has me gripping my throbbing cock.

I spot a pen and paper on her desk and move towards it. My hand shakes slightly as I scribble a note, the letters intentionally messy and unrecognizable. "You're so fucking beautiful. Look what you do to me." My cock jerks at the thought of her reading those words.

I glance around her room, my gaze landing on her dresser. That's when the idea comes to me. I open the top drawer and sift through her things until I find what I'm looking for—a small, instant camera. I smirk, already knowing what I'll capture with it.

With swift, deliberate movements, I snap a photo of my cock. It's still hard and leaking, ready to explode all over her again. I place the Polaroid with the note, ensuring it's visible, knowing the mystery will torment her.

Standing over her, I yearn to touch her one more time. I lean down, my lips ghosting over her ear. "You're mine, Lena," I whisper. "And I will haunt you to your grave if that's what it takes to keep you close."

Then, I leave her room, my heart pounding with anticipation. I can't wait for her to wake up and discover what I've done. The thought of her confusion, the stir of unwanted—or secretly wanted—desire, makes my chest tighten. She won't know who did this... for now. But one day, she'll figure it out. She'll realize it was me all along, and by then, she'll be mine, too obsessed and hooked on me to do anything but succumb.

LENA

I wake up feeling rested, the nightmare of my fiancé, David, fading from memory. But as I stretch, something feels off. I look down and see a crusty white substance on my chest. My heart lurches as the realization hits.

"Oh my God," I whisper, my eyes widening. Dried cum. How did I not wake up? I look over at the other side of the bed, but David's not there. I check the time. Almost seven a.m. I sit up, anger and disgust swirling in my stomach.

How could he?

I get up, the sheet pooling around my waist, and spot something on the desk. Cautiously, I walk over, my eyes narrowing at the sight before me. There's a note, and next to it, an instant photo. My breath catches as I see a large, erect cock, the edges of my desk visible in the background.

I pick up the note, my hands shaking.

"You're so fucking beautiful. Look what you do to me."

My eyes dart back to the photo, and I realize with a sickening lurch that it's not David in the picture. This guy's cock is thicker and much longer. Slowly, the implications sink in.

Someone broke into my home and masturbated over me while I slept. I back away, my heart pounding. Who would do this? How did they get in? Questions swirl in my mind, but one nameless, faceless man permeates my thoughts.

The masked man.

A chill runs down my spine as I reflect on the mysterious stranger at the club. His protective demeanor. The way he pulled me close, grinding against me. And why the fuck does it make my pussy wet?

I can't tear my eyes away from the photo. My cheeks flame with embarrassment, even as my body betrays me. I squeeze my thighs together, my breath quickening. God, this is so wrong.

The stranger's cock is thick and veined. I swallow hard, biting my lip as my eyes flick back to the note. *You're so fucking beautiful.*

My phone buzzes, interrupting my disturbed thoughts. It's David. *Staying at Pete's this weekend. Won't be back til Sunday night.*

Relief floods me. At least I don't have to deal with him until tomorrow night. I set the phone down, my gaze returning to the photo. Part of me wants to throw it away, disgusted and appalled by this violation of my privacy. But another part...

I lie back on the bed, reaching into the nightstand for my vibrator. My heart is pounding as I turn it on, closing my eyes as the familiar buzz fills the room. It's wrong, so wrong, but I can't stop thinking about that cock.

The vibrating toy reaches my clit, and my hips buck slightly as I press it against myself. I'm already wet, and the sensation sends a shiver through me. With my free hand, I pick up the photo, staring at it as I slowly circle my clit.

In my mind, I imagine it's not the vibrator touching me but him. His thick cock, sliding between my thighs. Pushing inside me. Claiming me. My breath hitches as I let out a soft moan, my hips moving involuntarily. The vibrator slips inside me, and I arch my back, biting my lip to stifle another moan.

I'm so wet, so ready, and my mind is filled with images of him. The stranger. His strong arms pull me close, grinding against me to that primal beat. And in my fantasy, the man behind the mask is Talon. The only man I've ever wanted.

My fingers tighten around the vibrator as I move it in and out, faster now. My breathing becomes ragged as I picture the stranger above me, his cock thrusting into me.

I'm so close, my body trembling with desire. I glance at the photo again, my eyes locking with the stranger's anonymous gaze. And then I come with a sharp cry, my body convulsing with pleasure.

As I lie there, panting, I realize with a jolt that this

whole time, my eyes were fixed on that photo, on him. Oh God, what is happening to me?

I lay in bed, my body still tingling from my release. The shame crashes over me as reality sets in. What kind of person gets off to evidence left by a stalker? But I can't deny the truth—it's the first time I've felt desire since Talon.

My hand traces over my collarbone where David left bruises last night. Since starting college, I've staved off his advances. But last night, it was like reliving being back in Mr. Wilson's clutches after Talon left. It feels like I'm broken now.

With Talon...sex had been different. Raw. Passionate. Caring. He'd awakened something in me I didn't know existed. The way his hands had explored my body, how he'd claimed me completely. Even now, the memory sends shivers down my spine.

David's touch last night was nothing like that. It was mechanical, painful, degrading. He didn't care about my pleasure or comfort. To him, I was just a toy to be used. And now it's happened once. It's bound to happen again. The thought makes bile rise in my throat.

I curl onto my side, wrapping my arms around myself. How did I end up here? Trapped in this nightmare with David, getting aroused by a stalker's photo while remembering the only man who ever made me feel truly alive? A man who should have been off limits, considering we grew up together.

The worst part is knowing that what happened with Talon wasn't just sex—it was a connection, an understanding that went soul-deep. Everything since then has felt hollow, especially David's violations now, that leave me feeling dirty and used.

I squeeze my eyes shut, trying to block out the memories of David's assaults. But they creep in anyway, making my skin crawl all over again.

I hurry to clean up, putting my vibrator away and wiping down my body. I feel ashamed, confused, and incredibly turned on all at once. I glance at the photo again before hiding it in my drawer and the note.

What have I become?

TALON

I stalk Lena across the college campus, keeping to the shadows as I observe her every move. The thrill of watching her pleasure herself with the image of my hard cock still lingers, stoking the flames of my twisted desire. My heart pounds with anticipation, knowing that soon, I will eliminate the obstacle standing in the way of our union.

As Lena enters the library, I quietly slip in behind her, blending seamlessly into the throngs of students. My eyes never leave her, memorizing her graceful movements and how the light plays across her features. She's utterly captivating, a delicate flower I long to possess and corrupt.

I follow her to the second floor, watching her settle into a quiet nook. Carefully, I position myself nearby, pretending to peruse the shelves with my hood hiding my face while keeping her firmly in sight. The knowledge that I hold such power over her, that I can manipulate and control her life, sends a jolt of exhilaration through me.

Lena appears focused on her studies, unaware of the predator lurking mere feet away. I allow myself a small, satisfied smile, reveling in my sense of control. Soon, I will move, eliminating the last obstacle standing in our way.

The thought of removing that pathetic excuse of a man from the equation fills me with a dark, primal excitement. He dares to touch what is mine, to taint the perfection of Lena Graves. I clench my fists, my knuckles turning white with the intensity of my grip. He will pay for his transgressions, for daring to lay a hand on what is rightfully mine.

As Lena packs up her belongings and heads for the exit, I trail behind her, keeping a safe distance. My eyes follow her every step, my mind already formulating the next phase of my plan.

I slink through the shadows of the campus quad, my gaze fixed solely on Lena's graceful form as she emerges from the library. The mere sight of her sets my blood aflame with an all-consuming desire that borders on madness.

However, the sudden appearance of that sniveling worm, David, shatters my possessive reverie. He strides toward Lena with an overconfident swagger, clutching a bouquet of cheap flowers that reek of desperation. My lip curls with disgust as he wraps his arms around her, planting a sloppy kiss on her cheek.

I bristle with barely contained fury, watching as Lena flinches ever so slightly at his touch. The motion is subtle, but it speaks volumes—that coward has dared to lay his hands on her in a way that has caused her distress. My fists clench at the mere thought, fighting the overwhelming urge to tear him limb from limb.

Lena forces a tight smile, her posture stiff and radiating discomfort as David loops his arm through hers, steering her across the quad. I follow at a discreet distance, my footsteps silent as a wraith, every fiber of my being attuned to the tension emanating from her rigid frame.

She doesn't want this. My Lena, trapped in the clutches of this pathetic excuse for a man, her light slowly being extinguished by his poisonous presence. Rage courses through my veins, scalding and all-consuming, as I vow to free her from his clutches, no matter the cost.

If that sniveling bastard has dared to harm a single hair on her head, he will suffer a fate worse than death itself. I will tear him apart, piece by agonizing piece, until he begs for the release of death. And when he finally draws his last, wheezing breath, I will cradle Lena in my arms and show her the depths of my devotion, love, and obsession.

I trail behind Lena and David, my eyes locked on their retreating forms. The urge to close the distance between us and rip him away from her is almost overwhelming, but I maintain my composure. Patience, I remind myself. The time will come.

They enter a small restaurant, the warm glow of the lights beckoning them inside. I pause, considering my next move. I can't simply barge in and create a scene—that would only alarm Lena and draw unwanted attention. No, I need to be more calculated and strategic.

Slipping into the shadows, I find a secluded table near the back, where I can observe them undetected. I am drawn to Lena as she hesitantly follows David to a cozy booth in the corner. She looks so small, so fragile, and my heart aches with the need to protect her.

David orders a bottle of wine, his arrogant grin making my blood boil. I watch as he pours Lena a generous glass, his hand lingering on hers for a moment too long. Lena flinches at the unwanted contact, and I must fight the urge to storm over and tear him away from her.

Forcing myself to remain calm, I observe as the evening progresses. David does most of the talking, his boisterous laughter grating on my nerves. On the other hand, Lena sits quietly, her eyes downcast as she sips her wine. I can see the tension in her shoulders, the way she shrinks into herself, desperately wishing to be anywhere but here.

The waiter arrives with their meals, and David immediately digs in, seemingly oblivious to Lena's discomfort. She picks at her food, her appetite clearly diminished by the oppressive atmosphere. I clench my jaw, my fingers itching to reach out and comfort her, to shield her from this nightmare.

As David leans in, his hand reaching across the table to grasp Lena's, I feel a surge of possessive rage. That should be my hand touching her, my fingers intertwined with hers.

Lena flinches away, her eyes wide with fear and revulsion.

Don't worry, princess. I'll free you soon enough.

I grip the table's edge, knuckles turning white as I watch David's hand snake across the table to grasp Lena's. She flinches away from his touch, her eyes sparking with a fear that sets my blood boiling. How dare he touch her like that! How dare he instill that look of terror in her beautiful eyes!

Forcing myself to remain still, to not storm over and rip his throat out right here and now, is one of the greatest challenges I've ever faced. But I know that if I act rashly if I reveal myself before the time is right, it could jeopardize everything. So, with a trembling breath, I tear my gaze away from the sickening sight before me and rise from my seat.

I can't stay here any longer, not without risking exposure. The need to act, to strike, to eliminate this pathetic excuse for a man is clawing at my insides like a rabid animal. If I remain, I may do something reckless that could compromise my carefully laid plans.

No, it's better to retreat, for now, to regroup and strategize. I slip out of the restaurant, my footsteps silent, and melt into the shadows of the night. The crisp evening air does little to cool the fire within me, but it provides clarity, allowing me to focus my thoughts.

As I move through the darkened streets, my mind races, formulating and discarding plans, weighing the risks and rewards of each potential course of action. I need to be smart about this and leave no stone unturned. David must be eliminated, that much is certain, but it needs to be done in a way that doesn't arouse suspicion, that doesn't lead back to me or Lena.

Perhaps a mugging gone wrong? No, too risky, too many variables that could unravel the whole operation. Maybe a tragic accident, a slip and fall that results in a fatal injury? But how to orchestrate such a thing without drawing unwanted attention?

The possibilities swirl through my mind like a tempest, each more twisted and intricate than the last. But through it all, one thought remains constant: Lena. She is the driving force behind every decision, every carefully calculated move.

As I retreat to the shadows, to the secluded sanctuary of my apartment where I can plan and strategize without interruption, I feel a renewed sense of determination coursing through my veins. David's days are numbered, and I will stop at nothing to ensure his permanent removal from Lena's life.

A twisted smile curves my lips as I envision our future, a dark and beautiful tapestry woven from the threads of my devotion. Yes, Lena Graves will be mine, and anyone foolish enough to stand in our way will suffer the consequences.

The game is afoot, and I am the master puppeteer, pulling the strings from the shadows. David's demise is inevitable, a mere formality in the grand scheme. All that remains is to decide how best to orchestrate his downfall.

LENA

I feel an unseen presence watching me again, prickling the back of my neck, but I can't place the source. The sensation follows me throughout the day, heightening my anxiety. David hovers over me, acting overly kind and solicitous after he raped me the other night. I shudder inwardly, repulsed by his attempt to make amends. His fake concern only serves as a reminder of his true, abusive nature.

As David drives me home from dinner, the tense silence in the car is suffocating. The moment we step inside, his façade crumbles, and he grabs me roughly, pushing me against the wall. "Time to show your gratitude for dinner," he demands.

So much for him attempting to make amends. Is this what I can expect every night from here on out?

I try to push him away, but his grip tightens. "No, I'm not in the mood," I say, hating the tremor in my voice.

David's hands are everywhere.

I struggle, but he's too strong. I can feel his arousal pressing into my thigh, and I know what's coming. "Please... I don't want to," I beg, my voice small and shaking.

"No one asked you," he growls, his breath hot on my neck. I try to twist away, but he slams me back against the wall, his mouth crushing mine in a brutal kiss. My heart sinks as I realize there's no escaping this. Not tonight.

He tears at my clothes, and I sob, turning my face away. I can't bear to look at him. David grabs my hips and pushes me toward my bedroom. His hands are rough as he forces me onto the bed and shoves my thighs apart.

I clench my teeth. I hate this. I hate him. I want to disappear, to be anywhere but here.

Somewhere in the back of my mind, I sense something else. A presence. As if someone else is watching in the room with us. But it's too late to stop what's happening.

David climbs onto the bed, covering me with his body. I will myself to disconnect, to leave my body and float above this sordid scene. Just like I did Friday night.

I can't breathe. David's weight crushes me against the bed as he fumbles to get his cock free. Tears stream down my face, but my pleas fall on deaf ears. I squeeze my eyes shut, trying to escape this nightmare.

Suddenly, there's a sickening squelch, and David freezes. His eyes widen in shock as a gurgling sound escapes his lips. Warm liquid splatters my face, and I open my eyes to see a knife protruding from David's throat.

He gapes at me, blood bubbling from his mouth before his body is violently shoved off mine. I try to scream, but a large hand clamps over my mouth, muffling my cries.

My assailant is a dark, imposing figure towering over me. The mask is the same one the man wore at the club.

I stare at the masked man, David's lifeless body crumpled at his feet. My heart pounds as I try to piece together what just happened. He removes his hand.

"Who... who are you?" I manage to choke out.

The man remains silent, his chest rising and falling with each breath. There's something vaguely familiar about his build and how he carries himself. An odd flicker of hope ignites in my gut. "Talon?" I whisper, hardly daring to believe it.

He doesn't respond, but I can feel the intensity of his gaze even through the mask. I search his face for any recognition, but he gives nothing away.

Before I can say anything else, he brings a damp cloth over my nose and mouth. A sickly sweet scent invades my senses, making my head swim.

I thrash wildly, trying to break free, but his grip is like iron. Black spots dance before my vision as the world starts to spin. My eyelids grow heavy, and I feel myself slipping away into unconsciousness.

The last thing I see is his striking blue eyes glinting through the mask's eyeholes, watching me as the darkness claims me.

32

TALON

*L*ena's chest rises and falls softly as the drugs pull her into unconsciousness. My hands shake with adrenaline, blood dripping from my fingers onto the hardwood floor. David's corpse lies twisted at my feet, his vacant eyes staring at nothing.

A surge of satisfaction courses through me at the sight. He got what he deserved for daring to touch what's mine. The knife in my hand feels heavy with righteous purpose. No one will ever hurt my girl again.

I need to focus. The body won't dispose of itself, but my gaze keeps drifting back to Lena, vulnerable and perfect. The urge to claim her wars with my need to protect her. Not yet, not like this. First, I have work to do.

Grabbing my latex gloves, I slip them on. I take David's cell phone, I grab my knife, peel up his eyelids, and use his vacant gaze to unlock the phone. And then, I enter the settings and remove the lock from his screen so that I can send a text to Lena from another location, placing him elsewhere. Pocketing the phone, I focus on the body.

I wrap David's body in a shower curtain, using duct tape to seal him inside. The copper tang of blood fills my nostrils as I scrub the floor. Each swipe of bleach erases the stains of his existence. Good. Let him fade away like he never existed.

My hands work methodically, cleaning every surface while my mind races. The cemetery will be the perfect place—poetic justice for him to rot among the other dead in an unmarked grave. I've already picked out the spot.

I pause to brush a strand of hair from Lena's face. "Sleep well, princess. He'll be nothing but a bad dream when you wake up." The possessive fire in my chest burns brighter. Soon, she'll be mine completely, just as it was always meant to be.

Time to move. I hoist David's body over my shoulder, triumphant at how limp and powerless he is now. No more will his hands bring bruises to her skin. I've made sure of that.

The night awaits, ready to swallow all evidence of what transpired here. By morning, no one will know what happened to David Collins. But I'll know. And I'll savor the memory of his final breaths.

I carry David's body to my waiting van, having already lined the cargo area with thick plastic sheets. Months of planning have prepared me for this moment. The wrapped corpse lands with a satisfying thud as I slide it inside.

My tool kit waits beside the body—everything

needed to ensure no trace remains. Latex gloves, industrial-grade cleaning supplies, bone saw, and containers of acid. Nothing left to chance.

First, I need to text Lena from his cell and ditch it at the club. So, I drive to one of the clubs I know David often goes to and slip the van down a back alley behind it, ensuring that the security camera to view the dumpster is blocked by the van. I send Lena a text, ensuring it sounds genuine to David.

Going out. Won't be back until late.

Keeping the engine running and the hood over my masked face, I get out and toss the cell phone into the dumpster before sliding back into the van on the other side.

From there, the drive to the cemetery takes fifteen minutes. I've mapped every security camera and potential witness location. The route I'm using avoids them all. The van's plates are stolen, and they are switched regularly. The vehicle itself is unremarkable—just another work van in the night.

The grave I've prepared sits in a remote corner, disguised as fresh maintenance work. The hole is deep— eight feet down. Deeper than standard plots. I drag David's body to the edge and roll it in. The acid comes next, carefully poured to accelerate decomposition. The chemicals will destroy DNA, dental records, and anything identifying him.

Thankfully, this graveyard is out of the way and there are no residential buildings nearby. Rushing to the equipment shed, I jump onto the mini backhoe I used the other night to dig the hole. Hotwiring it, I drive it toward the hole and use it to layer dirt and quicklime as I fill the grave. Each shovelful is calculated to look natural when the ground settles. I've even brought matching grass sod to lay over the top. By morning, it will look undisturbed.

Back at the van, I strip off my clothes and seal them in a bag for burning later. The tools get cleaned meticulously. I wear new clothes and fresh gloves. Everything that touched the body or grave site goes into industrial waste containers, to be disposed of across different locations over the next week.

One final area sweep with a UV light confirms no blood trail remains. The ground is smoothed, and grass is in place. Even knowing where to look, I can barely spot the grave. Perfect.

I allow myself a small smile as I drive away. They'll never find him. And even if they somehow did, there's nothing to connect it back to me or Lena. I've made sure of that.

33

TALON

I slip back into their apartment like a shadow, the UV light heavy in my pocket. The mask and hood shield my identity from any prying eyes or cameras. However, I've already disabled the building's security systems.

My boots barely whisper against the floor as I move through the darkened space. Lena's still unconscious on the bed, exactly where I left her. Her chest rises and falls in a steady rhythm that pulls at something deep inside me. Focus. I'm here to clean, not watch her sleep.

The UV light casts an eerie blue glow as I scan the hardwood. A few drops near the doorway glow bright—I missed them earlier. I pull out fresh cleaning supplies and get to work. The wood grain fights me, trying to hold onto its secrets, but I'm thorough. No evidence can remain.

Moving methodically across the floor, I check every inch. There is a smear here, a spatter there. Each spot gets the same treatment—bleach, scrub, dry, repeat. The chemical smell burns my nose through the mask. It is a small price to pay for perfection.

My knees ache from crawling around, but I don't stop until the UV reveals nothing but a clean floor. One final sweep, to be certain. Nothing glows except the natural oils in the wood grain. Good.

Lena stirs slightly in her sleep, drawing my attention. The drugs will keep her under for a while longer.

I run the bath, testing the temperature with my hand. It's not too hot, not too cold—perfect. The gentle sound of running water fills the master bathroom as steam rises in lazy curls.

Moving back to the bedroom, I strip Lena while she's lying down, adding the clothes to the pile I'll need to burn. The blood on her clothes has dried to a rusty brown, staining the delicate fabric. My jaw clenches at the sight. And then, once she's naked I lift her carefully from the bed. She's light in my arms, head lolling against my chest.

I lower her into the warm water. Her dark hair fans out around her like ink, and I can't help but stare at her peaceful face. My hands shake slightly as I begin washing away the blood, moving with careful precision. The water turns pink.

That bastard was so close to entering her against her will, but thankfully I stopped her.

Using a soft washcloth, I clean every trace of tonight's events from her skin. My breathing grows ragged as I work, heat coursing through my veins. I force myself to focus on the task at hand.

Once clean, I lift her from the tub and wrap her in a thick towel, gently patting her dry.

I carry her to the small sofa in her bedroom, arranging her carefully on the cushions. A strand of damp hair falls across her face, and I brush it with trembling fingers.

Turning away, I gather the bloodied sheets and clothes into a large black bag. Everything must be destroyed. But first, I need to shower and then bleach the bathroom.

I step out of the steaming shower, my skin scrubbed raw. The bathroom gleams from floor to ceiling, every surface bleached twice. Not a trace remains of what happened here.

Moving through the apartment, I double-check my work. The new sheets on the bed are pristine. The floor shows no hint of struggle. Even the air smells clean, pine cleaner masking any lingering metallic traces.

Satisfied with my inspection, I return to where Lena rests on the sofa. Her chest rises and falls steadily, her face peaceful in a drug-induced sleep. The towel has slipped, exposing one delicate shoulder.

My hands clench at my sides. She looks so vulnerable, so perfect. Mine to protect. Mine to possess.

I lift her gently, cradling her against my chest. Her damp hair leaves wet spots on my shirt as I carry her to the freshly made bed. Laying her down carefully, I arrange her limbs in a comfortable position.

The drugs will keep her unconscious for a while. Plenty of time to have some fun before she wakes. I trace a finger along her jawline, relishing the softness of her skin.

"Time to play," I whisper, sitting beside her on the bed. My hand hovers over her sleeping form, anticipation building in my veins.

I hover over her. My eyes take in every inch of her body, savoring the sight as my hands explore her curves. Her skin is soft under my touch, and I ache to mark it with my mouth.

Lena's scent fills my lungs as I lean down, inhaling deeply. My tongue darts out, tasting her neck, trailing down to the valley between her breasts.

My mouth waters as I move lower, my tongue painting swirls on her smooth skin. Her taste lingers on my tongue, and I growl softly, the sound vibrating against her stomach.

I can't resist any longer. My mouth finds Lena's core, and I lick her slowly, savoring the sweetness of her arousal. Her lips are soft against mine while I feast on her, wanting to devour her.

Lena moans in her sleep, her hips lifting slightly off the bed. The sound goes straight to my cock, making me throb with need. I rub myself against her thigh, desperate for relief.

But I want to be inside her more than anything. I position myself at her entrance, the tip of my cock teasing her wet heat. With a gentle thrust, I slide into her, groaning as her tightness envelopes me.

Her body accepts me, and I sink deeper, filling her fully. My hands grip her hips as I begin to move, slowly at first, but soon, my restraint breaks. I pound into her, my breath coming in sharp pants.

Lena's breath catches, her body tensing around me. Her eyes flutter open, unfocused at first, but then—

She sees me. Her eyes widen, pupils dilated with desire and confusion. "Talon?"

My name on her lips drives me crazy. "Fuck, Lena," I grit out.

Her eyes lock onto mine, the realization sparking something dangerous in their hazel depths. Her slender body arches beneath me, the muscles in her thighs tensing as she takes me in deeper.

"Talon?" she breathes again, her voice a mix of shock and desire.

I can't stop. My princess's body feels too good around mine, and I'm gripped by an urgent need to claim every inch of her. "Yeah, baby. It's me."

Lena's hands reach up, her fingers digging into my shoulders. "Oh God," she moans, her hips moving against mine in a sensual rhythm. "It's really you. Talon."

When she utters my name again, it sends a spark of arousal straight to my cock. I thrust harder, my breath laboring. "You have no idea how much I've fucking missed you, Lena."

She arches her back, offering herself to me as my hands glide down her body. Her skin is hot to the touch, her nipples tightening beneath my palms.

I squeeze her breasts and lean down, biting gently at her neck as I thrust into her again and again. "It's been so hard, watching you, wanting you. Did you fucking miss this?" I growl against her skin, my teeth grazing her neck.

Lena gasps, her back arching as my fingers tighten on her hips. "Yes," she whispers, the word a barely audible admission. "I did. Oh, God, Talon."

Hearing that confession sends a spike of possessive satisfaction through me. I pull out of her slowly, the slick sound fueling my desire.

"Get on your hands and knees," I command, voice hoarse with need.

Lena obeys, positioning herself on the bed, her perfect ass raised in invitation. Her skin is flushed, a sweet bite mark darkening on her shoulder.

Mine.

I want to take my time and savor every moment, but the desperate need to claim her overrides all else. Gripping my cock, I rub the tip up and down her slit, spreading her arousal.

Lena moans, her head hanging down as she braces herself on her forearms. "Talon, please."

I don't keep her waiting. With a fierce thrust, I drive into her, claiming what's mine. Her tightness envelops me, and I groan at the sensation.

"Fuck, Lena," I grit out, beginning to move. "You're so fucking tight."

Lena cries out, her fingers digging into the bedsheets. "Harder, Talon. I need more."

Hearing that desperate plea, I lose all restraint. Grabbing her hips, I slam into her with force, my cock driving deep.

"Again," she pants, her body rocking back to meet my thrusts. "Harder, Talon. Fuck me harder."

Her words spur me on, and I deliver what she craves. My hands dig into her soft flesh, holding her in place as I pound into her relentlessly. The bed creaks with the force of our passion.

"That's it, baby," I grunt. "Take it all. Only me inside you now, Lena."

Lena's breath comes in sharp gasps, her back arching as pleasure overtakes her. "Yes, Talon. Only you. Oh, God..."

Her pussy clamps down on my cock, and I know she's close. I reach between us, my fingers finding her swollen clit. "Come for me, Lena. Let me feel you squeeze my cock."

My words push her over the edge, and she cries out, her body convulsing around me. I keep thrusting through her orgasm, prolonging her pleasure.

Lena's cries fill the room, her nails digging into the sheets as her body milks my cock. Her juices flow, coating my thighs as I continue to move inside her.

"Milk my cock. Make me come inside you," I encourage.

Her body tightens again, a second orgasm rippling through her. "Talon!" she cries, her voice full of wonder and pleasure. "I'm coming again."

Feeling her contract around me again pushes me over the edge. "Fuck, Lena," I grit out, my body tensing. "I'm gonna come, baby. Gonna fill your tight little pussy."

With a few more fierce thrusts, I spill myself into her,

groaning as my release washes over me. Lena's body shudders with the force of my climax, her inner walls pulsing around me.

Collapsing onto my back, I hold her tight, my face buried in her neck. Our bodies are drenched in sweat, our hearts pounding in unison.

Lena's fingers trace lazy patterns on my chest, her breath evening out. "Wow," she whispers, a smile in her voice. "That was..."

"Incredible," I finish for her, lifting my head to meet her gaze.

I feel Lena's body tense against mine as reality crashes over her. She bolts upright, yanking the sheet to cover herself.

"Oh God. This wasn't—I thought it was a dream." Her eyes dart around the room, panic setting in. "You killed David. You actually killed him."

I reach for her, but she flinches away. Keeping my voice steady, I explain, "He was trying to rape you, Lena. I watched that piece of shit force himself on you while you begged him to stop."

"But you—you stabbed him. I remember the blood..." Her voice breaks.

"He deserved worse for touching what's mine." My jaw clenches at the memory. "He's gone now. Forever. No one will ever hurt you like that again."

Lena's hands shake as she grips the sheet tighter. "You killed someone, Talon. You actually murdered him."

"To protect you." I move closer, careful not to startle her. "Everything I do is to keep you safe. David won't ever lay his hands on you again. He can't hurt you anymore."

I pull Lena into my arms as her shoulders shake with sobs. She doesn't resist, instead collapsing against my chest. Her fingers dig into my skin like she's afraid I'll disappear.

"He made me feel so powerless," she sobs. "The first time he did it was Friday night, and then after dinner he..."

"Shh." I stroke her hair, breathing in her scent. "He can't touch you ever again. No one will hurt you like that again."

Her body trembles against mine. I hold her tighter, letting her release everything she's bottled up. My Lena, so strong for so long, letting those walls crumble.

"I hated being under his control," she whispers into my chest. "The way he'd smile while hurting me like he enjoyed my fear..."

"Everything will be fine now," I murmur against her hair. "I'm here. I'll always protect you, always keep you safe. No one else will ever lay a hand on you."

Her sobs gradually quiet, her breathing steadying as she stays wrapped in my embrace. I continue running my fingers through her hair, feeling her relax against me.

"Thank you," she breathes, her voice barely audible. "For saving me from him."

I press my lips to her forehead. "Always, Lena. I'll always save you."

LENA

*J*olt awake, my head fuzzy with fragments of memories that feel like a nightmare. The bedroom is pristine—no blood, no signs of struggle. Nothing to confirm the violent scene from last night.

"Did I dream it all?" I whisper to myself, running my fingers through my tangled hair. The sheets beside me are cold and empty. No trace of Talon.

My heart pounds as I scan the room. Everything looks normal—too normal. The picture frames still hang straight on the walls, and David's clothes still lie scattered across the floor where he left them.

David. My stomach lurches as fragments of last night flash through my mind—his cruel grip, the masked figure, the knife...

The bedroom door swings open with a creak. I gasp, pulling the sheets up to my chin as Talon appears in the doorway. His presence fills the room, dark and intense.

"You're really here," I breathe. "Last night... it wasn't a dream?"

"No dream." His voice is low and controlled.

"What—" My voice cracks. I clear my throat and try again. "What am I supposed to do? People will ask questions. The police... his family... How do I explain David's disappearance?"

Talon steps closer, his blue eyes boring into mine. "You don't explain anything. You're the grieving fiancée who has no idea where he went. He was acting strange lately, distant. Maybe the pressure of graduation got to him. Maybe he needed space."

"But—"

"The less you know, the more genuine your reactions will be." He perches on the edge of the bed. "Trust me, Lena. I've taken care of everything. No one will ever find him."

A shiver runs through me at his words. I should be terrified. I should be running. Instead, I reach for his hand, craving his dark comfort.

I stare at Talon's hand, his touch comforting and dangerous. His thumb traces circles on my palm, but his words slice through the quiet morning air.

"Who's next, baby? Mr. Wilson, perhaps?" His eyes darken with an intensity that makes my breath catch. "He hurt you. Made you feel worthless. Don't you want him gone too?"

My stomach churns at the mention of our foster father. Years of abuse flash through my mind—the bruises, the cruel words, the way he'd drink himself into violent rages. And his violation, worse than David's, occurred twice after Talon was gone.

"I—" The words stick in my throat. Part of me

wants to say yes, to watch Mr. Wilson suffer like he made us suffer. But another part remembers how it felt when Talon left before. The emptiness. The abandonment. "What if something goes wrong? What if they catch you?"

Talon's grip tightens. "No one will catch me. I'm careful. Methodical." His free hand cups my cheek, forcing me to meet his gaze. "Don't you trust me?"

"Of course I do," I lean into his touch. "But I can't lose you again. The last time you disappeared..." Tears burn behind my eyes. "Eight months, Talon. It felt like an eternity."

"That was different. I was protecting you then." His thumb wipes away a tear that escapes. "Now I'm strong enough to keep you safe. To eliminate anyone who ever hurt you."

"Please. Not yet. I just got you back." My fingers clutch his shirt. "Can't we just... be together for a while? Figure out what this is between us?"

His jaw clenches, and that familiar darkness swirls in his eyes. I can see the battle raging inside him—the need to hurt, to destroy, warring with his desire to give me what I want.

"For now," he finally growls. "But he'll pay eventually. They all will."

I push away the memories of David, of last night's violence. My heart hammers as I look up into Talon's stormy eyes. I can't bear the thought of losing him again, tugging him close. His solid body presses against mine. His lips find mine, fierce and urgent. The kiss is a spark that ignites the smoldering heat between us. And he lifts me as if I weigh nothing. My legs wrap around his waist, instinctively opening for him.

The wall behind me bites into my skin as he pushes me against it. Talon's mouth trails down my neck, his teeth nipping at the sensitive skin, claiming me. I arch against him, craving more.

"You're mine," he growls, his breath hot against my ear.

"Yes," I whisper, surrendering to the wildness within me. I've locked these desires away for so long, afraid to unleash them. But with Talon, I can embrace the dark, erotic impulses that surge between us.

His need for me is as raw and urgent as my own. My hands explore his back, his shoulders, and the scars that mark him. We're both scarred, damaged by our pasts. But in this moment, we're connected, vibrant, and alive.

Talon lines himself up and thrusts into me, filling me completely. I gasp, my head falling back against the wall. The friction of his body against mine sends sparks of pleasure through me. It's primal, intense, and so different from my imagined fantasies.

He sets a relentless pace, his gaze never leaving mine. His eyes reflect the same pleasure and torment I feel, and we have an unspoken understanding.

"Look at me, baby," he grunts. "I want to see your eyes when I make you come."

I'm consumed by the raw passion of the moment, the feral heat in his eyes. His body perfectly syncs with mine as if we're two halves of a whole, finally reunited.

The tension coils tighter and tighter within me, a building pressure seeking release. Talon's thrusts grow harder, faster, pushing me closer to the edge. He knows exactly what I need, how to drive me wild. His hands grip my thighs, lifting me higher, driving deeper.

Our eyes lock, and I see the moment the pleasure overtakes him. His back arches, his breath catching. "Lena," he groans, and I feel his release, triggering my own climax. My body pulses around him, waves of pleasure washing over me.

For a moment, we stay connected, our breathing heavy. His forehead rests against mine, our sweat-dampened skin sticking together. Then he gently lowers me to the ground, his eyes shining fiercely.

TALON

I watch Lena from across the street as she speaks to David's parents on her phone. Her performance is perfect—her voice trembling with worry, she asks if they've heard from him. Pride swells in my chest. She's following my instructions exactly.

"No, I haven't heard anything since he went out Friday night," she says, pacing by her window. "I thought he was just staying at Mark's place, but when he didn't come home yesterday..." Her voice catches. "I'm really getting worried."

I slip deeper into the shadows as a police cruiser approaches her building. Two officers step out, notepads ready. Lena meets them at the door, wringing her hands —another nice touch.

Through my scope, I watch her invite them inside. She sits primly on the edge of the couch, eyes wide and innocent, as she recounts the story we crafted. David went out drinking with friends. He never came home.

There were no calls or texts after his brief text to Lena. It is so unlike him to disappear without a word.

The cops take notes and ask routine questions. When was the last time she saw him? Did they have any fights recently? Has he ever disappeared before? Lena answers each one perfectly, revealing enough anxiety to be believable while maintaining composure.

I have to stay away now. Let the investigation run its course. But watching her perform for them, I know I chose well. She's mine in every way that matters. The darkness in her matches my own.

One of the officers places a comforting hand on her shoulder. My fingers twitch, wanting to break each digit for daring to touch her, but I remain still and patient. This is all part of the plan.

The police leave after taking her statement. Lena closes the door behind them and sinks against it, shoulders slumping. Even from here, I can see this performance's toll on her. But she'll endure it. She's stronger than she knows.

I'll keep my distance, watching over her from the shadows while she plays her part. The grieving fiancée is worried sick about her missing husband-to-be. If only they knew the truth—that she's always belonged to me. And that sad son of bitch took his last breath while he tried to rape my precious girl and bled out on the floor of the apartment.

I text her burner phone, my fingers tapping out a quick message: "Cemetery. Midnight. Come alone."

Her response is immediate: "Why there?"

"It's a surprise. Trust me."

I can picture her biting her lip, weighing the risks. But I know she'll come. The darkness in her calls to mine.

"Ok. Midnight," she replies.

I smile, tucking the phone away. My revenge on that piece of shit David isn't complete yet. Killing him was just the start. He needs to understand, even in death, that Lena was never his. She will never be his.

I want to claim her over his grave, mark her as mine where his rotting corpse lies eight feet below. Let his spirit watch as I take what he thought belonged to him. The thought makes my cock throb with anticipation.

The hours crawl by until midnight approaches. I pace between the headstones, the moonlight casting long shadows across the grass. This spot where he's buried is perfect—secluded enough that no one will interrupt us.

Footsteps crunch on gravel. Lena appears through the darkness, wearing a black dress that makes her look like a gothic angel. My angel of death.

"You came." I reach for her hand, pulling her close.

"Of course I did." She swallows hard. "Now tell me why we're here."

I lead her to David's fresh grave, unmarked still since his body won't be found. "Because our revenge isn't complete yet, precious girl. Not until I fuck you right here, over his worthless corpse."

I trace my finger along Lena's jawline as she stares at me, shock evident in her widened eyes. Her pulse races beneath my touch, a mix of fear and desire.

"You think I'm crazy." I press my lips to her neck,

breathing in her scent. "But deep down, you feel it, too. That darkness inside you, begging to be set free."

"This is insane," she whispers, but her body betrays her, leaning into my touch. "We can't—not here."

"We can. We will." My hands slide down her sides, gripping her hips. "Stop fighting what you are, precious girl. I've seen the shadows in your eyes when you thought no one was looking."

Her breath catches as I nip at her throat. "Talon..."

"Remember how good it felt when he died? When his blood spilled across the floor?" I press against her, letting her feel how hard I am. "You weren't disgusted. You were relieved. Excited even."

"That's not—" She starts to protest, but I silence her with a kiss, rough and demanding.

"Don't lie to me." I break away, staring into her eyes. "Don't lie to yourself. The darkness has always been there, waiting. Just like I've been waiting."

My hand tangles in her hair, tugging her head back. Her resistance wavers, and her body softens against mine. I can feel her walls crumbling, that carefully maintained facade of normalcy starting to crack.

"Let go," I whisper against her skin. "Let me show you how beautiful the darkness can be."

She shudders, fingers clutching my shirt. "You're insane," she says again, but there's less conviction now, her voice breathy with need.

"Maybe." I slide my hand under her dress. "But you're just like me. Two broken pieces that fit perfectly together."

It's time for her to accept what she is—what we are

—and embrace the darkness that's been there all along. I need to mark her with my initials so everyone knows she belongs to me.

"Take off your dress." My voice is a command, brooking no refusal.

She looks at me, eyes flicking to the knife in my hand, and obeys. Slowly, teasingly, she peels the fabric away, revealing her body to the night. The moonlight makes her skin glow silver, accentuating her curves.

"On all fours." I gesture to the ground above David's grave. "Over his dead body."

Lena bites her lip, a mix of apprehension and desire flitting across her face. But she complies, getting down on all fours, ass raised invitingly.

The knife glints in the moonlight. As I step closer, she tenses, anticipation and fear dancing in her eyes. "Trust me," I whisper, carding my fingers through her hair.

My free hand slides over her ass, caressing the soft skin. Then, with the tip of the blade, I begin to carve. Slowly, meticulously, I etch my initials into her flesh — TV, for Talon Voss.

She gasps as the blade bites but doesn't pull away. Instead, her body relaxes into the touch, accepting the pain. I carve deeper, ensuring the mark will scar, wanting everyone to know she's forever mine.

"Do you see how good it feels to let the darkness out?" I murmur, trailing kisses along her spine.

"Yes." Her voice is hoarse with desire.

"Tell me how much you've been craving this?"

"So much," she breathes. "More, please."

"Your wish is my command, precious girl." I set the knife aside, positioning myself behind her.

With a sharp thrust, I enter her, claiming her body as my own. Lena moans, her head falling forward as she pushes back against me. "Fuck, yes," she breathes. "Harder, Talon."

I grasp her hips and thrust again, deeper this time, relishing the feel of her tight heat around me. "You like it rough, don't you, princess?"

"Yes," she pants. "Always knew I was a little fucked up."

"Not fucked up, beautiful." I nibble her shoulder, then bite down gently.

"You wish I hadn't killed him." I grip Lena's hips, pulling her back to meet my thrusts. "Don't you, baby? You wanted to watch him suffer while we fucked."

"No." Her breath comes in short gasps as I pound into her. "I—I mean, yes. Fuck, Talon."

I lean down over her back, my mouth close to her ear. "Admit it. You wanted to ride me while he watched, helpless to do anything. To see the fear in his eyes as I made you scream."

"Yes," she moans, her body moving in rhythmic circles against mine. "God, yes."

Pulling out, I grab her and push her against a headstone beside us. "I knew you were a freak like me," I growl, plunging back inside her. "I should've let him live long enough to see it."

Lena's head falls back against the stone. Her eyes are closed, lips parted as she pants my name.

"You wanted to watch him bleed while I made you

come, didn't you?" I grip her throat, squeezing lightly, as I slam into her.

Her nails dig into my arms. "God, Talon, please. Harder."

I groan, the pleasure curling through my body. This is what I've fantasized about for years. Her begging for it. Me, giving it to her.

"You want me to mark you?" I bite her ear, sucking gently. "Make it so everyone knows you're mine?"

"Yes." Her fingers tangle in my hair, pulling me closer. "Please, mark me. Everywhere."

"Only if you promise to be a good girl." I ease out of her, stroking her slick folds with my thumb. "If you let me take you wherever and however I want."

"Yes." Her voice is a desperate plea. "Anything, just don't stop."

"That's my girl." I thrust back inside her, setting a brutal pace. "Remember this moment, right here, right now. The moment you became irrevocably mine."

Lena's back arches, her body tense as she rides the wave of her orgasm. I spill inside her, groaning her name. We're both breathless for a moment, our hearts pounding in unison. Then, gently, I lower us to the ground, pulling her onto my lap, her back against my chest. She shivers in the night air, and I wrap my arms around her, feeling a sense of possessiveness like never before.

"Are you cold?" I murmur, kissing her neck.

"A little."

I hand Lena her dress, watching as she slips it over her marked body. The moonlight catches on the fresh cuts—my initials forever etched into her skin. Pride and possessiveness surge through me at the sight.

"Ready to go?" I ask but pause before we leave. "Actually, there's one more thing I want to show you."

Taking her hand, I lead her to three empty plots beside David's grave. "See these? I've already reserved them." My fingers trace through the air, mapping out the spaces. "One for Jamie, one for Mr. Wilson, and one for Mrs. Wilson. A family reunion of sorts."

"No." Lena's grip on my hand tightens painfully. "You can't hurt Jamie."

I turn to face her, surprised by the steel in her voice.

"He protected me when you weren't there, Talon. Multiple times." Her eyes flash with determination. "And Mrs. Wilson—Jamie needs some family. You can't touch her, either."

The fierce protectiveness in her tone catches me off guard. I hadn't expected her to defend them, especially not after what we just did over David's grave. But there she stands, chin lifted defiantly, daring me to argue.

"Jamie showed me kindness when no one else would," she continues. "He doesn't deserve to end up here."

I study Lena's face in the moonlight, processing her fierce defense of Jamie and Mrs. Wilson. My jaw clenches.

"What about Mr. Wilson?"

Lena's shoulders tense. She stares at the empty plot I indicated for him, a slight tremor running through her body. After a long pause, she gives a single nod.

"He deserves it because..." Her voice trails off, hands twisting in the fabric of her dress.

"Tell me." My tone brooks no argument. "What did he do?"

Lena wraps her arms around herself, taking a shaky breath. "After you left—when he caught us and threw you out... he..." She swallows hard. "When everyone was gone, and he was drunk, he... he raped me. Two times."

White-hot rage floods my system. My fists clench at my sides.

"Jamie stopped him other times when he tried," she continues, voice barely above a whisper. "If Jamie hadn't been there..."

A growl rips from my throat. The world takes on a red tinge as I imagine that bastard touching her. Hurting her. My Lena.

"When?" I demand through gritted teeth.

"A few weeks after you left."

My chest constricts painfully. If I hadn't left... if I'd stayed...

I clench my jaw, fury and frustration warring inside me. "He would have made sure I rotted in prison," I tell Lena. "A troubled foster kid against an upstanding member of the community? The cops would've laughed."

Mr. Wilson had connections throughout Salem—the police chief played golf with him, and the DA attended the same church. Meanwhile, I was just another damaged kid with a record of fighting and "behavioral issues."

"That bastard probably saw something he liked and that's why he kicked me out," My fists clench at my sides. "He could have done it years before, but after seeing you in that way he wanted you to himself." The rage I feel is impossible to tame.

I remember the look in Mr. Wilson's eyes that last evening—cold calculation. He knew exactly what he was doing when he caught me with Lena. If I hadn't left, he would have found a way to get rid of me permanently anyway.

"One phone call to his buddy at the precinct," I continue, "and I'd have been charged with assault or something worse. My word against his about what really happened."

Lena's fingers brush my arm. "You can't blame yourself for his actions."

"But I can destroy him now." I meet her gaze in the moonlight. "I'll ensure he's eight feet under, just like his no longer future son-in-law."

The rage still burns hot in my chest, but it's focused now. Controlled. Mr. Wilson's time is coming, but it has to be perfect. Calculated. I won't let him get away with what he did to Lena.

LENA

*D*ark memories flood my mind while I lie in bed, staring at the ceiling.

The image of David's shocked expression as the knife plunged into his throat while his body weighed me down. The way Talon's masked face appeared like a demon from my nightmares or perhaps dreams. How he took me over David's fresh grave.

My stomach churns. Any sane person would run screaming. But I can't forget how safe I felt in Talon's arms at the cemetery, how right it felt when he claimed me. The way his possessive touch ignited something primal inside me.

I roll over, burying my face in the pillow. "What's wrong with me?"

Talon killed a man. He's obsessed, dangerous, unhinged. And yet... I've never felt more alive than when I was with him. Maybe I'm just as broken. Losing my parents, followed by years of mental and physical abuse from the Wilsons, twisted something inside me, too.

I think back to the scared nine-year-old girl who first met Talon. Even then, there was something magnetic about him. Through all the beatings he took for me and the silent ways he protected me, I fell in love with his darkness.

"I love him," I whisper into the darkness. The truth of it settles heavily in my chest. "God help me, I love every twisted, violent part of him."

Because Talon understands me in ways no one else ever could. He knows my pain, my rage, my desire for revenge against those who hurt us. He's the only one who's ever truly seen me.

The bathroom door creaks, and I jolt upright in bed. Steam billows from the doorway as Talon emerges, water droplets trailing down his sculpted chest. The towel hangs dangerously low on his hips, and I can't help but trace the defined V of his muscles with my eyes. Scars mark his skin—a testament to all the abuse he endured protecting me and perhaps before the Wilsons, too. I know very little about his former life.

"What were you saying?" His voice is rough, sending shivers down my spine.

I clutch the sheets tighter, averting my gaze. "Nothing. Just talking to myself."

He stalks toward the bed like a predator, muscles rippling with each step. His eyes narrow, piercing straight through me. "Tell me what's going on in your pretty head."

My heart pounds against my ribs. Even after everything we've done, the intensity of his presence still overwhelms me. Water drips from his dark hair onto my arm as he leans closer, and I resist the urge to reach out and touch him.

"Lena." His tone carries a warning. He won't let this go—he never does. Talon's possessive nature means he needs to know every thought and every feeling that crosses my mind.

I take a shaky breath, meeting his intense gaze. "I was just thinking about us. About everything that's happened."

Talon's eyes darken as he sits on the edge of the bed. His fingers trace along my jaw, and I fight to not lean into his touch. "Having second thoughts?"

"No." The word comes out stronger than I expected. "That's what scares me. I should be horrified. I should want to run screaming after what happened with David. But instead..."

"Instead?" His grip tightens slightly.

"Instead, I've never felt more alive." The confession tumbles from my lips. "When you killed him, then claimed me in the cemetery—I know it's wrong, but it felt right. Like everything finally clicked into place."

A dangerous smile spreads across his face. "My beautiful, dark girl." His thumb brushes across my bottom lip. "You're finally embracing who you really are."

"And who is that?"

"Mine." He leans closer, his breath hot against my ear. "The darkness inside you matches mine. That's why we fit so perfectly together."

I shiver at his words, knowing they're true. The years of abuse and pain have shaped us both. Where others would see a monster in Talon, I see my protector, my salvation.

"I love you," I whisper, the words falling between us like a confession.

His eyes flash with something primal. Before I can react, he has me pinned beneath him, the towel forgotten. Water drips from his hair onto my face as he stares down at me with an intensity that steals my breath.

"Say it again."

"I love you," I breathe.

His eyes glint with a fierce intensity, and his thumb grazes my bottom lip, sending shivers down my spine. "Say it like you mean it."

I swallow, feeling a heady mix of desire and fear. "I love you, Talon. Every dark and twisted part of you."

A feral grin spreads across his face, and he lowers his head, his lips claiming mine in a fierce kiss. His tongue invades my mouth, demanding and possessive. I melt into him, my hands tangling in his damp hair as I surrender to the onslaught of his mouth. His kiss is hungry and desperate.

Talon's hands roam impatiently over my body, igniting fiery trails of desire in their wake. He tugs at the edges of my shirt, impatient to tear it away and bare my flesh to his hungry gaze. I gasp into his mouth as the fabric pulls taut across my breasts, then sigh as he rips it open, buttons popping off, exposing my lace bra.

His lips trail down my neck, leaving a trail of fiery kisses along my shoulder. I squirm beneath him, craving more of his intense touch. Talon's hands roam lower, slipping beneath the elastic of my pajama pants, his fingers stroking the sensitive skin of my inner thighs.

"You're so wet for me, baby," he murmurs against my skin, his hot breath sending shivers down my spine.

"Please," I whisper, my breath heavy. "I need you."

His chuckle vibrates against my neck, sending delicious shivers through me. "Tell me what you want, Lena."

My cheeks heat up. I've never been one for dirty talk, but something about Talon brings out my inner vixen. "I want you inside me." I rock my hips against him, needing to feel him buried deep. "I need to feel you claim me again."

A growl rumbles in his chest, wasting no time he peels off my pants and tosses them aside. His eyes scorch a path down my body, taking in my nakedness with raw hunger.

"You're so fucking gorgeous," he says, his fingers tracing the curve of my breast before tugging at my bra. "All mine."

I arch my back, allowing him to free me from the delicate lace, exposing my erect nipples to his hungry gaze. "All yours," I agree, my voice husky.

With a groan, he lowers his head, his tongue teasing one tight peak while his fingers pluck at the other. My back bows off the bed as electricity shoots through me. "Talon, please," I beg, my body on fire.

He chuckles, the vibrations dancing across my sensitive skin. "My greedy girl. Want it all, don't you?"

I nod frantically. "Please, Talon. Take me. Make me yours."

His eyes darken to a deep, fathomless blue as he positions himself between my thighs.

I grasp his shoulders, pulling him closer. "Don't hold back."

His lips crash down on mine as he drives into me in one swift thrust. We both groan, our bodies uniting with a fierce intensity. Talon begins to move, his hips snapping as he sets a brutal pace. I meet his rhythm, my body welcoming his possession.

"That's it, baby," he growls against my ear. "So greedy for my cock."

He groans, his body tensing above me as he thrusts harder. "Take it all, baby. Take your fill."

His words send a fresh wave of desire coursing through me, and I wrap my legs tighter around his waist, urging him deeper. Talon holds me in place as he pounds into me relentlessly.

"That's it, take it all," he grunts, his eyes fixed on where our bodies join, watching his length disappear inside me over and over. "You love it, don't you? My cock filling you up."

"Yes," I whimper, my head tipping back as pleasure skyrockets through me. "God, yes."

Talon's mouth finds my neck, his teeth grazing my sensitive skin as his thrusts become more urgent. "Say my name."

"Talon," I moan, my fingers digging into his shoulders. "Talon, please."

His pace becomes even more frenzied, his grunts

filling the room. "I can feel you squeezing me, baby. You're so tight around me."

I cry out as he hits a sweet spot deep within me. "There, there!"

He chuckles, the sound vibrating through his chest. "Like that, do you?" He shifts his hips, repeating the motion, driving me wild. "God, you're so responsive."

"Yes!" I'm a mess of need, bucking my hips to meet his. "Harder, Talon. Fuck me harder."

With a feral growl, he pulls out, causing me to whimper at the loss. Then he flips me over, pressing me into the mattress. He grips my hips, pulling me up onto my knees as he drives into me from behind.

"You like it like this, don't you?" he grunts, his breath hot against my neck. "On your knees, taking it like a good girl."

I moan, my head falling forward as he pistons in and out of me. "Yes, fuck, yes!"

Talon's hand lands on my ass, giving it a sharp smack. "That's my good girl." He repeats the action, his rhythm never faltering. "Always so wet and eager for me, baby."

My breath catches as he slaps my ass again, sending a bolt of pleasure straight to my core. "More," I beg.

He chuckles, the sound sending delicious shivers down my spine. "Such a dirty girl. Want me to mark you up, don't you?"

"Yes, please." My cheeks burn with shame, but my body craves his touch. "Please, Talon."

He obliges, his hand raining down sharp slaps that leave my ass cheeks stinging. I cry out with each blow, the pleasure and pain mixing in a heady cocktail that pushes me closer to the edge. His finger traces the brand he etched into my skin with his knife.

"That's it, take it," he growls, his fingers digging into my hips as he thrusts into me with abandon. "Take all the pain and pleasure I give you."

I sob with each slap, my body shaking as the pressure builds. "Talon, I'm close," I pant.

"Come for me, baby," he grunts, his thrusts becoming more erratic. "Come on my cock."

His command pushes me over the edge, and I cry out as my orgasm washes over me. Talon lets out a ragged groan, his hands gripping my hips tightly as he empties himself inside me with a few more sharp thrusts.

We collapse onto the bed, our bodies damp with sweat. Talon kisses my shoulder, his hands gently stroking my hair.

"That was—intense." I turn my head to look at him, my voice breathless.

He chuckles, the sound rumbling through his chest. "I aim to please, baby."

I nuzzle closer to him, my fingers tracing the scars on his back. Memories of his protective actions over the years flood my mind. "You know, you're the only one who's ever seen all of me," I whisper.

He goes still, then slowly turns his head to look at me, his eyes filled with a fierce intensity. "You know I'd do anything for you, right?"

My heart twists at the raw emotion in his eyes. "I know."

His hand reaches for mine. "I'm yours forever."

My breath catches at his words, the depth of his devotion overwhelming me. No one has ever loved me with such fierce, uncontrollable passion. It scares me, excites me, and fulfills me all at once.

"Can I—" My voice falters as I swallow, suddenly shy. "Can I carve my initials in you like you did to me?"

His eyes darken. "Where do you want it?"

I bite my lip, a mix of anticipation and nerves coursing through me. "Here." I trace a spot above his heart. "I want my mark right here."

A slow, sinful smile spreads across his face. "Whatever my dark angel wants."

He kisses me softly, his tongue tangling with mine in a sweet, intimate caress that contrasts sharply with our previous rough passion. Then he gets up, going to his bag and retrieving a small, sharp knife.

He hands it to me, his eyes sparkling with dark desire. "Make your mark, Lena."

My fingers tremble as I take the knife from him, the blade glinting menacingly. I hesitate, my breath catching as I realize what I'm about to do.

"Don't hold back," he whispers, his voice thick with anticipation. "Make it deep. I want to feel it."

I take a steadying breath, my fingers tightening around the knife's handle. Talon's chest rises and falls with his rapid breaths, his eyes glittering with anticipation. I lean down, pressing a soft kiss to the spot above his heart.

"Tell me if it hurts too much," I whisper, my voice laced with concern.

His fingers thread through my hair, holding me in place as he captures my mouth in a searing kiss. "It won't." His voice is confident, his lips moving against mine. "Do it, Lena."

My heart hammers in my chest as I drag the tip of the blade lightly across his skin, watching the first bead of crimson form. Talon inhales sharply at the contact, his eyes flashing with dark pleasure. I bite my lip, steeling myself, then slowly begin to carve.

The knife bites into his flesh, and he arches his back with a sharp hiss. I pause, my body going tense. "Are you okay?"

"Fuck," he gasps, his eyes squeezed shut as he savors the sensation. "Keep going."

I swallow and continue, dragging the blade slowly through his skin. Talon lets out a low growl, his hips bucking upwards, seeking friction. I look down, my eyes widening at the sight of his straining erection. A surge of desire courses through me, and I shift my position, straddling his waist.

His eyes fly open, pupils dilated with hunger. "What are you doing?" he rasps.

Instead of answering, I sink down onto him, his length filling me with exquisite slowness. We groan at the intimate connection, our bodies fusing together once more.

"Fuck," he grunts, his head falling back as he grips my hips.

I begin to move, riding him with slow, torturous strokes as the knife continues its steady journey across his skin. The rhythm of our bodies sets a spellbinding pace. His pain is my pleasure, our breaths mingling in a symphony of panting need.

"Keep going," he grits out between clenched teeth. "Don't stop."

I comply, my body moving with a will of its own. The knife slices through his skin as I rise and fall, my inner muscles clenching around him with each descent. Talon's fingers dig into my hips, holding me in place as he thrusts upwards to meet my downward motions.

"Faster, baby," he pants, his eyes locked on mine. "I need it harder."

I quicken my pace, my breath coming in short gasps as I bounce on his lap. He fills me completely, his length stroking all the right places. My inner walls squeeze around him, desperate to prolong this moment of perfect unity.

"Your pussy was made for my cock," he grunts, his head thrown back in abandon.

My fingers tighten around the hilt of the knife as I move faster, the blade finishing the first initial. I start on the second with renewed vigor, wanting to brand him as mine. Talon's teeth grit, his jaw clenching from the pain and pleasure.

"Seeing my initials on you turns me on," I confess, my eyes never leaving the marks I'm carving. "Knowing you'll carry my initials forever."

"Fuck," he groans, his eyes rolling back in his head. "No going back now, is there?"

"Never," I breathe, leaning down to nip at his earlobe. "You're mine forever, Talon. My soulmate in darkness."

"Yes," he hisses, his body arching off the bed as he seeks deeper contact. "Do it harder, Lena. I want to feel it."

My heart soars at his words, and I drag the knife more firmly across his skin, leaving a deep impression of my love. "Are you sure?"

"Fuck, yes. Don't hold back," he hisses, eyes burning with raw desire.

I grin, my cheeks flushing with excitement as I add more pressure to my strokes. The knife bites into his flesh, leaving a permanent mark of my initials on his chest. "LG," I breathe, my voice thick with satisfaction.

"Together in darkness," he agrees, his eyes burning with feral intensity. "Nothing can break this bond."

Our gazes lock, our bodies moving in perfect unison as if choreographed. The knife falls from my hand as I move forward and lick the bloody wound. My walls clench around him as my pleasure builds, an exquisite torture that demands release.

"I'm close," I whisper, my body tightening around him.

"Come for me," he growls, his voice deep and commanding. "Come on my cock, baby."

His words send me spiraling over the edge, and my orgasm crashes over me.

Talon growls, his hands digging into my hips as he bucks upwards, burying himself deep within me. His body goes taut, his release pulsing inside me.

We ride out our dual release, our bodies slick with sweat as our hearts pound in rhythm. When we come down from our mutual high, I kiss the initials on Talon's chest, his blood fresh and warm.

"Perfect," he murmurs, his eyes half-lidded with satisfaction. "Just like you, Lena."

I trace my fingers over the fresh carving on Talon's chest, watching the way his blood glistens in the dim light. My initials, permanently etched into his skin—a dark mirror of the mark he left on me. The metallic scent of blood mingles with our sweat and sex, creating an intoxicating cocktail that makes my head spin.

Who would have thought that scared little foster girl would end up here?

But there's something right about this—about us. Two broken pieces that fit together perfectly in their jagged edges. Others might call our love toxic, danger-ous, or wrong. They don't understand that some flowers only bloom in darkness.

I press my palm against his chest, feeling his strong heartbeat beneath my initials. This is real. This is forever. No more David, no more Wilson family trying to control us. Just Talon and me, bound together by blood and darkness and an obsessive love that consumes everything in its path.

For the first time in my life, I feel truly powerful. Not the victim, not the good little foster daughter trying to please everyone. Here, in Talon's arms, covered in his blood, I am exactly who I was always meant to be.

My dark protector. My perfectly twisted other half.

I smile, letting my fingernails dig into the fresh wounds on his chest. His sharp intake of breath sends a thrill through me. Yes, this is exactly where I belong.

TALON

J watch Lena sip her coffee across the breakfast table. The morning light streams through our Boston apartment windows, casting a warm glow on her skin. Two months have passed since David's disappearance, and the investigation has hit dead ends despite the Collins family throwing their wealth at it.

"The heat's died down," I say, setting down my mug. "It's time we deal with Wilson."

Lena's hand trembles slightly as she lowers her cup. "Are you sure?"

"He deserves what's coming after what he did to you." My jaw clenches at the memory of his violation. "When he kicked me out, he took advantage of you. That was his final mistake."

"I wanted to forget that." Her voice wavers. "But every time I close my eyes..."

"He won't hurt you again." I reach across the table and take her hand. "I've planned everything. The

Collins family can't find David, and they never will. Mr. Wilson will meet the same fate."

"What if something goes wrong?" Her hazel eyes meet mine, filled with concern.

"Nothing will go wrong. I've been watching his routine for weeks. He's predictable—same schedule, same habits." I squeeze her hand. "He thinks he's untouchable because of his connections. That's what will make this perfect."

"The system failed us back then," Lena whispers.

"And now it's time to get our revenge." I trace circles on her palm. "Do you trust me?"

"With my life." She nods. "When?"

"Tonight. I'll need your help, though." I stand and move around the table to her. "No one will ever hurt you again. I promise."

Mr. Wilson thinks he got away with it—hurting Lena and abusing his power. But tonight, that power dynamic shifts. I've watched, waited, bided my time, and meticulously planned our revenge.

"You'll need to arrive around seven when it's getting dark." I outline the plan as Lena listens, her eyes unwavering. "Come to the front door; I'll watch through the kitchen window. Knock three times, and Mr. Wilson will answer. He'll be alone and likely drunk, so you must be careful. Act vulnerable, play into his sick fantasies."

Her jaw tightens at the thought, but she remains resolute. I know this isn't easy for her, but we both understand the necessity.

"What then?" she asks, her voice steady.

"Let him believe you're willing. Draw him to your old room, and I'll take care of the rest."

Lena's eyes glint with mixed emotions—fear, anger, and determination. "And then?"

"I'll make him pay for what he did to you for what he tried to do again." A cold smile stretches my lips. "I've waited a long time for this."

She swallows, her expression conflicted. "What exactly do you mean by 'pay'?"

Leaning forward, I whisper, "I'll make sure he suffers. He'll never lay a hand on you or anyone else ever again. Trust me."

Lena's gaze drops to her hands, and she takes a steadying breath. "What about you? Are you sure you want to do this?"

"I'm sure." I pause, searching her eyes. "This isn't just about revenge for me; it's about ensuring your safety. He can't be allowed to hurt you again. Ever."

"Okay." Her voice is soft, but her tone is resolute. "I trust you."

Lena's eyes shine with a mixture of emotions as she leans into my kiss. I taste her hesitation and growing desire, the clash of her innocent self with the darkness bubbling inside her. She wants to embrace it; I can feel it. But fear holds her back, the remnants of her innocence, afraid to fully surrender to this new, intense world we've entered together.

"He deserves it," I murmur against her lips, my hands pulling her closer. "After what he did to you, the pain he caused."

I feel her shudder at my words, her breath catching

in her throat. "I know," she whispers. "It's just... so dark. So final."

I pull back slightly, brushing a stray strand of hair from her face. "You wanted revenge, and I'm giving it to you. Together, we'll make him pay for his sins against you."

She bites her lip, her eyes darting away before returning to meet mine. "What exactly are we going to do to him?"

A slow smile spreads and twists my lips. "We'll tie him up. This time, the power will be in our hands. He'll be helpless while we do whatever we please."

Lena's eyes widen at the imagery my words evoke. "And then?"

Stepping closer, I whisper, "Then we'll take our time. We'll make him watch as we revel in each other, joined as one, while he slowly bleeds out. Alone and helpless, he'll realize too late that his power is gone."

She swallows, her chest rising and falling with the rapid beat of her heart. I see the conflict in her eyes, the battle between her darker impulses and her lingering innocence. "Are you sure about this? About me?"

Leaning down, I capture her lips in a searing kiss that conveys all the certainty I feel. "You're mine, Lena. Embrace it. Embrace the darkness, and let it consume you. Together, we'll burn brighter than ever before."

Her arms wrap around my neck, her body pressing against mine as she returns my kiss with equal fervor. I feel her hesitation melting away, replaced by a fierce hunger. Lena is fully present in this moment, her eyes filled with determination and a dark, alluring light.

"I'm ready." She breathes the words, her fingers threading through my hair. "Let's show him what happens when he messes with us."

Her voice holds a confident edge that sends a rush of satisfaction through me. I pull her closer, our bodies aligning, our hearts pounding in unison.

"Tonight," I promise. "Tonight, we set our plan in motion, and Wilson gets what's coming to him."

The darkness inside me pulses with anticipation as I watch Lena. Her hands tremble slightly as she applies makeup, but determination burns in her eyes. She's embracing the shadows now, letting them seep into her soul like they did mine all those years ago.

Mr. Wilson thought he could break us. He used his power and his connections to keep us under his thumb. But he never understood what he was creating. Every blow, every cruel word, every time he touched her—it all fed something deeper, darker within me.

I remember the first time I saw him lay hands on her. The rage that filled me wasn't just protective—it was possessive. Primal. She was mine to protect, control, and love in my own twisted way. That bastard's greatest mistake was thinking he could take what belonged to me.

David's death was just the beginning. I can still feel the satisfaction of driving the blade into his flesh, watching the realization in his eyes of what happens when you touch what's mine. But Mr. Wilson deserves something special that will make him understand the true meaning of powerlessness.

Watching Lena now, I see the same darkness

reflecting in her eyes. She's no longer that innocent girl he tried to break. She's become beautiful and deadly, like a rose with poisoned thorns. My perfect match in this dance.

How she moves, preparing herself for our performance tonight, sends electricity through my veins. She knows what's coming, knows the role she has to play, and still chooses this path—chooses me. The monster turned out to be her salvation.

Mr. Wilson has no idea what's coming for him. He'll open that door expecting to find a vulnerable girl he can manipulate. Instead, he'll find the instrument of his destruction wrapped in a package of false innocence. And I'll be there, waiting for the perfect moment to strike.

Tonight, we'll paint our love story in shades of crimson, and our abuser's screams will be our symphony.

LENA

*M*y knuckles rap against the wood, echoing through the still evening air. I stand before the familiar door, my heart hammering against my ribs as the clock strikes seven. My cell phone is in the apartment back in Boston as I couldn't have my cell place me here on the night Mr. Wilson goes missing. But I feel oddly vulnerable without it.

Inside, I hear Mr. Wilson's heavy footsteps and grumbling. The floorboards creak under his weight. Each step closer sends ice through my veins as memories of his hands on me resurface. I wrap my arms around myself, fighting the urge to run. Talon's presence somewhere in the shadows steadies me.

The door swings open. Mr. Wilson's bulky frame fills the doorway, his beady eyes widening. The stench of whiskey wafts from him, making my stomach turn.

"What the hell are you doing here?" His words slur together, his face reddening.

I force my voice to remain steady. "I don't have classes tomorrow. With everything that's happened with David, I just..." I swallow hard, channeling the grief I'm supposed to feel. "I needed something familiar. Somewhere that feels like home."

His eyes narrow, scanning me up and down in a way that makes my skin crawl. The porch light casts harsh shadows across his face, deepening the cruel lines around his mouth.

"You look different," he says, leaning against the doorframe. "City life's changed you."

I drop my gaze to the ground, playing the part of the broken foster daughter. "Everything's changed since David disappeared. I just... I don't know where else to go."

The lie tastes bitter on my tongue, but I keep my expression vulnerable. Open. Just as Talon and I planned.

Mr. Wilson steps aside, waving me in with exaggerated courtesy. The familiar musty smell of the house hits me—stale cigarettes and cheap bourbon. His hand brushes against me as I pass, making my skin crawl beneath my sweater. I clench my jaw, fighting back bile.

"Been a while since you've been home." His words drip with something dark. "Must be lonely without David around."

I wrap my arms tighter around myself, keeping my eyes down. "I need to freshen up. Maybe take a shower."

A predatory grin spreads across his face. "I could

join you. We're all alone here tonight. Mrs. Wilson has her weekly book club meeting. I could make sure you don't slip." He leans closer, alcohol heavy on his breath. "Give me a little show like the old days."

My hands shake as memories flood back—the terror, the pain, being trapped in this house with nowhere to run. But now it's different. Talon is waiting upstairs, climbing the familiar route to my old bedroom window.

I stay calm, remembering our plan. Every degrading comment and violation leads exactly where we want it to.

I climb the familiar stairs, my footsteps light against the worn carpet. Mr. Wilson's heavy breathing follows close behind. The sound makes me jumpy, but I keep moving forward.

My old bedroom door looms ahead. Everything looks smaller now, less intimidating than when I was a child. I reach for the light switch with trembling fingers, flicking it on. The yellow glow fills the room as I step inside.

Mr. Wilson stumbles in after me, his eyes glazed from the whiskey. The door slams shut behind him with a thunderous bang. His head whips around, face contorting in shock as he spots Talon.

"What the—" His meaty hand fumbles for his cell phone.

I snatch it from his grasp before he can get his fingers around it. The device feels cold and heavy in my palm.

"What is this?" Mr. Wilson's voice rises to a hysterical pitch. His eyes dart between Talon and me like a cornered animal. "What are you doing in my house?"

Sweat beads on his forehead as he backs away from the door. His chest heaves with panicked breaths.

"You can't... you're not supposed to be here." He points a shaking finger at Talon. "I got rid of you. I made sure you were gone!"

The confidence and cruelty from moments ago evaporate as Mr. Wilson realizes he's the one trapped and at our mercy for once. His face drains of color when he notices the knife in Talon's hand, leaving him pale and sickly under the harsh bedroom light.

The air feels heavy, pregnant with the promise of violence. Talon's eyes meet mine, his expression dark and unyielding. Mr. Wilson's eyes dart between us like a trapped animal, his face a mask of fear.

Talon moves with lightning speed. He grabs Mr. Wilson by the collar, pushing him face-first onto the bed. Before he can struggle, Talon has him tied up, gagged, and trussed like a pig ready for roasting. His clothes are gone, and my former abuser is left naked and vulnerable, just as I was when he forced himself inside me.

This is it.

My heart pounds in my chest, a mixture of adrenaline and something else... excitement. I try to tamp down the rebellious thrill coursing through me, but it's no use. A deviant smile tugs at my lips.

Talon hands me the knife. It's cold and heavy in my palm, a weighty promise of retribution. My breath catches as Mr. Wilson's eyes meet mine, pleading and terrified.

I remember the nightmares, the bruises, the sheer terror he instilled in me. But now, the power dynamic has shifted. I'm in control.

With steady hands, I bring the knife to his shoulder, drawing a shallow line across his skin. A bead of red rises to the surface, trickling down his arm. He thrashes against his restraints, his muffled whines filling the room. But Talon and I only smile at each other.

Talon takes over, slicing with precision and delight. Soon, Mr. Wilson is painted with his own blood, his breath coming in ragged gasps. He's aware and suffering, but he's not yet done. We're just getting started.

My inhibitions melt away as I watch Talon's back flex with each cut, his muscles taut with concentration. I've wanted this for so long. To see this bastard broken, begging for mercy.

The knife slips from Talon's hand, landing on the tarp with a soft thud. I reach for it, but Talon shakes his head. He grabs my hand, pulling me to meet his lips for a hungry kiss.

We fall onto the bed together, our feverish need for each other overcoming us. Mr. Wilson's eyes bulge as he watches, his mouth working silently around the gag. He wanted a show, and he's going to get one.

Talon enters me, filling me with his hardness. I cry out, biting my lip to stifle the sound. Talon whispers, his breath hot against my ear.

"Let him hear you," he urges me. "Let him know what he's missing."

I moan, my head falling back as Talon thrusts into

me. "Is this the show you wanted?" I call out, addressing Mr. Wilson. "How does it feel to be on the other side?"

He tries to speak, but the gag silences him. His eyes burn with hatred, but he's powerless to stop us. I lean forward, pressing my lips to Talon's ear.

"Make me yours," I whisper. "Right here, in front of him."

Talon's hips move faster, his breath coming in sharp gasps. "This is what you get for hurting her," he growls at Mr. Wilson. "A front-row seat to your worst nightmare."

Our movements become frantic, driven by the darkness within us and our shared desire. Mr. Wilson's eyes glaze over as his life slips away, his body bloody and broken. But Talon and I are lost in each other, our climax washing over us like a tidal wave.

As we come back to earth, we realize Mr. Wilson's lifeless gaze is fixed on us, his eyes wide and unblinking. Talon's hand trails down my back, resting on my hip.

"Fuck, that was hot," he groans.

I sink my teeth into my bottom lip because it is shockingly arousing. What that says about me and my mental state, I don't know. All I know is that I love Talon so fucking much. "I love you."

The words hang heavy in the air between us. "Fuck, do you know how long I wanted you to tell me that? I fucking love you too, princess. Always have and always will."

We kiss then, but it's slower and more heartfelt than before. When we break apart, Talon rests his forehead against mine. "We need to start the cleanup. Shower first."

I nod in reply and get off the bed, heading into the bathroom. The shower's hot spray washes away blood and sweat, turning pink as it swirls down the drain. Talon's hands move methodically over my skin, ensuring no trace remains. His touch is clinical now, focused on the task at hand.

"Turn," he instructs, and I comply as he scrubs my back.

We dry off quickly and seal our clothes and the towels we dried off with in black garbage bags.

Back in the bedroom, I help Talon wrap Mr. Wilson's flaccid, naked body in heavy black plastic. The tarp beneath him made cleanup easier, catching most of the blood. We secure the wrapping with duct tape, working in silence.

"Hold the light," Talon says, handing me a UV flashlight.

I sweep the blue beam across the floor and walls. At the same time, he follows with a cleaning solution, methodically removing any traces we might have missed. The metallic smell of blood mingles with harsh chemicals.

"Clear," I whisper after triple-checking every surface.

We carry the wrapped bundle down the stairs, careful not to bump the walls. My arms strain under the weight. Outside, we check there's no one about. The night air is cool against my damp skin as we load Mr. Wilson into Talon's trunk.

I slide into the passenger seat, exhausted but alert. Talon starts the engine and pulls away from the curb. As we begin the long drive back to Boston, the house disappears in the rearview mirror.

The highway stretches empty before us, streetlights casting intermittent shadows across the dashboard. In the trunk, our cargo lies silent. My foster father's final resting place awaits; in a fresh grave beside David.

TALON

*I*t's midnight, and we stand over the open grave—the fresh earth mocking us. Lena's eyes glisten with unshed tears, haunted by the ghosts of our past. I pull her close, and she leans into me, seeking comfort in my embrace. Tonight, we lay our demons to rest.

We lower Mr. Wilson's body into the grave, the moonlight casting an eerie glow on the black plastic shroud. I pour the acid in next, ensuring that his body will decompose quickly. The weight of his sins presses down on us as we begin to fill the hole with shovelfuls of dirt and lime layers. Each clump of soil echoes our determination to bury the pain and suffering he inflicted. We work in silence, lost in our own thoughts.

As the grave fills, I feel a sense of closure. The man who abused us, who tried to break us, is now nothing more than a memory. We stand united, stronger than ever, telling the world we will not be victims. Mr. Wilson's legacy ends here.

I level out the ground with a few passes of the backhoe tracks before running a rake over the grass placed back over the top. Ensuring we leave no obvious disturbance here. The moon reflects off the freshly replaced grass sections—the only living witness to our actions here tonight. I step back, and Lena moves closer, our shoulders brushing. At this moment, we are bound by more than just our shared trauma—we are connected by our strength and determination to forge a new path.

She whispers, "It's done." Her voice is thick with emotion. I nod, unable to find the words to describe the tempest of feelings inside me. We stand side by side, staring at the grave, reflecting on the journey that brought us here. It's not just Mr. Wilson's body we've buried but also the remnants of our childhood fears and the shadows that haunted us.

"We did what we had to," I finally say, my voice hoarse. "He'll never hurt anyone again."

Lena nods, her eyes never leaving the grave. "I hope he rots in hell." Her tone is fierce, a fire that wasn't there before.

I step closer to Lena, my gaze intense. "There's one more thing we need to do." I glance at the graves, then back at her. "Let me make you forget them completely."

Her eyes widen, and she bites her lip. "What do you mean?"

I move closer, my body inches from hers. "We're already stained by their touch. But there's a part of you they never claimed." I brush her hair back, my fingers lingering on her neck. "Let me take it. Let me brand you as mine."

My cock twitches in excitement to be the one to claim her pucker, that tiny hole between her smooth cheeks, for the first time.

Lena's breath quickens, and she pulls away slightly. "I... I don't know, Talon. What if it hurts?"

I shake my head, my eyes never leaving hers. "I would never hurt you. I'll go slow, and I have lube." I pull a small bottle of lube from my pocket, offering it to her. "We don't have to, but I want to know that part of you, too, belongs to me."

She clears her throat. "You really want me, don't you?"

"More than anything." I step forward, pressing my body against hers. "You're the only light in my dark world, and I'll always keep you safe and make you mine."

Lena's eyes search mine, her lips parting slightly. "Here? Over their graves?"

I nod. "It's just us, Lena. And it'll be a real 'fuck you' to those assholes."

She shivers, and I see the desire warring with her nerves. "Okay," she whispers, her voice laced with uncertainty. "But you have to promise to be gentle."

"I promise." I cup her face, my thumbs brushing her cheeks. "It might be uncomfortable initially, but I'll take care of you. Always."

Lena nods, and I pull her against me, my lips capturing hers in a possessive kiss. Her hands tangle in my hair, and she responds with a hunger that matches mine.

I position Lena on the fresh grave, her hands and

knees sinking into the soft earth as she assumes the doggy position. Her back arches, offering herself to me, and I can't help but admire the gorgeous curves of her body. Her skin glows in the moonlight, starkly contrasting the darkness surrounding us.

I kneel behind her, taking a moment to appreciate the view. Slowly, I start to prep her, drizzling an ample amount of lube on her asshole before using my fingers to gently loosen her up. She lets out a soft moan, and I pause, worried I might be hurting her. "You okay?" I whisper.

"Keep going," she replies, her voice laced with anticipation.

I oblige, my fingers working her slowly, deliberately. I want to make sure she's ready and desperate for me. It's not just about the physical act but the emotional connection that comes with it. I take my time, enjoying her body responding to my touch.

I slip my pinky in and feel her relax around it. Slowly, I slide in, one knuckle, then two, then all the way. I thrust my pinky into that perfect, pink starfish, groaning, knowing I'm her first... and her last.

I bite her ass as I trade my pinky for my thick middle finger. She adjusts to my size with a sharp intake of breath.

"That's my good girl," I murmur, so turned on I can barely think straight. I want to fuck her ass so badly. I need it.

I know she's ready for something bigger when she's squirming and breathless. I pull my fingers away and reach into my pocket for the small dildo. It's not much, but it'll do the job to help stretch her, get her ready for my cock. Adding more lube, I press it inside her gently, and she moans deeply. Her hips rock back, seeking more, and I thrust it slowly, building a steady rhythm. Her moans fill the night air, and I revel in her sounds.

Finally, when she's begging for more, I ease the dildo out and line myself up to her entrance. "You ready for me, Lena?" I ask, coating my dick in lube.

"Please, Talon," she whispers. "I need you."

With a gentle but firm thrust, I ease myself inside her. She takes the head of my cock like a woman starved. I pause, seeing the shadows of her breasts swaying as her breathing hitches. I growl as I fight the urge to push into her ass all at once. I feel her back up onto my cock as her ass swallows me, inch by inch. She's tight, and I pause again, allowing her to adjust to my size.

"You feel so fucking good," I murmur, my hands gripping her hips.

"More," she urges, pushing back against me.

I oblige, pulling out slowly and then thrusting back into her. This time, I go deeper, claiming her fully. She lets out a sharp gasp, and I stop, concerned I might have hurt her. "You okay?"

"Don't stop," she pants. "It's just—intense."

Smiling, I begin to move, my hips finding a steady rhythm. I go slow at first, but the urgency builds, and soon, I'm thrusting harder, deeper. The night air is filled with the sounds of our passion—the slick sound of flesh sliding together, our heavy breathing, and Lena's soft whimpers.

I lean over her, my chest pressing against her back as I reach around to caress her breasts. She arches into my touch, her body responding to mine.

I love how her body yields to mine, accepting me in ways she never has before. Her sweet cries fill the air as I thrust into her with abandon. Our bodies move as one, a savage symphony of need and desire. The ground beneath her knees is unforgiving, but she doesn't seem to notice, caught up in the moment's intensity.

"You like that, don't you?" I growl in her ear. "You like being taken like this over their fucking corpses."

"Yes," she pants. "Harder, Talon. Claim me."

I grip her hips tighter, my fingers digging into her soft flesh as I thrust deeper. "You're mine, Lena. Never forget that. Mine to take, to protect, to keep safe."

She moans, her head hanging low as her hair falls forward. "Yours," she agrees. "Only yours."

Hearing those words sends a rush of possessiveness through me, and I pound into her with increased fervor. Our flesh slaps against each other, the force of my thrusts causing the sensual curves of her flesh to jiggle with each impact. I want to mark her, brand her as irrevocably mine, so no one else can ever claim her again.

"You're such a bad, bad girl," I groan, my breathing becoming labored as the pleasure builds.

"It's all for you," she whispers, her voice hoarse. "Always for you, Talon."

I grab her hips roughly, pulling her back onto me as I drive forward with renewed force. Lena lets out a hiss of pleasure, and I know I've found that sweet spot inside her ass. I focus my thrusts there, wanting to give her as much pleasure as she gives me. Our grunts and moans fill the air, mingling with the earthy scent of dirt and the heady fragrance of our desire.

The night breeze caresses our heated skin, but it does nothing to cool the fire burning between us. Lena's body is smooth and pale, her back glistening in the moonlight. I lean over her again, my mouth close to her ear. "You're making me forget everything, Lena," I murmur. "All the pain, all the darkness—it fades when I'm inside you."

"Then stay," she begs. "Stay with me forever."

"Forever," I promise, my voice thick with emotion. My finger finds her clit as I hover over her, flicking and rubbing. "You and me, Lena. Against the world."

Our passion builds to a crescendo, the pleasure becoming all-consuming. I feel her ass tighten around me, her cries becoming more desperate. I know she's close, and the knowledge sends me hurtling over the edge.

"Come for me," I demand, reaching around to pinch her swollen clit. "Come with my cock deep in that tight little ass."

She obliges, her body shaking as her ass swallows me whole. I thrust a few more times, riding out her orgasm before I let myself find release. I bury myself inside her, my hands gripping her hips as I fill her with my essence. I groan, my eyes squeezed shut as I savor the feel of her. "Lena," I breathe, my voice hoarse.

She collapses forward, and I gently ease out of her. I pull her against me, and she turns in my arms, her eyes shining with unshed tears. "That was..." She trails off, unable to find the words.

"Perfect," I finish for her, brushing her hair back from her face. "You were perfect."

I help Lena stand on shaky legs, retrieving her discarded panties from beside the grave. With gentle care, I slide them back up her thighs. Her skin feels cold in the night air, so I shrug off my leather jacket and wrap it around her shoulders. The jacket engulfs her small frame, and she burrows into its warmth.

I zip up my jeans and adjust my clothes. "Let's go home," I say softly, pulling her close. She nods against my chest, and I can feel the tension leaving her body.

We walk away from the graves together, our footsteps crunching on the frost-covered grass. The weight of our past is lying buried beneath the earth behind us. Mr. Wilson and David can never hurt her again. Their control over our lives is finished.

Lena's hand finds mine in the darkness, our fingers intertwining. Each step takes us further from the shadows of our past and closer to our future together. The crisp night air feels cleansing, washing away the last remnants of fear and pain that have haunted us for so long.

The moonlight guides our path through the cemetery, casting long shadows between the headstones. But these shadows hold no power over us anymore. We are free.

LENA

*M*y cell phone's ringtone jolts me awake. My stomach dips when I see Mrs. Wilson's name on the screen. Taking a deep breath, I answer.

"Lena? Oh, thank goodness." Mrs. Wilson's voice trembles. "Richard's missing. He didn't come home last night. I-I need you to come back. Please."

My fingers tighten around the phone. Talon shifts beside me, his eyes opening to study my expression.

"He's just... gone?" I keep my voice steady, channeling the innocent concern I've practiced my whole life.

"The police are here. They're asking questions. I don't know what to do." She breaks into sobs. "Jamie's too far away to get back this weekend. He got a job in Los Angeles. I need you, dear. You're part of this family."

Family. The word tastes bitter in my mouth after everything they put me through. But I have to play my part.

"Of course, I'll come right away." I glance at Talon, who nods slightly. "Give me a couple hours to drive up."

After hanging up, I press my forehead against Talon's chest. "I have to go back."

"Be careful." His fingers trace my spine. "Remember what we practiced. You're worried and confused. You haven't heard from him."

"I know." I pull away and start gathering my things. "But facing Mrs. Wilson... after what we did..."

"You can handle this," Talon's voice says with absolute certainty. "You've fooled them your whole life. One more performance."

I pack clothes for two days, my makeup bag, and toiletries. My hands shake slightly as I zip up the overnight bag, but I force them steady. Over the years, I've gotten good at controlling my reactions.

"They won't find anything." Talon's voice carries from the doorway, where he leans against the frame, arms crossed. "We were thorough."

I nod, thinking of the fresh grave next to David's. Mr. Wilson's final resting place is marked only by disturbed earth that will soon settle and grow over with grass. No one will think to look there.

"I know." I check my phone, watching the Uber's arrival time tick down. "It's just... seeing Mrs. Wilson again. After everything."

"Remember who you are now." Talon crosses the room and cups my face in his hands. "You're not that scared little girl anymore."

His touch grounds me and reminds me of my strength and what we've accomplished together. I lean into his palm momentarily before pulling away to grab my bag.

My phone buzzes telling me that the Uber has arrived. A black Toyota Camry idles outside our building, ready to make the hour-long drive to Salem—to the house where I endured years of abuse and control. Talon stretches his hand out to me and I pass him my cellphone.

"I'll be watching," Talon says as I head for the door. "Always."

I shoulder my bag and step out into the morning sun. The Uber driver pops the trunk, and I place my bag inside. As I slide into the backseat and give the driver Mrs. Wilson's address, I glimpse Talon in our apartment window. His presence, even from afar, steels my resolve.

Mr. Wilson won't be coming home. His body will stay buried deep in that Boston cemetery, his sins covered by six feet of earth. And I'll play my part as the concerned foster daughter, returning from college to comfort her grieving foster mother.

The Uber crawls to a stop in front of the Wilsons' house. My stomach churns at the sight of the familiar white colonial with its perfect lawn and manicured hedges. A police car sits in the driveway.

Before I can grab my bag from the trunk, the front door flies open, and Mrs. Wilson rushes out, her silk robe fluttering behind her. Her face is streaked with mascara, and her hair is disheveled—a far cry from her usual polished appearance.

"Oh, Lena!" She throws her arms around me, her

designer perfume choking me. "Thank God you're here!"

Her embrace feels hollow, like every time she's hugged me over the years. I pat her back awkwardly, noting how her shoulders shake with exaggerated sobs.

"I just don't understand," she wails, pulling back to dab at her eyes with a monogrammed handkerchief. "Richard would never just disappear like this. He always tells me where he's going."

I force my features into a mask of concern, though my skin crawls at her touch. "When did you last see him?"

"Last night, before I went to my book club. He said he was staying home." She clutches my arm, her manicured nails digging into my skin. "But when I returned, he was gone, no note, no text. The police say there's no activity on his credit cards, and his car is still parked in the drive..."

Her voice cracks on the last word, and she collapses against me again. I hold her up, playing the role of the supportive foster daughter while my mind flashes to Talon's bloody hands, to the fresh dirt of the grave.

"Come inside, dear." Mrs. Wilson straightens up, suddenly remembering we have an audience. She smooths her robe and attempts a watery smile. "The detective wants to speak with you."

I follow her up the front steps, my overnight bag heavy in my hand. The house looms over us, holding years of dark secrets behind its pristine facade, just like Mrs. Wilson herself.

Inside, two detectives wait in the living room—a tall

woman with cropped gray hair and a younger man taking notes. Mrs. Wilson hovers nearby, wringing her handkerchief.

"Miss Graves?" The female detective extends her hand. "I'm Detective Morris. This is Detective Chen. We'd like to ask you a few questions about Richard Wilson."

I shake her hand, maintaining the right balance of concern and composure. "Of course. Anything I can do to help."

"When was the last time you spoke with Mr. Wilson?" Detective Morris's sharp eyes study my face.

"About two weeks ago." I twist my hands in my lap. "He called to check how I was settling in at the new apartment. The conversation was brief—five minutes at most."

Detective Chen's pen scratches across his notepad. "And what was his demeanor during that call?"

"Normal, I guess." I furrow my brow as if trying to remember. "He asked about my classes and told me to study hard. Nothing seemed off."

"When did you last see him in person?"

"Before I left for MIT two months ago," I say, letting my voice waver slightly. "At the goodbye dinner."

I pick a loose thread on my sleeve, remembering that last dinner. Mr. Wilson had been drinking heavily, his face flushed as he lectured me about making the family proud at university. The bruises from his last "lesson" were still yellowing on my ribs.

"And how would you describe your relationship with

your foster father?" Detective Morris leans forward, her eyes intent.

My fingers are still on the thread. I've rehearsed this answer countless times with Talon, crafting the perfect mix of gratitude and distance.

"The Wilsons took me in when I had nowhere else to go," I begin, meeting Mrs. Wilson's tearful gaze across the room. "Mr. Wilson was... strict. But he wanted us to succeed. He pushed us to excel in school, to be responsible."

The words taste like ash in my mouth. I think of the countless nights spent trembling in my room, listening to his heavy footsteps in the hall. He'd grab my arm hard enough to leave marks when I "disappointed" him. And I try not to think of his weight crushing me into the mattress when he raped me that first time.

"Did he ever mention wanting to leave? Any problems at work or at home?" Detective Chen's pen hovers over his notepad.

I shake my head. "No, nothing like that. He was proud of his position at the bank, always talking about his latest deals."

Mrs. Wilson dabs at her eyes again. "That's right. Everything was fine. Perfect, even. I just don't understand..."

I watch her performance with detached fascination. She'd always been good at playing the devoted wife who turns a blind eye to her husband's cruelty, but now she plays the grieving spouse just as convincingly.

"Is there anything else you can tell us?" Detective

Morris asks. "Any detail, no matter how small, could help."

"I wish I could be more helpful," I say softly, letting my shoulders slump. "But I've been so focused on starting classes, getting settled in Boston. I haven't been home much."

As they leave, the front door shuts behind the detectives, and Mrs. Wilson's shoulders straighten. Her tear-stained face hardens as she turns to me, all traces of grief vanishing.

"Have you seen Talon lately?" Her voice carries an edge I remember too well.

My heart pounds, but I keep my expression neutral. "Talon? No, not since you kicked him out."

She studies my face, perfectly manicured nails drumming against her silk robe. "Really? Because Jamie mentioned seeing someone who looked like him near here last month."

"It couldn't have been him." I shrug, forcing myself to meet her gaze steadily. "I haven't heard from him."

"Hmm." She crosses to the drink cart and pours herself a generous measure of gin. "You always were close to him. As we found out, finding him defiling you that night." She takes a long sip, ice cubes clinking against crystal. "Well, if you hear from him, you'll let me know immediately. Won't you, dear?"

The threat in her voice is clear—the same tone she used when covering up her husband's abuse. I nod, playing the role of the obedient foster daughter one more time.

"Of course, Mrs. Wilson. You'll be the first to know."

I follow Mrs. Wilson into the kitchen, my stomach churning as she pulls containers from the fridge. The familiar space feels different now—tainted by what Talon and I did to Mr. Wilson. His favorite chair sits empty at the head of the table.

"I made too much chicken marsala last night," Mrs. Wilson says, her voice brittle as she transfers food to plates. "I keep forgetting to cook for two."

The microwave hums as she heats our dinner. I grip the counter's edge, remembering how Mr. Wilson complained that his food wasn't at the perfect temperature. How his rage would build over the smallest things.

But killing him... the violence of it floods back. The way Talon's knife slid into him and mine, the gurgling sounds he made. We should have planned better and been more careful. What if someone saw something? What if they find evidence we missed?

"Sit, dear." Mrs. Wilson sets the steaming plates on the table. "You must be hungry after the journey."

I sink into my old spot across from where Mr. Wilson always sat. The chicken marsala smells rich and buttery, but my appetite has vanished. Each bite feels like sawdust in my mouth.

"I just keep thinking he'll walk through that door," Mrs. Wilson says, pushing food around her plate. "Demanding his dinner, complaining about work..."

The weight of our actions settles over me like a heavy blanket. We acted on rage and impulse, and now we must live with the consequences.

TALON

I watch the video feed intently as Lena helps Mrs. Wilson prepare another bland casserole. My fingers drum against the steering wheel of my parked car, three blocks from the Wilson house. Every muscle in my body tenses when Mrs. Wilson gets too close to Lena with that kitchen knife.

"Just chop the onions finer, dear," Mrs. Wilson instructs in that saccharine voice that makes my skin crawl. I hear rhythmic chopping sounds through the hidden microphone in Lena's necklace.

The weekend crawls by at an excruciating pace. I barely sleep, constantly monitoring the feeds. Mrs. Wilson cycles between weeping dramatically about Richard's disappearance and passive-aggressive comments toward Lena. The detectives come and go, asking more questions. Lena plays her part perfectly— the concerned foster daughter who just wants to help find Richard.

My hands clench the steering wheel tighter when

Detective Chen suggests Lena stay longer to support Mrs. Wilson. Relief floods through me as Lena declines, citing college commitments.

"I really should get back to college," Lena tells them. "But please call me if you hear anything."

Finally, Sunday evening arrives. I trail the Uber safely as it winds through the streets toward Boston. Lena stares out the window, her shoulders relaxing with each mile that takes her further from Salem. The hidden camera in her coat button gives me a clear view of her expression as the coat is tossed on the seat beside her—a mixture of exhaustion and satisfaction.

I always keep three cars between us, watching carefully for any signs of surveillance. But the detectives seem to have bought her story. They're looking in all the wrong places, just as planned.

The Uber pulls up to our building. I park across the street, hidden in the shadows, and watch through my windshield as she exits the car. Her steps are steady as she walks to her door. She is almost home, safe, and almost back in my arms, where she belongs.

I slip out of my car, following Lena's silhouette as she approaches the apartment entrance. Her keys jingle in her hand, echoing through the empty hallway. My footsteps are silent against the carpet as I close the distance between us.

She fumbles with her keys at the door, and I seize my moment. In one fluid motion, I wrap my arms around her waist from behind. Lena lets out a surprised squeal that makes my heart race.

"Miss me?" I whisper against her ear.

She spins in my arms, her hazel eyes bright with recognition. "You scared me half to death!"

I capture her lips with mine, feeling her body melt against me as she responds with equal fervor. Watching her from afar has left me starved for her touch. With one hand, I help her unlock the door while keeping her pressed close.

We stumble through the doorway, neither willing to break the kiss. I kick the door shut behind us, echoing through our apartment. Lena's fingers thread through my hair as I back her against the wall, deepening our kiss.

"I hate being apart from you," she breathes against my lips.

"Then let's never be apart again," I respond, pulling her closer.

The weekend of pretense falls away, replaced by the raw truth of us—together, united, exactly as we should be.

I kick the door shut, my eyes never leaving Lena's. Hunger consumes me as I take in her flushed cheeks, swollen lips, and the desire burning in her eyes. She wants me as badly as I want her.

My lips crush against hers, claiming her mouth with an urgency that reflects our separation. Her fingers tug at my hair, sending a ripple of pleasure down my spine. Every kiss, every touch, ignites the flame between us. I push her toward the bedroom, needing to feel her skin against mine.

Inside the room, I push her gently, and she falls onto the bed, her eyes sparkling with anticipation. I climb onto the mattress, pinning her beneath me, reveling in the feel of her curves against my hard frame. My hands slide under her sweater, my thumbs grazing the sensitive skin of her waist. Her breath catches as I lift the fabric over her head, baring her to me.

"You're so fucking beautiful," I whisper, capturing her lips in a kiss that steals the breath from her lungs. My hands explore the soft contours of her body, reveling in her responsiveness. She arches into my touch, craving more.

With gentle force, I roll her onto her stomach, running my hands over the curves of her hips and thighs. I bind her wrists with a soft silk scarf from the dresser. She looks at me over her shoulder, her eyes flickering with surprise and something more—a spark of desire fueled by surrender. I secure her arms behind her back.

"Talon," she breathes.

The sound of my name on her lips sends a primal rush through my veins. I trace the length of her body with my hands. My lips move from the back of her neck to her spine while my hands explore lower. Her breath hitches as I slip my fingers into the waistband of her pants. With deliberate slowness, I tease her, sliding her pants over her hips, baring her to my gaze inch by inch.

"Please," she whispers, her back arching.

I give in to her soft plea, sliding her pants down her legs and off. My fingers trace the curve of her ass, my fingers brushing over the carving of my initials down to the soft skin of her inner thighs, making her shiver. She's vulnerable, exposed, and mine.

Her submission fuels my lust, and I feel the primal need to claim her, to brand her as mine in the most elemental way. I want to thrust into her, marking her body with mine. But first, I want to savor her.

I kneel beside her bound form, trailing kisses along her spine as my hands continue their exploration. She squirms beneath my touch, a soft moan escaping her lips. Her responsiveness only fuels my hunger.

My fingers dip lower, finding the wet heat between her thighs. She's ready for me, dripping with desire. I brush my thumb over her swollen center, making her body tremble. Her hips push back, seeking more.

"You like that, baby?" I murmur, my lips moving against her shoulder. "You like it when I touch you here?"

"Yes," she pants. "Talon, please."

My cock throbs with need as I position myself behind her. Her bound arms excite me, knowing she's completely at my mercy. I hold my length in my hand, rubbing the tip against her slick entrance. Our eyes lock over her shoulder, and with one smooth, powerful thrust, I fill her. Her cry of pleasure is music to my ears. Then, with a slow rhythm, I move.

I bury myself deep within her, my hips slamming against her ass. Her entire body shifts forward with each thrust. Her moans fill the room, urging me on.

"That's it, take it all," I grit out. "Your cunt is so fucking tight around my cock."

My hands grip her hips as I piston into her. Her body is a vessel for my pleasure, and I use it shamelessly.

With each thrust, I claim her a little more, branding her as mine.

"You're mine, Lena," I growl. "My little tied-up fuck toy."

Her breathless cries fill the room as I plunder her body. I feel her walls tighten around me, her pleasure building. I want to draw this out, take her to the edge and back again. I slow my rhythm, drawing her pleasure out in an attempt to tease and torture her.

"T-Talon," she stammers. "Please, I'm so close."

"Not yet," I whisper, my lips brushing her ear. "I'm not ready for you to milk me yet."

With renewed fervor, I drive into her, my hips a blur. Her cries fill the room, a symphony of pleasure and need. I feel her body tighten like a coiled spring, ready to snap.

"Come for me, Lena," I demand. "Let me feel it."

Her body convulses around me, her climax tearing through her. She cries out, her voice echoing off the walls. I continue to thrust, riding out her waves of pleasure. My release coils within me, held in check by sheer force of will.

With a final, powerful thrust, I spill myself into her, filling her with my seed. My vision blurs as I bury my face in the curve of her neck, panting.

"That's it, baby," I whisper, my lips brushing her skin. "Take every goddamn drop of my cum in that perfect pussy."

I let my spent body collapse onto hers, still joined as one. Our hearts pound in unison, the rhythm of our love song. In this moment, we are one—completely, perfectly united.

"Talon," she says, her voice trembling. "Untie me, please."

I hold her tightly, slowly pulling out of her body. The threads of our connection feel unbreakable as she turns her head and captures my gaze over her shoulder, her brown eyes shimmering with emotion. This is what I've craved—total devotion. I carefully untie the scarf, freeing her wrists. She shifts onto her knees before me and winds her arms around my neck, tangling her fingers in my hair.

I pull Lena closer, breathing in her scent as she nestles against my chest. Her fingers trace patterns on my skin, sending shivers through my body. The moonlight filtering through the window casts a silvery glow across her face, highlighting the curve of her cheek.

"I've loved you since that first day at the Wilsons," I whisper, running my fingers through her dark waves. "Even when I tried to push you away, you were already under my skin."

Lena lifts her head, her hazel eyes meeting mine. "I think I fell for you when you took that beating for me. No one had ever protected me like that before."

My arms tighten around her. "I'll always protect you, Lena. You're my reason for breathing, my purpose."

"Promise you'll never leave again?" Her voice carries a hint of vulnerability that makes my heart clench.

"Never." I press a kiss on her forehead. "You're stuck with me forever, baby. No force on earth could tear me away from you now."

She smiles, tracing my jawline with her fingertips. "Good, because I love you more than anything, Talon Voss. Even when you're being overprotective and possessive."

"That's just part of my charm." I capture her hand and bring it to my lips.

"I wouldn't have you any other way," she murmurs, already drifting toward sleep.

I watch as her eyes flutter closed, her breathing evening out. Holding her like this, feeling her heartbeat against mine, I know with absolute certainty that everything I've done has been worth it. Every dark deed, every violent act—it all led me back to her.

LENA

I sit at my kitchen table, reading the headlines about Richard Wilson's disappearance on my cell phone. The words blur together as Detective Chen's business card catches my eye for the hundredth time. He's been calling daily, asking the same questions with increasing suspicion.

"We need to leave." Talon's voice breaks through my thoughts. He stands by the window, scanning the street below.

"They're watching the apartment." My fingers trace the rim of my coffee mug. "I saw an unmarked car this morning."

"David vanishing was one thing. But Richard?" Talon moves behind me, his hands settling on my shoulders. "They're connecting dots we can't afford them to connect."

The weight of our actions presses down on me. Every knock at the door sends my heart racing, and every phone call could bring out whole world crashing down.

"I could transfer," I whisper, thinking of the acceptance letter from the University of Texas sitting in my drawer. "Start fresh somewhere else. I got accepted to the University of Texas."

"Austin would work. Big city, easy to blend in." His thumb traces circles on my neck. "We could leave tonight. I've got cash, new IDs..."

A police siren wails in the distance, and I tense. Talon's grip tightens protectively.

"What about Mrs. Wilson?" The guilt gnaws at me. Despite everything, she'd been kinder than Richard.

"She'll survive." Talon's voice holds no sympathy. "But we won't if we stay here. The cops are building a case, Lena. They've interviewed your classmates about David. They know about our connection."

He's right. With each passing day, the noose tightens. The questions get more pointed, and the stares are more suspicious. My carefully crafted responses feel thinner and more transparent.

"Pack light," Talon says, kissing my temple. "Only what we absolutely need. We'll get new everything in Texas."

I nod, my decision made. Boston holds too many ghosts, too many secrets buried in shallow graves.

I stuff clothes and essentials into a small duffel bag, my hands shaking with each item. The apartment feels different now—every shadow holds a threat, and every sound could be approaching footsteps. Talon moves silently through the rooms, methodically erasing traces of our presence.

"Leave the phone," he instructs as I reach for it. "They can track it."

The hours crawl by like years. We sit in darkness, watching the street below through a gap in the curtains. The unmarked police car remains stationed at the corner, its occupants probably drinking coffee to stay awake.

At eleven thirty, Talon's hand finds mine in the dark. "The night shift change happens soon. That's our window."

I nod, though he probably can't see it. My heart pounds so hard that I worry the cops might hear it from the street.

Minutes tick by. The surveillance car's headlights finally flicker to life, and it pulls away from the curb.

"Now," he whispers, handing me my mask and hoodie.

We can't risk being picked up by cameras. Once my mask and hoodie are in place, the hood drawn up, we move like ghosts through the building, taking the back stairs to avoid the lobby cameras. We emerge into the alley behind the building. Talon's car sits three blocks away, parked in a blind spot between security cameras.

My legs feel weak as we walk, trying to appear casual. Every passing car makes my stomach lurch. But we make it to his vehicle without incident. The engine purrs to life, and Talon pulls onto the empty street.

"Don't look back," he says as we pass the city limits sign. "Just keep your eyes forward."

As Boston disappears behind us, I sink into the passenger seat, the highway stretching endlessly south into the darkness.

The headlights cut through the darkness as we pull into a deserted motel parking lot. My muscles ache from sitting so long, and exhaustion weighs heavy on my eyelids. Four hours of watching trees and road signs blur past has drained me.

Talon kills the engine, plunging us into silence broken only by crickets chirping in the distance. "We should get some sleep here. Can't risk using cards or leaving a paper trail. And we've got cash, but we must be careful about spending it."

I turn to him. The dim parking lot lights cast shadows across his face, but I can still see the weariness in his eyes. He's been driving nonstop, keeping us moving forward while I dozed on and off.

"I love you," I whisper, leaning across the center console to press my lips against his. "Through everything, I love you."

His hand cups my neck, pulling me deeper into the kiss. His familiar taste grounds me, reminding me why we're here and running. For all his darkness, for all the blood on our hands, he's my anchor.

"Back seat," he murmurs against my mouth. "More room to stretch out."

We climb over the seats, arranging ourselves in the limited space. Talon pulls me against his chest, and I curl into his warmth. His heartbeat thumps steadily under my ear as his fingers trail through my hair.

The leather seats creak as we settle in. It's uncomfortable, but I feel safer with him than I've ever felt.

I can't sleep. My mind is a mess of thoughts and worries, each knotting my stomach. The steady rhythm of Talon's heartbeat eventually draws my eyes open. The car interior is almost pitch black, illuminated only by the faint glow of the parking lot lights through the windshield.

We're pressed together, his body curled around mine, with my ass snuggled against his hard dick. I shift slightly, needing some relief from the pressure building between my legs. His hand settles on my hip, his thumb making lazy circles on my skin.

"Can't sleep?" he murmurs, his warm breath tickling my ear.

I shake my head, not trusting my voice. Being this close to him, skin to skin, has my heart thumping erratically.

His hand slides down to cup my ass, giving it a gentle squeeze. "Horny?"

I swallow. "Kind of."

"Mmm, me too." His hand moves lower, fingers dipping between my legs. "You're so wet."

I nod, biting my lip to hold back a moan as he teases my clit. "Your fault," I whisper.

"My fault?" He chuckles, his free hand tightening on my hip. "Baby, this is all you. I can't help it if my girl likes to rub her ass against my cock."

I can feel the smile stretching my lips as he continues to play with me, his fingers slipping deeper. "I didn't think we'd end up fucking in my car."

He thrusts his hips gently, his cock sliding along the cleft of my ass. "There's a lot of things I never thought we'd do, but somehow we keep surprising each other." His fingers curl inside me, hitting just the right spot.

"Oh, fuck," I breathe, my nails digging into his arm.

"My thoughts exactly," he says, lips trailing down my neck. "Gonna make you come all over my hand, baby. And then, I'm gonna fill you up and make you scream."

His thumb presses against my clit, sending sparks through my body. "Talon," I gasp, my back arching against him.

"That's it," he groans, kissing my shoulder. "Let go for me."

His fingers curl and pump, his thumb working in perfect rhythm. I can't think, can't breathe, can only feel. I'm tumbling over the edge, dragged under by his whispered encouragements.

"That's my girl," he breathes, kissing my ear as my body shudders through the aftershocks. "I need to bury myself deep inside that tight pussy."

His dirty talk sends sparks straight to my core, desire coiling low in my belly again. "Fuck, yes," I manage to whisper.

He pulls his hand away, and I whine at the loss. "You're insatiable tonight."

I roll my eyes, even though he can't see me in the dark. "Says the guy with the raging hard-on."

His chuckle vibrates against my back. "Fair point. Guess it's my turn to take care of this problem."

The car creaks as he shifts, and then I feel him lining up at my entrance. He pushes inside, filling me in one smooth stroke. I cry out, my body adjusting to his size. He feels so good, stretching me in all the right ways.

"Jesus, Lena," he grits out, his hips beginning to move. "So fucking tight. I love your greedy little pussy."

My back arches as he begins to thrust. I bite my lip, trying to keep quiet, but it's impossible with the way he's pounding into me. My body rocks with each snap of his hips, the car bouncing slightly in time with our rhythm. His hands grip my hips, guiding me into each stroke, his cock slamming deep.

His fingers dig into my flesh, his movements becoming more urgent. "I'm not gonna last, baby. Your pussy milking me dry."

The filthy words push me over the edge again, and I come with a cry, my body clenching around him. "Talon, yes!"

He groans my name, his release pulsing inside me. He stills, his forehead dropping to my shoulder as he rides out the waves of pleasure.

Talon's arms tighten around me as we drift in the afterglow, his softening cock still buried inside me. "I want to keep my dick warm, and where better than your pussy?"

I giggle, my fingers tracing random patterns on his arm. "Yeah, I'll keep it warm."

His hips give a slight thrust, sending tingles through my sensitive flesh. "Maybe I'll just stay inside you like this forever."

I consider this, my hand moving to rest over his, where it's draped around my hip. "Could be worse places."

He chuckles, nuzzling his face into the back of my neck. "Much worse places."

We settle into silence, my eyes closing as I try to chase sleep. But my mind won't calm, images and memories flashing behind my eyelids. I shift slightly, trying to find a more comfortable position without detaching from him.

"You okay?" His voice rumbles through his chest, vibrating against my back.

"Yeah." I hesitate, not wanting to voice my fears and break the moment's peace. "Just trying to clear my head a bit."

He gets it without me needing to say more. "They'll find the bodies eventually," he says, his tone matter of fact. "But by the time they do, we'll be long gone."

I draw small circles on his arm, my heart heavy. "I know. They were monsters. But it doesn't make this easier."

His lips press a kiss to my shoulder. "You're feeling guilty, but I'm not. I'm glad they're dead. I'm glad we did it."

Those words lift some of the weight from my chest. I sink into his embrace, grateful for his unwavering strength. "I guess I am glad, too. I just... I don't want the police to think I had something to do with it."

"They won't." His free hand covers mine, lacing our fingers together. "They don't have anything to link us to the deaths, and that's if they even find the bodies."

His reassurance soothes some of my fears, and my eyes finally drift shut.

TALON

Finally, after a long drive, I pull into the parking lot of our new apartment complex in Austin, stretching after the long drive. The building's beige exterior and simple landscaping won't win any beauty contests. Still, it's far from Boston, and that's what matters.

"Home sweet home," I say, helping Lena grab her bag from the trunk. The Texas heat hits differently than Massachusetts—more intense, like it's trying to burn away our past.

Our second-floor unit has basic furnishings—a worn couch, kitchen table, and queen bed. The AC unit rattles but pumps out cold air. The walls need a fresh coat of paint, and the carpet's seen better days, but it's ours. No one knows us here.

"I need to head to UT," Lena says, pulling out her acceptance letter. Her eyes sparkle with determination despite the exhaustion from our three-day journey. "The sooner I get enrolled, the better."

I nod, grabbing my keys again. "I'll drive you." The campus isn't far—another reason I chose this location. I can keep watch over her between job shifts once I find one.

The university sprawls across downtown Austin, its limestone buildings gleaming under the brutal sun. Students mill about, wrapped up in their normal lives. They have no idea what darkness Lena and I carry.

I park near the admissions office. "Want me to come in?"

"I've got this," Lena says, squeezing my hand. She steps out into the heat, the acceptance letter clutched to her chest. I watch her walk away, her shoulders straight and head high. Even after everything, she still carries herself with that quiet grace that first drew me to her.

I'll wait here until she's done, scanning the crowds for any signs of trouble. Old habits die hard. But for now, we're safe. We made it.

I watch Lena practically skip back to the car, her face lit up with that radiant smile that makes my chest tighten. She slides into the passenger seat, clutching a stack of papers.

"They're letting me transfer!" She bounces in her seat. "I can start next week. The admissions officer said my grades from MIT were exceptional."

"Of course they were." I brush my thumb across her cheek, pride swelling in my chest. My brilliant girl, already carving out her place here.

"What about you?" She turns those hazel eyes on me. "Have you thought about where you'll work?"

"Got a few leads." I start the car, letting the AC blast

away the Texas heat. "There's a construction company hiring near downtown. Manual labor pays well, and they don't ask many questions." The less attention we draw, the better. "Also spotted a warehouse looking for night shift workers."

"You should apply to both." Lena reaches over, squeezing my thigh. "The sooner we get settled, the safer we'll be."

I cover her hand with mine. She's right—we need to establish ourselves quickly and build a routine that looks normal to anyone watching. The construction job would let me keep my nights free to spend with Lena, while warehouse work would give me the days to watch over her.

"I'll head over to the construction site first now," I say, pulling onto the main road. "Then check out the warehouse. One of them's bound to work out."

Lena nods, already flipping through her university paperwork. The sunlight catches her hair, highlighting those natural waves I love running my fingers through. Everything I've done—everything I'll continue to—is to keep her safe, to give her this chance at a real life. Even if that life will always be shadowed by my darkness.

I pull into the dusty construction site, gravel crunching under my tires. Workers in hard hats and reflective vests mill around a half-finished apartment complex. The site manager's trailer sits near the entrance, its metal walls reflecting the harsh Texas sun.

Inside, the AC barely takes the edge off the heat. A burly man with salt-and-pepper hair looks up from his paperwork.

"Can I help you?"

"Looking for work," I say, relaxed but confident. "Got experience with heavy lifting, concrete, basic carpentry."

He leans back in his chair. "We might have something. When can you start?"

"Next week. My girlfriend and I just moved here from Boston. Pretty desperate for steady work."

"Boston?" He raises an eyebrow. "Long way from home."

I shrug. "Needed a change of scenery."

"Well, we're always short-handed in this heat. Pay's eighteen an hour, overtime available. Show up Monday at six a.m., and we'll get your paperwork sorted."

"Appreciate it." I shake his hand, relieved at how easy that was. A normal day job means I can keep my nights free for Lena.

But when I return to the car, my heart stops. The passenger seat is empty. My pulse spikes as I scan the lot, fighting down panic. Where is she? Did someone—

Then, I spot her sitting on a low concrete wall near the site entrance. She's gazing at the Austin skyline, her hair catching the sunlight. My racing heart steadies.

"Got the job," I call out, walking over to her. "Start Monday."

She turns, flashing that smile that makes everything else fade away. "I knew you would."

I pull Lena into my arms, breathing in her familiar scent. She fits perfectly against me, her head tucked under my chin. The construction site's noise fades away as I focus on her warmth, her steady heartbeat.

"I love you," she whispers against my chest. Her fingers trace patterns on my back, sending shivers down my spine despite the Texas heat.

"Love you more." I kiss the top of her head, savoring this peaceful moment. After everything we've been through, these simple touches mean everything.

Lena tilts her face up, those hazel eyes sparkling. "Show me."

I capture her lips, pouring all my devotion into the kiss. She melts against me, her hands sliding to tangle in my hair. The rest of the world disappears—there's only us, only this.

When we finally break apart, both breathless, I rest my forehead against hers. "Let's head home."

She nods, a soft smile playing on her lips. I keep her hand in mine as we walk back to the car, unwilling to break contact. The afternoon sun bathes everything in golden light, making Lena's skin glow.

Opening her door first, I help her before sliding behind the wheel. The AC hits us with blessed relief from the heat. Lena immediately reaches for my hand again, lacing our fingers over the center console.

"We have the whole weekend to get settled," she says, squeezing my hand. "Just us."

"Just us," I echo, bringing her hand to my lips. The promise of uninterrupted time together makes my heart race. No more running or looking over our shoulders.

I pull out of the construction site, heading toward our new apartment. Lena hums along to the radio, her thumb stroking my palm. This is what peace feels like, I realize. This is what I've fought so hard for.

TALON

Three weeks later…

Something's been bothering Lena these past weeks. Her eyes dart away when I catch her staring. She squirms in her sleep, whimpering my name. Tonight, I'm getting answers.

"Talk to me," I say, cornering her in our kitchen after dinner. "What's going on in your head?"

Lena's cheeks flush pink. She fidgets with her sleeve, avoiding my gaze. "It's nothing."

"Bullshit." I step closer, tilting her chin up. "You've been off for weeks. Tell me."

She swallows hard. "I've been having these dreams..."

"What kind of dreams?"

Her voice drops to a whisper. "About you. That night. With David."

My pulse quickens. "Go on."

"You're wearing the mask." Her breathing gets shallow. "There's blood everywhere. You're... taking me. Even when I beg you to stop."

Heat courses through my veins at her confession. "And these dreams... do they scare you?"

"That's the thing." Lena's eyes finally meet mine, dark with something between shame and desire. "They don't. I wake up wanting them to be real so badly it hurts."

"These aren't just dreams, are they? You fantasize about it, too."

She nods, trembling slightly. "I can't stop thinking about it. About you like that—dangerous, covered in blood. Taking what you want from me."

My grip on her chin tightens. "You want me to be the monster?"

"Yes," she breathes.

I study Lena's flushed face and trail my hand lower to cup her neck, noting how her pulse races beneath my fingers. "I have an idea."

Moving to our closet, I pull out the black mask from that night and a bottle of stage blood leftover from Halloween. Her eyes widen with recognition.

"We could recreate it. Make those dreams real." I hold up the items. "Safe, controlled. With boundaries."

Lena's breath catches. She nods slowly, biting her lip. "How would we...?"

"We establish a safe word first. Something you'd never say during play. If you say it, everything stops immediately. No questions asked."

"Pineapple," she suggests quickly.

I arch an eyebrow. "Been thinking about this, have you?"

Her cheeks darken further. "Maybe."

"Good girl." I trace her jawline. "I'll wear the mask, use the fake blood. Make it feel real for you. But you'll always be safe with me."

"I know." She steps closer, pressing against me. "I trust you completely."

"Even when I'm being a monster?"

"Especially then." Her eyes gleam with anticipation. "When do we start?"

I check the time. "Give me thirty minutes to set up. Then come upstairs." I pull her into a deep kiss before releasing her. "And Lena? Remember—pineapple if you need to stop."

She nods eagerly. "Thirty minutes."

I watch her leave, my blood pumping with anticipation. I knew Lena's innocent exterior concealed a darker side, a side only I could truly unleash. Setting to work, I strip off my shirt. I dress in black sweatpants and a tight-fitting shirt, ensuring my arms and chest are exposed. The skull mask soon follows, covering my face, obscuring my identity, and freeing the monster within.

Taking the stage blood, I smear it across my chest and arms, emphasizing the contours of my muscles. I wipe my hands with it, feeling the cool liquid contrast against my heated skin. Every action heightens my arousal, knowing this isn't just about sex. It's about trust, surrender, and the dynamic power shift between us. I prepare the room, the mask heightening my senses, making my heart thunder in my chest.

I stand by the door, listening for her soft footsteps. Before I see her, her perfume hits me first, a sweet, floral scent. She's breathtaking, her eyes sparkling with nervous excitement.

Moving swiftly, I grab her, one hand over her mouth to stifle her cry, the other around her waist, pulling her to me. I feel her initial struggle, testing the waters of this new dynamic. She's trembling, and I realize my grip is tight, my body pressed threateningly close.

I keep my hand over her mouth, silencing the scream caught in her throat. She writhes in my grasp, panic flashing in her eyes, and I feel her hot breath against my palm. Her struggles only fuel my urgency. She kicks out, her foot connecting with my shin, but it does little to deter me.

With my free hand, I reach down and squeeze her inner thigh, digging my fingers in roughly. I relish her sharp intake of breath. "You think you can fight me, little Lena? I'd be careful if I were you." I tighten my grip warningly, and she stills.

I step back, pushing her toward the bedroom, and she stumbles, her eyes wide. "Please—stop," she whispers, her voice shaking. "This isn't what I—"

I slam the bedroom door shut with my foot, cutting off her protests. Her eyes flick to the mask, and I see the moment her arousal battles with her fear. "No," she breathes, taking an instinctive step back. "No, don't do this."

"You wanted me to be the monster, baby. And monsters don't ask permission," I purr.

She shakes her head, her eyes shining with fear and desire. "I've changed my mind. I don't want this."

A low laugh rumbles in my throat. "You don't get to change your mind."

I back her against the wall, and she lets out a startled cry. Quickly, I grab her wrists, pinning them above her head with one hand, holding her in place. With my free hand, I grasp her thigh and lift it, baring her to me. She whimpers, arching her back, her chest rising and falling rapidly. I stroke her inner thigh with my thumb, dip my head, and bite the sensitive skin of her neck, marking her.

"No, please," she whimpers, closing her eyes. "Let me go."

I nip at her jaw. "Afraid, baby? You can use your safe word." My tongue darts out, tasting her skin, and she moans, her hips jerking. "But you won't, will you? Because this is what you want."

She tries to deny it, but her body betrays her, pressing into my touch. I grind against her, my hard length pressing against her soft core. "Admit it," I growl, nipping at her ear. "Admit that you want me to take you. That you've been waiting for this."

"No," she gasps, trying to deny it even as her hips rock against mine. "Stop, please. I don't—"

I crush her mouth with mine, devouring her lips, cutting off her words. She tastes of heat and desire, and I groan, my control slipping. I release her hands and tear at her shirt, popping buttons in my haste. It falls open, baring her breasts, and I lean down, licking her hardened peaks with my tongue. Her back arches, and I suck one peaked nipple into my mouth, biting gently.

"Stop," she whispers, digging her fingers into my hair. "Please."

I lift my head, staring at her through the mask, my eyes burning into hers. "Do you really want me to stop, Lena?" I rub my hard length against her core, letting her feel my arousal. "Because I can stop. I can leave you here, wet and aching."

She shakes her head, moaning as I rub against her. "Stop," she gasps. "I—I want you to stop."

I release a harsh breath, my control hanging by a thread. With a quick movement, I hoist her onto the bed, pushing her back. She lands on the mattress, her hair tumbling around her, her chest heaving. Her eyes are wide, full of anticipation and fear, making me harder.

I climb onto the bed, looming over her. "Tell me what you want, Lena. Tell me you want me to fuck you."

Her mouth opens, and I see the struggle within her. "Say it," I growl, nipping at her neck, sucking a bruise just above the pulse point. "Tell me what a filthy girl you are."

"Stop," she breathes, but it lacks conviction. "Get off me. Please, I—"

I grip her thighs, spread her open, and growl at the sight of her soaked panties. "Such a liar, baby. Your body betrays you."

"No." Her chest heaves as I hook my fingers into the waistband of her panties. "Please, I don't want this."

I tear her panties away, baring her to me. She tries to

cover herself, but I grab her wrists, holding them above her head. "So fucking wet for me. And now you're mine." I grind my hardness into her core, reveling in her gasp. "Tell me how much you want it."

She bucks against me, seeking friction, and I smile behind the mask. "Don't," she whimpers. "But don't— ah!"

With one hand, I grasp my length, rubbing the tip through her slick folds, coating myself in her arousal. "I'll give it to you, baby. Exactly how you want it."

She nods frantically, her eyes dark with need. "No, please. Stop, don't—"

I thrust into her, claiming her with a brutal stroke. She cries out, her back arching, her inner walls pulsating around me. I freeze, feeling her hot, tight pussy quiver around me. I trail my fingertips down her side, sliding them beneath her, cupping her soft ass. She bucks against me, meeting my hips, and I withdraw before snapping my hips forward, claiming her again.

She pants, her hair wild around her, her body sheathed in a thin layer of sweat. "No more," she begs, even as her hips circle, seeking more friction. "Get off me. Please, stop."

My lips twist in a dark smile, and I reach down, slipping my fingers between us, teasing her clit. "You want me to stop, baby? Like this?" I stroke her in time with my thrusts, feeling her inner walls clench around me. "Or this?" I brush her nipples with my thumb, flicking them and rolling them between my fingers.

She whimpers, arching off the bed, her hips stuttering against mine. "Please," she keens, her body tightening around me. "Please, Talon, I'm—"

I withdraw, pulling almost all the way out, and then snap my hips forward, filling her completely. Her inner walls clench convulsively, milking my length, and I groan, my control shattering. I thrust into her, my hips a blur, seeking my own release. Her keening cries fill the room, her body bowing, her head thrashing as she breaks apart around me. I feel her inner walls spasming, rippling around me, and it's enough to push me over the edge.

With a low growl, I spill myself into her, marking her completely mine.

I watch her, basking in the afterglow of our intense fucking. Her chest rises and falls rapidly, her skin gleams with a sheen of sweat, and her eyes shine with a mixture of satisfaction and wonder.

"That," she says softly, her voice full of awe, "was the best orgasm I've ever had."

My eyes narrow at her words. With a gentle movement, I wrap my hand around her throat, squeezing just enough to assert my dominance. "That's what you wanted, wasn't it? To be taken. To be raped." I tighten my grip, savoring the feeling of her delicate throat beneath my hand. "You're a naughty girl, Lena."

She swallows, her eyes flicking to my hand before meeting my gaze. "Did it make you hard?"

I chuckle darkly, my thumb stroking her pulse. "Harder than I've ever been. Couldn't think of anything but taking you, claiming you as my own." My thumb brushes over her rapidly beating pulse. "I couldn't stop myself."

Lena bites her lip, her eyes sparkling with unspoken desire. "I liked it," she admits softly.

Hearing those words sets something off within me. With a low growl, I rip my mask off and crush my mouth to hers, tasting her thoroughly, marking her as mine. Her lips are soft and pliant beneath mine, and she melts into me, her arms wrapping around my neck, pulling me closer. Our tongues dance, passionately entwined, each tasting the other, clinging and claiming.

When we finally part, breathless, she rests her forehead against mine, her eyes searching mine. "You're dangerous," she whispers.

I smirk. "But you like that."

She nods slowly. "I like it a lot."

I release her throat, trailing my fingertips down her neck, enjoying the little shivers I elicit. "Do you want me to tie you up next time? Restrain you so you're completely at my mercy?"

Lena's breath catches, and she bites her lip. "Yes," she breathes, her eyes dark with anticipation. "I want you to do whatever you want with me."

Hearing those words sends a shot of desire straight to my groin. "You're mine, Lena. Always remember that." I brush her hair back from her face, my thumb tracing her jawline. "And I'm yours."

She leans into my touch, her eyes softening. "Yours," she echoes.

Wrapping my arms around her, I pull her close, and she settles into my embrace, resting her head on my chest. We stay like that for a while, enjoying the quiet intimacy of the moment, the sound of our heartbeats slowly returning to normal.

I kiss the top of her head, breathing in her sweet scent. "I love you, Lena."

"I love you too, Talon," she murmurs, her voice warm and content. "I love you so much."

I hold her close, grateful for this moment of peace. I know the storm of our pasts will always loom on the horizon. But for now, we're safe—together.

EPILOGUE

Eight months later...

*J*gaze out the window of Talon's truck as pine trees whiz past, their branches casting dancing shadows across the dashboard. The winding road leads us deeper into the Hill Country wilderness, far from the bustling streets of Austin.

"You're being mysterious about this cabin," I say, glancing at Talon's strong profile. His jaw tightens slightly as he concentrates on navigating the rough dirt road.

"That's the point of a surprise." A hint of a smile plays at the corner of his mouth. "Eight months of city life—thought we could use some time away from everything."

I nod, understanding the unspoken meaning. Away from prying eyes, away from having to maintain appearances. Out here, we can truly be ourselves.

The cabin appears through the trees—rustic but

well-maintained, with a wraparound porch and large windows. As we pull up, memories of the past year flash through my mind—the darkness we've shared and the way Talon helps me process my trauma by giving me back control in ways I never expected.

"What's going on in that head of yours?" Talon asks as he kills the engine.

"Just thinking about how far we've come. How you understand me in ways no one else does." I reach for his hand. "The way you help me feel safe to explore the darker parts of myself."

He brings my knuckles to his lips. "You're mine to protect. To help heal." His eyes darken with promise. "And to push your boundaries when you need it."

A shiver runs through me, equal parts anticipation and trust. Out here in the wilderness, surrounded by trees and silence, we can fully embrace our shared darkness without judgment or restraint.

Talon grabs our bags from the truck bed. "Let's get settled in. We have the whole week ahead of us."

I follow him up the porch steps, my pulse quickening. In this secluded cabin, we can explore our twisted desires freely—finding healing through carefully orchestrated chaos and processing past trauma through consensual power exchange.

The cabin's interior is cozy, with rustic wooden beams and a stone fireplace dominating the living room. I finish unpacking our bags in the bedroom, hang up our clothes, and arrange toiletries in the adjoining bathroom.

"Talon?" I call out, expecting to find him stoking a

fire or preparing dinner. The living room stands empty, shadows lengthening across the hardwood floors as dusk settles in. "Are you in the kitchen?"

Silence answers me. My heartbeat quickens - not from fear, but from the electric anticipation whenever Talon disappears like this. I check each room, finding no trace of him.

The porch creaks under my feet as I step outside. The air has grown cool, pine needles rustling in the breeze. "Talon?" My voice carries through the trees, met only by chirping crickets and distant bird calls.

I wrap my arms around myself, scanning the darkening tree line. The forest feels alive with secrets, but I know better than to venture into its depths alone at nightfall.

A large hand clamps over my mouth from behind. I inhale sharply, recognizing Talon's familiar scent— cedarwood and something distinctly male—even as an unfamiliar, distorted voice growls in my ear.

"Don't make a sound."

My heart hammers against my ribs as I feel the warmth of his body against my back. Talon spins me around, and I bite back a gasp. I know this is him, yet I can't help the adrenaline rush that comes with seeing his eyes hidden behind the mask, his face marked with fake blood.

He holds a knife loosely, the blade glinting in the fading light. Goosebumps rise on my skin, and I struggle to catch my breath as my eyes flick down to the bulge in his sweatpants.

"Turn around and put your hands behind your

back," he growls, the rough edge to his voice sending a thrill through me. Obeying without hesitation, I feel the soft give of the porch beneath my bare feet as I turn. I bring my wrists together, anticipation coursing through my veins.

The clink of metal makes me stiffen. I hear the rattle of chains as he wraps them around my wrists, binding them together. I hold my breath, part of me anticipating the cool bite of the metal, but instead, I feel the soft fabric of a blindfold. He's going to blindfold me first.

The fabric brushes my eyelids, then settles gently over my eyes, blocking the world around me. I'm aware of Talon standing behind me, his breathing heavy, his desire for me tangible. I shift my stance, the porch's wooden planks creaking beneath my feet.

"Comfortable?" he asks.

I nod. "Yes." My voice comes out raspy, my throat dry.

"Good." He steps closer, his body heat enveloping me. "You know the safe word."

"Yes." I trust him implicitly. Even in this vulnerable state, with my wrists bound and my vision obscured, I know that he would never truly hurt me. This is about giving me back control, about exploring the darkness within myself in a safe environment.

The knife scrapes lightly against my skin, trailing down the side of my neck and onto my shoulder. Goose-bumps erupt across my skin.

Terror pulses through me as I feel Talon's body press against my back. I struggle, knocking against his arms, but he's too strong. He grunts his hot breath on my neck, sending shivers of fear down my spine. I know it's him, but the mask distorts his voice.

"Come on, sweetheart. You know you want it," he says, his voice rough and unrecognizable.

I shake my head, hair tumbling over my face, obscuring my vision even more. "No, get off me!"

He grabs a handful of my hair, yanking my head back and exposing my throat. My heart is hammering, my breath coming in short gasps. Despite knowing it's Talon, my body is responding as if it were a stranger violating me.

The knife presses into my throat, sending a chill through me. "Such a pretty neck. It'd be a shame to ruin it."

His erection presses against my lower back, his intention clear. I squirm, trying to throw him off balance, but he predicts my moves, holding me effortlessly.

"Please, stop!" I cry out. My fear is genuine even though I love my would-be attacker. I can feel his excitement and desire for me, which fuels my resistance.

I consider using the safe word, but I don't want this to end. Not yet. I want to see how far he'll take this fantasy.

The knife leaves my throat, and his arms wrap around me. His breath is hot in my ear as he murmurs crude promises of what he plans to do to me.

I try to wriggle free, kicking out, but he's expecting this. He slams me against the cabin wall, the impact rattling my teeth. My struggles weaken as he continues to overpower me.

"That's it, fight me," he snarls, his lips brushing my ear.

The knife is back at my throat, and I can't help the whimper that escapes my lips. Fear and desire flood my senses as I realize that my aggressive, fantasized stranger is about to take what he wants—me.

"Please, don't," I beg, my voice breaking. I don't want Talon to stop.

He chuckles, low and dangerous, his hot breath tickling my ear. "Don't fight it. You want this. You've always wanted it."

I shake my head vigorously, causing my hair to tumble over my shoulders and the blindfold to slip slightly, granting me a hazy view of the darkening trees surrounding us. "No," I whisper.

His free hand grabs my ass, squeezing hard enough to make me yelp. "You've been waiting for this, haven't you, slut?"

I can feel his eyes on me, even through the mask. He knows my deepest, darkest secrets, my forbidden desires. I hate him and crave him in this moment.

"This ass has been waiting for a real man to fill it," he growls, his fingers teasing the edges of the butt plug nestled inside me. I moan softly, torn between fighting him and surrendering to the pleasure. "Did you bring this, hoping some guy would bend you over and see how fucking desperate you are for an ass fucking?"

"No," I whisper, even as my body yearns for exactly that.

I feel the twist of the plug, the stretch as he slowly pulls it from me, and then the cold night air on my exposed skin. Embarrassment wars with arousal as my muscles clench around the emptiness he's left behind.

"Liar," he snarls, yanking my hair hard enough to bring tears to my eyes. "You knew this is what I'd do to you, and you still came out here."

I nod, the movement making my hair fall forward, obscuring my face. I want him to see the truth in my eyes, to understand that my desires are just as depraved as his.

His hands grip my hips, and he pulls me back against him, the hard length of his erection pressing into the cleft of my ass. "Beg me to fuck you. Beg, and maybe I'll give you what you want."

"No," I whisper again, my chest heaving.

The knife presses into my throat, and I freeze, remembering our safe word. I don't want this to end.

"Last chance," he warns, his voice harsh.

Desire courses through me, and I tilt my head back, baring my throat to him. "Fuck my ass. Take what you want. I've been waiting for it."

He growls his approval, his fingers biting into my hips. I feel the head of his cock press against my stretched asshole, and then he's pushing inside, filling me in one smooth stroke. I cry out, a mix of pain and pleasure, my body stretched around his girth.

He stills for a moment, his breath hot on the back of my neck, then begins to move with slow, deep thrusts. "That's it, take it. Take all of me, you filthy little slut."

I moan, my body moving with his, my shoulders thrust helplessly against the cabin wall with my head turned to one side. His rhythm becomes relentless,

307

pounding into me with hard, fast strokes that send shocks of pleasure through my body.

"You like that, don't you? Like getting your ass destroyed by a stranger?"

"Yes," I sob, surrender and rapture mixing in my voice.

His pace quickens, his hips slapping against my ass as he drives into me with fierce, primal need. I'm lost in the whirlwind of sensations, craving more, needing release.

"Come for me," he demands, nipping at my shoulder. "Come with my cock in that beautiful fucking ass, and I might let you breathe."

My body clenches around him on command as I shatter into a million pieces. I cry out, my voice echoing through the trees, my orgasm pulsing through me in waves.

He comes with a growl, his release flooding me, marking me as his.

We stand there, joined together, our breathing harsh and labored. Slowly, he pulls out of me, and I struggle to hold myself up. He unfastens the handcuffs and then yanks the blindfold off. Suddenly he pulls me face him, and Talon stands before me, his mask hiding the full extent of his expression, but his eyes—piercing and intense—give him away. This game of ours is just as much for him as it is for me.

I step forward into his arms, and he holds me tightly, his face buried into my hair. "I love how fucking kinky you are," he whispers. "I just fucking love you more than anything on this godforsaken earth."

I close my eyes, savoring the moment of vulnerability. "I love you, too."

He lifts and carries me, still naked, to the cabin's porch swing. His fingers trace lazy patterns on my arm while the gentle breeze carries the scent of pine needles.

"I never thought I'd find peace after everything," I whisper, listening to his steady heartbeat. "But here, with you, I finally feel whole."

Talon's arm tightens around me. "You saved me too, Lena. Before you, I was lost in darkness. You showed me there could be light, even for someone like me."

I lift my head to meet his gaze. Those piercing blue eyes that once terrified me now hold nothing but devotion. "We saved each other," I say softly. "All those years in that foster home, enduring the Wilsons' abuse—it led us here. Together."

He cups my face gently, his thumb brushing my cheek. "You're my redemption, Lena Graves. My reason for being better."

Tears well in my eyes as I think about our journey - from scared foster kids to survivors who found love in the darkest places. "Promise me we'll always have this," I whisper. "Just us, against the world."

"I promise." He kisses my forehead tenderly. "You're my home, Lena. My everything."

We fall into a comfortable silence, watching the last rays of the sun disappear behind the trees. The stars emerge one by one, twinkling in the velvet sky. In this moment, our past trauma and pain feel distant. We've found healing in each other's arms and turned our shared darkness into something beautiful.

"I love you, Talon Voss," I murmur, snuggling closer.

His lips brush my hair. "I love you too, always."

The porch swing creaks softly as we rock, two broken souls who found wholeness together. Our love may not be a fairytale, but it's ours—fierce, dark, and eternal.

THE END

ABOUT THE AUTHOR

I've always been drawn to the dark side of fiction. My stories? They're an exploration of that darkness, filled with mysterious masked men, fearless heroines, and spice that'll set your Kindles ablaze.

Ever since I can remember, I've been captivated by the darker side of romance. It's necessary to add I don't condone these kinds of relationships in real life. However, the intoxicating chase, the deadly dance, the heart-racing fear, and an irresistible attraction I adore writing.

I exclusively publish on Amazon, providing a thrilling escape for those who dare to venture into the dark side of love and lust. If you've read my book and found yourself wanting more, follow me on Amazon or social media for updates on my next dark novella release. Your adventure is only a page flip away.

Printed in Great Britain
by Amazon

54152453R00182